DREAMING ANASTASIA

JOY PREBLE

sourcebooks
fire

Published by Sourcebooks Jabberwocky, an imprint of Sourcebooks, Inc.
P.O. Box 4410, Naperville, Illinois 60567–4410
(630) 961–3900
Fax: (630) 961–2168
www.sourcebooks.com

Library of Congress Cataloging-in-Publication Data

Preble, Joy.
    Dreaming Anastasia / Joy Preble.
        p. cm.
    Summary: In alternating voices, sixteen-year-old Chicagoan Anne and
handsome, magical Ethan tell of their fated quest to rescue Russian Grand
Duchess Anastasia, who tells of her long captivity in the hut of legendary
witch Baba Yaga.
    1. Anastasiia Nikolaevna, Grand Duchess, daughter of Nicholas II, Em-
peror of Russia, 1901-1918--Juvenile fiction. [1. Anastasia, Grand Duchess,
daughter of Nicholas II, Emperor of Russia, 1901-1918--Fiction. 2. Fate and
fatalism--Fiction. 3. Dreams--Fiction. 4. Magic--Fiction. 5. Baba Yaga (Legendary character)--Fiction. 6. Witches--Fiction. 7. Russia--History--Nicholas
II, 1894-1917--Fiction.] I. Title.
    PZ7.P90518Dre 2009
    [Fic]--dc22
                                2009023659

Printed and bound in the United States of America.
        VP 10 9 8 7 6 5

For Michelle Andelman—
You pulled me out of the slush pile
and allowed me to follow my dream.
I wouldn't be here if not for your wisdom and encouragement.

And for my mother, Rose Brown—
Who believed I could do anything
if only I'd just shut up and get to work.

The Forest, Late Evening,

Anastasia

I DIDN'T ALWAYS DREAM ABOUT MY FAMILY. STILL, THEY haunted me for the longest time. Their smiles. Their voices. How they looked when they died. But of all the things I remember, the strongest memory is a story.

Of the stories my mother told me, only one did I love hearing over and over. I had not known it would become my story—the one I would live day after day. Here in the small hut with its tiny windows and smooth, wooden floor. The small bed in which I sleep, its blue and red cotton quilt tucked neatly around me. My *matroyshka* nestled on the soft goose-down pillow. The *matroyshka*—the doll my mother gave me near the end, the one she told me to hold tight, even though she knew I was seventeen and far, far too old for such things. A wooden nesting doll, its figure repeated itself smaller and smaller, each hidden inside the other, the last one so tiny it almost disappeared in the palm of my hand.

I understand now what it is to be hidden like that—so tucked away that no one even knows I am here.

In the story, there was a girl. Her name was Vasilisa, and she was very beautiful. Her parents loved her. Her life was good. But things changed. Her mother died. Her father remarried.

And the new wife—well, she wasn't so fond of Vasilisa. So she sent her to the hut of the fearsome witch Baba Yaga to fetch some light for their cabin. And that was supposed to be that. For no one returned from Baba Yaga's. But Vasilisa had the doll her dying mother gave her. And the doll—because this was a fairy tale and so dolls could talk—told her what to do. Helped her get that light she came for and escape. And when Vasilisa returned home, that same light burned so brightly that it killed the wicked stepmother who sent Vasilisa to that horrible place. Vasilisa remained unharmed. She married a handsome prince. And lived happily ever after.

When I listened to my mother tell the story, I would pretend I was Vasilisa the Brave. In my imagination, I heeded the advice of the doll. I outwitted the evil Baba Yaga, the fearsome witch who kept her enemies' heads on pikes outside her hut. Who rode the skies in her mortar and howled to the heavens and skittered about on bony legs. Who ate up lost little girls with her iron teeth.

But the story was not as I imagined. Not as my mother told it. I am not particularly brave. And it was not an evil stepmother who sent me to this hut in the forest. I came because I believed *him*. The man I trusted with all my heart. The one who told me I was special. That I alone would save the Romanovs by letting him save me.

Oh, yes, I believed. Even as the Bolsheviks forced us to the house in Ekaterinburg. Even as I sewed jewels into my clothing so no one would find them. And even on that July day when we were all herded like cattle down into that basement.

Because that is what seventeen-year-old girls do. They believe.

But that was all so long ago. At least, I think it was. In the hut, it is hard to say. Time works differently here. We are always on the move. The two hen's legs that support the hut are always scrabbling for a new destination. Keeping us from whoever might be searching. If anyone still cares to search.

At first, I thought I'd go mad. And perhaps I have. But most days, I convince myself that I do not mind it so much. I sweep and sew and fill the kettle in the fireplace and bring sweet, hot tea to Auntie Yaga. Auntie, who rocks in her chair, her black cat settled in her lap, and smiles with those great iron teeth—and sometimes, as my mother did, tells stories.

"They don't really know me," Auntie says. She takes a long sip of tea and clasps the cup with two huge, brown, gnarled hands. It is those hands that scare me most—that have always scared me—and so my heart skitters in my chest. The fear is less now than it used to be, but its fingers still run along my belly until I want to scream and scream even though I know now that it will make no difference. That what I did, that what brought me here, made no difference. But that, of course, is yet another story.

"They say they know what evil is," Auntie Yaga continues. "But they do not. They think it is all so very simple. That I am a witch, and that is that. But it is not as they tell it. I am not what they think I am."

Listening to Auntie Yaga now, I really do understand. None of it is simple. It is not like the stories my mother told. Not like what *he* told me.

"You will save them, Anastasia," he said. "You just need to be brave. I'll take care of the rest."

Only that wasn't simple either. Or perhaps it was. A simple revolution. A simple set of murders. My family, destroyed one by one in front of my eyes. Their screams. Their cries for mercy. And a storm in a room where no storm could exist. A thick, black cloud that deepened and swirled and cracked open the ceiling. A giant pair of hands—the same hands that now clutch a cup of sweet tea—that closed about me and carried me here. And suddenly, I knew how not simple it all really was.

Downtown Chicago,
One Week Ago

SUNDAY, 1:40 PM

ANNE

I DON'T NOTICE HIM LOOKING AT ME. NOT RIGHT AWAY. I mean, by the time Tess and I hike our way up to row 16, seats D and E, of the nosebleed section and squeeze past everyone else who's already seated—because, obviously, they have their own transportation and don't have to wait for my father to get done with his Sunday morning golf game to drive them downtown for the matinee of *Swan Lake*—it's almost curtain time.

So we're already at our seats before I feel some sort of weird, prickly tingling on the back of my neck and turn around to find him standing there staring.

I elbow Tess. "Look behind us," I whisper. "That guy. The tall one wearing the blazer. He's watching us."

"Guy?" Tess is not whispering. Tess never whispers. I'm not sure she actually can. "Where?" She cranes her neck in the wrong direction.

Tess is many things. Subtle is not one of them.

"God, Tess. Lower your voice. About four rows behind us. To the left."

"Not us," she says when she finally figures out where to look. "You. He's staring at you, Anne. And he's wicked hot."

I narrow my eyes at her as we plop down in our seats. "You promised," I say. "I mean, seriously, Tess. No human being uses that word so much. Not to mention we're in Chicago, not Boston. So enough already."

"Sorry," she says—although she's grinning, so I'm pretty sure she's not. Tess visited her Boston cousins this summer and has developed a single-minded devotion to the Bostonism *wicked*. As in, "That test was *wicked* hard." "That pair of jeans is *wicked* cute." "Heather Bartlett"—who sleeps with any guy who can fog a mirror—"is *wicked* slutty."

Or, "Using a word so much that you kill the effect is *wicked* annoying."

Besides, I'm not sure I agree with her anyway. He's cute and all, and the blazer look works on him, but he's standing so still and looking at us so closely that I'm thinking *stalker* might be a better description than *hot*. And anyway, I'm surprised Tess thinks so. Tess is usually more about the piercings and the tattoos—the whole bad boy thing.

I sneak another look.

Stalker guy's no bad boy. At least not the parts of him I can see. He's about my age, maybe a little older. And he's tall, a little over six feet or so, with this shaggy, brown hair that he really should brush off his forehead. He's wearing khaki pants and a white shirt topped with the brown corduroy blazer. Pretty normal, other than the fact that he's a guy and he's at a ballet and he's alone. Not that I'm judging or anything.

But the thing is, he's still watching me. Okay, make that openly staring. And even from here, I can see that his eyes are this fierce, startling blue.

I stare back. He's not flirting. But he's not dropping his gaze either. And for a second, it feels a little more dangerous than flirting. More like crazy reckless.

And then honestly, because I'm me and not my best friend, Tess—who's blond and tall and has guys trailing after her like puppies—I'm just sort of irritated. Why can't some normal guy find me attractive? Someone who just wants to go for coffee at Java Joe's and maybe to a movie or something and not stare at me until I can actually feel my face getting a little warm?

"Do we know him?" I ask Tess.

She shakes her head. "Don't think so," she says as the lights dim, the music cues up, and *Swan Lake* begins.

I swivel in my seat to look at Mr. Blue Eyes again, but the auditorium is so dark that all I can see is his silhouette, which is pretty neutral on the hot or not scale.

On stage, handsome Prince Siegfried falls in love with the beautiful but doomed Odette. By intermission, they've danced their *pas de deux,* and old Sieg has promised to save Odette from her midnight-to-dawn swan enchantment—even though I seriously want to tell her to fly off and find some other guy who'll actually manage to help her. I've seen *Swan Lake* before. Twice—because even though I hate the ending, there's just something about it that makes me want to see it again. So I know the evil Rothbart has enchanted Odette. And that all Siegfried has to do is vow eternal love for her to break the spell.

Only come the end of intermission, he'll screw it up, just like always. Rothbart will enchant his own daughter, Odile, to look like Odette, and stupid Siegfried is gonna fall for it. He'll pledge his love for the wrong girl, Odette will stay doomed, and the only way out of the whole mess will be for Siegfried to die for her.

5

I mean, come on—how stupid is this guy that he can't tell a black swan costume from a white one?

The house lights flick on. Tess and I look behind us. Staring guy is gone.

"Too bad." Tess rummages through the little plaid Burberry bag she'd recently snagged from her mother's closet. She fishes out bronze lip gloss and applies some to her already sufficiently glossed lips.

"His loss," she says as we snake our way to the lobby so I can plunk down four dollars for a miniscule plastic cup of Diet Coke. "Mr. Stealthy just doesn't know what beautiful little birdies he's missing out on." She flutters her way—swan style—to the concession stand.

I grin. Encouraged, she flutters some more.

"Enough," I tell her. If I don't, the fluttering will go the same way as the whole *wicked* thing, and pretty soon, she'll be fluttering everywhere she figures I think it's funny.

"Tight-ass." Tess makes a face. "And ooh, that reminds me. I wonder if he has one." She waggles her eyebrows at me. "You so want to know. Admit it."

I just shake my head. I'm not admitting anything. Besides, he'd never turned around.

"You know you do." Tess grabs my cup and helps herself to a few swallows. Translate—she gulps down the rest of it.

"Whatever." I hold out my hand for my empty cup, sigh, and toss it into the nearby trash can. "It's not like we're ever going to see him again."

"You just never know," Tess tells me as the house lights blink. "You just never know."

6

Sunday, 1:50 pm

Ethan

I KNOW I'M TOO CLOSE. THAT I NEED TO BE CAREFUL. THAT I should look away.

But I don't.

She brushes some of her auburn hair out of her eyes, then leans over and whispers to the tall blond girl next to her. And then, as though she feels my gaze, she turns.

She's the one, I realize as we look at each other. After all these years, after all the times I've been wrong. This sixteen-year-old girl with the laughing brown eyes and the posture of a prima ballerina—she's the one.

Of course, there is only one way for me to know for sure. Until then, I can only go on instinct. And here, two weeks after I've first begun to follow her, that instinct is telling me I'm right.

Her instincts are telling her something too. Even in the darkness once the lights have dimmed, I know she is still looking at me, still wondering why I'm looking at her.

And for a few seconds, Brother Viktor's words echo in my mind.

"There will be a girl," he had told me. I was not called Ethan then, but Etanovich. "The books say she will bear our bloodline.

She will be young, and she will be fiery. She will not know her destiny. But when you look into her eyes, when you touch her, the signs will be clear. You will know she is the one."

Just before intermission, I slip away. To stay now that Anne—that is her name, Anne, which surprised me at the same time as it seemed fitting—had seen me would be too dangerous.

So I will just keep watching. Soon it will be time to find her again. Time to know for sure if what the documents say is true. Time to know if my long, long wait is finally about to end.

Sunday, 7:30 pm

Anne

T HANKS FOR THE PIZZA," TESS SAYS TO MY MOTHER. SHE'S flopped next to me on the family-room floor, her empty plate in front of her.

"Sure thing, sweetie." From her seat on the couch, my mom gives Tess a smile, then goes back to watching whatever it is she's watching on the Travel Channel—something about the top-ten romantic getaways, which is a bit of a stretch these days since my parents aren't exactly on a romance kick. My father is currently out on his post-dinner jog while my mother is curled up on the couch with the show.

The two of us—Tess and I, that is, since both my parents are avoiding wheat, and pizza is far off their list—just chowed our way through most of a medium Lou Malnati's cheese and tomato. This means we'll be sluggish and heavy when we tie on those pointe shoes tomorrow afternoon at Miss Amy's, where we're both in advanced ballet—but Lou's pizzas are worth it.

At least that's the story I'm telling myself.

But I've got some kind of crazy nervous energy zipping through me, and I think my metabolism is going to take care of most of the excess calories anyway. I've felt this way ever since *Swan Lake* that afternoon. The feeling stayed with me on the drive home from the city and didn't even go away when Tess and I worked on our world history homework while we waited for my dad to come back with the pizza. Which surprised me, because normally, world history is not exactly a subject that makes me do handsprings. Not that I don't like knowing about the stuff. I actually do. But Coach Wicker—who pretends to teach the class when he's not too busy figuring out football plays on the computer—is the most singularly boring individual I've ever met. He can take something that I find interesting—like, say, Henry VIII and all those wives—and turn it into something so ridiculously dull that suddenly, I can't remember which wife he divorced and which one he had beheaded, and I really don't care in any case.

"She looks good," Tess says after we've carried our plates into the kitchen and I'm wiping up the stray strands of cheese that dripped to the counter when I plated up the pizza from its Lou to-go box.

"Who?"

Tess frowns. "Who do you think?"

"Oh." I realize she means my mother. "Really?"

"Yeah," Tess says. "Not so thin, maybe. Not so—I don't know, fragile."

I shrug. "Maybe," I tell her.

It's something I try not to dwell on. Not that I'm successful at it or anything. But I do try, just like I've been trying for almost two years, and sometimes, it *is* getting better. Except for the part where my older brother, David, is no longer my older brother, because he's dead from cancer, and the rest of us—my mother, my father, and me—are still trying to pick up the pieces.

Which is why it helps to have a friend like Tess who can shift from where she's been—talking about how my mother barely eats anything these days—to where she heads now, so quickly, actually, that it takes a few seconds before I catch up with her.

"Well, anyway," Tess says. It's one of her favorite ways to jump topics. "He really was hot, wasn't he?"

"*He* who?"

"Ballet guy," she says. "Thick hair. Blue eyes. Serious studly goodness going on there."

I shrug again. "I guess," I tell her. "But that whole staring thing—what was up with that?"

"Doesn't matter. Doesn't diminish him on the hotness scale. Note, by the way, how I did not just say *wicked hot?*"

"Progress. That's good. Maybe you do have a learning curve."

"Funny. You are oh so funny, Annie. But I mean it. There was just something about him."

"Something annoying, maybe."

"You mean it? You didn't find him, like, way attractive?"

"I didn't find him *not* attractive. But it's not like he's going to keep me up nights. Like I said—all that staring. And his posture. He was so—I don't know, straight. So formal or something."

"Huh," Tess says. "Hadn't thought about that. But you're right. He was standing up pretty straight. Geez, Michaelson, give me a break. No wonder you ended things with Adam Green three months ago and haven't replaced him with anyone. You are seriously too picky."

"First, it's not like I'm ever going to see this guy again. And second, I ended things with Adam because all he was interested in doing was feeling me up and hoping I'd let him do more. Which, let me say, is not what I consider even slightly romantic."

"Someone's standards are awfully high."

"Ha, ha." I reach into the pocket of the jeans I'd changed into once we got back from downtown and pull out my cell phone. "Should I get Neal on the phone? Tell him you've changed your level of expectation?"

Neal Patterson is Tess's ex. If she had her way, he'd be ex to the entire world as well. Their breakup was, in a word, legendary.

"Whatever," she says. "But the guy at the theater was cute. And he's got that whole mystery man thing going for him. That's gotta count for something."

"Only if he drops back out of the sky and starts stalking *you* next time."

"It could happen."

"Oh, yeah," I tell her. "I'm sure. You want to study some more before my dad gets back and drives you home?"

"If we have to," Tess says.

"Thought you bombed that last quiz. That one on all the royal families?"

"Who can remember all that crap? Plus it's sort of sick that they were all, like, intermarried to each other. That was one small royal family tree they had going there in Europe."

"Nothing like keeping it in the family," I tell her. And then we get back to work.

Chicago,
The Present

TUESDAY, 5:55 AM

ANNE

Anne." My father bends over my bed, gently shaking my shoulder until I open my eyes. He's turned on the lamp on my nightstand, and I can see that he hasn't combed his hair yet, so it's standing up all spiky. He's still in a T-shirt and the plaid Old Navy sleep pants my mother bought him so he wouldn't wander around in his boxers and make us both uncomfortable, even though with all the jogging and avoiding wheat, he's in decent shape.

"You were screaming," he says. "You must have been dreaming."

"Don't know," I tell him. "I don't remember."

My father studies me, but he doesn't push the issue. "I'm going to shower," he says eventually. He gives my arm a rub, lets his hand rest there for a bit. "And your alarm is about to ring, so you might as well get up. You sure you're okay?"

"Absolutely," I tell him. I sit up and give him my best smile. And then I keep smiling until he walks out of my room and back down the hall. Until I hear him turn on the shower in the master bath and hear the TV click on in my parents' bedroom, which means my mother is watching the news or whatever while she gets dressed.

And then I stop smiling and concentrate on getting my heart to stop racing in my chest and my pulse to stop doing the cha-cha in my veins.

But I know that's not going to happen anytime soon. It never does. Not when I have the dream—the same dream I had Sunday night after Tess went home. The same one I've had too many nights to count in the past three years since I first had it, right after we found out David was sick—which doesn't even make much sense, since it's not a dream about him.

Truth is, I've always had strange dreams. Particularly because sometimes—a lot of the time, actually—when I dream, I'm not me. It's like watching a movie through someone else's eyes or something. While I'm saying stuff and doing stuff, I'm pretty clear that in the dream, I'm this other person, not myself.

Once, I even dreamed as a guy—not that I woke up with any stunning insights about the male psyche or anything, which certainly doesn't surprise me. Tess says with guys, it all comes down to three things—sports, sex, and food. Not necessarily in that order. For example in junior high, I was trying to write a short story, and I asked my brother David what he and his friends said when they thought a girl was hot. His response was, "I'd do her." Then he grabbed the bag of Cheetos, snagged the remote, and flipped between ESPN and ESPN 2 for the next thirty minutes.

But these past few nights, I've just been her. The girl who haunts my dreams but whose face I never see. The one who refuses to leave me alone.

As always, I was trapped in this little cabin. That's the way it goes in these dreams. A pattern I've grown used to—like how I know Adam Green can never carry on a conversation with a girl without his eyes straying to her chest, or how my father simply cannot make it through dinner without checking his Treo, as though his law firm will simply curl up and die during the time it takes him to eat a plate of meat loaf.

And as always, I felt like I'd been there a while—days, maybe longer. I knew every inch of the room: tiny little windows, wooden floor, huge stone fireplace with a massive rocking chair next to it, and, tucked into the far corner, a bed with a quilt, a pillow, and a little wooden doll with red painted lips. Same stuff I always saw. The same feeling of watching it through a stranger's eyes.

She's so damn lonely. That's what I felt when I was her— this emptiness inside me, like someone's fist had burrowed its way into me and left a gaping hole. Like I'd done something—or had something done to me—that was so brutal and so awful I couldn't even think about it. I just felt sad. And sometimes, when I dreamed I was her, I woke up with my face wet with tears.

Normally, that's pretty much it. Which is probably why I've never told anyone about it. I mean, what would I say? That I keep dreaming I'm some girl I can't really see and I'm trapped somewhere and I feel sad? Yeah, right.

But this time, the dream changed. This time, *she* was doing the dreaming. And it was a dream she was struggling *not* to have. But let me say, she was spectacularly unsuccessful at stopping it. And so was I.

I was in a bigger room then, packed with people—adults and children. All talking a mile a minute in a language I couldn't understand. All clearly frightened out of their minds. And there was this one girl in particular, with long, brown hair and a white dress. She was my age, I think, sixteen or seventeen, or something close. I couldn't take my eyes off her. Or rather, the girl I am when I have this dream—she couldn't. Because she knew she was looking at herself. That whatever was about to happen to the brown-haired girl and all these other frightened people actually happened to *her*, and now she was dreaming about it, even though she'd clearly rather not. And honestly, neither would I. But I did.

My pulse quickened, and my heart started to beat so fast that I thought it was going to hammer up my throat and out my mouth. And then the shooting began. Men—some in uniforms, some in regular clothes—were shooting and shooting, and the people—they were screaming and falling. And there was blood everywhere—rivers of it running slick over the floor.

I kept watching the girl in the white dress, knowing it was me I was watching, even as a part of me knew I was dreaming as someone else. She screamed, then tried to run, only she saw she had nowhere to go. Nowhere, that is, but into—and this is the part that still has me feeling like I was sucked into a Stephen King novel or something—a giant pair of hands that swooped down out of a black cloud and scooped her up and out of the room.

Normally, this would be where I'd wake up. Or where the dream would finally change, and I'd be eating Thai food with Adam and he'd refuse to let us order extra spring rolls. Or I'd be making out with Johnny Depp in the frozen-foods aisle while my mother asked him to pass her the Lean Cuisine sesame chicken, because the sign said they're five for ten dollars.

But this time, I just kept on dreaming.

And things shifted back to the tiny little cabin.

18

There was an old woman sitting by that huge stone fireplace. She was rocking and sipping something from a mug. Her skin was brown and wrinkled, and she was wearing a long, brown dress that brushed the wooden floor as she rocked. She had some kind of red kerchief thing tied around her head and a black cat curled up in her lap. And compared to the room where everyone was getting shot, this seemed rather tame. The girl whose head I just couldn't exit seemed to know the woman. She wasn't exactly happy to see her, but she didn't seem frightened anymore either.

And that's when it happened. When the old woman in the rocker looked up. And suddenly, dream girl and I separated. I wasn't dreaming as her anymore. I was me, and she was standing next to me. But I didn't have time to look at her, because I was too busy looking at the woman in the rocker, who was now staring straight at me, her dark eyes burning, each pupil a tiny skull.

She smiled. Her teeth were metal—iron maybe, or silver. And then her mouth sort of dropped down and unhinged. Opened wider and wider, those metal teeth gleaming, until, just as I was sure she was going to swallow me whole, I finally woke up.

Which is why I'm sitting here in my bed, my heart still flopping around in my chest like a hooked fish and my T-shirt plastered to my back with sweat.

I'd like to blame it on the sushi we ate last night at that new place on Central Avenue.

But I can't.

So I do what I've done before. I get out of bed, pick out some clothes, and start getting ready for school.

And then I head into my bathroom, close the door, strip off my sweat-dampened T-shirt and underwear, climb into my shower, and hope that eventually the hot water will take the chill off my skin.

My dearest Alexei—

I am putting these words to paper to prove that beyond all reason and beyond all understanding, I am still here. I am still alive. I have pieced together what has become of me and why. And in telling each of you, my family, my dear ones, I will help myself understand—or, at least, that is my hope.

You will note, by the way, little brother, that I am writing in English, even if this sometimes makes my words clumsier than I would like. It is a tribute to our dear mama, who made sure we learned that language, and although this first entry is for you, the words honor her too, and let her live on in that way. She was at times a foolish woman, but her heart was good. And as our blood goes back on her side to the English and Queen Victoria, it seems fitting.

Blood, my Alexei, is of course no laughing matter to you. And certainly, there was more than enough of that at the end, but I'm certain I do not need to remind you of that. It is why Mama trusted Father Grigory—the one the people called Rasputin—because he promised that he would cure you. And it is, I realize now, the blessing and the curse of your birth, because, as we learned, hemophilia is passed down from mother to son. So it happened with you and Mama, even though she had prayed and hoped for a boy to join us girls and had finally gotten her wish.

But I digress. Or rather, I have yet to get to my true point. There is still more to say about blood—not yours, Alexei, and not mine—and I will try to say it here. And as we should with all good stories, I will attempt to start this one at the beginning.

The first memory I have of him was when I was about five. You were just a little, little boy then, two years old and toddling around after me. Father and I were walking in the park that afternoon, and this young man—a boy still, really, although I suppose at fourteen, most boys think they are men—with his dark hair and dark eyes came up to us.

"Hello," he said to me, and he reached out to shake my hand.

"Hello," I told him back, and I remember that suddenly I felt very shy, which, as you know, is not like me at all but really more like you. Remember how we always said that sometimes you just seemed to know things? Well, that was how I felt then—that this boy was important, even if I didn't understand how. I

22

tucked myself behind Papa and clung to his legs and waited to see why this boy was here.

"Hello, sir," the boy said to Papa, and he held out his hand to him as well.

But Papa wouldn't shake it. "You cannot be here," Papa told him. "You simply cannot."

"I am strong," the boy said. "And I'm smart."

"Even so," Papa told him, "it does not matter."

"She sends you her love," the boy said then. "She knows you have another son now. And she's heard he is ill. She wishes you only the best. And the boy too."

"And she sent you as her messenger?"

"So you could see me," the boy said to Papa. "So you could remember that I am here also."

"You do not exist," Papa told him. Then he took my hand, and we walked across the park, back to the Imperial Palace.

"Who was that?" I asked our father.

"No one," Papa said. "It was no one, Anastasia. That is all you need to know."

But of course, that was not the truth. And although many things have passed from my memory, that day has not. "Another son," the boy told our father. Another son. And I think if I am honest with myself, those two words were truly the beginning of the end.

But I do not want to get ahead of my tale, Alexei. And I want to write to the others as well. So I will close this for now and leave you what I have left, which is just that I remain

Your loving sister,

Anastasia

TUESDAY, 10:45 AM

ANNE

SKIN, ANNE, SKIN." MRS. KAPLAN, MY FRESHMAN-YEAR biology teacher, who's four-foot-eleven and so old she probably debated the theory of evolution with Darwin himself, jabs a bony, formaldehyde-smelling finger at my midsection. Actually, what she does is poke me in the belly button—which, by the way, is completely covered by my sweater—but I let it go since, let's face it, anyone who has supervised the dissection of so many frogs is probably a little loony at this point.

It's passing period between third and fourth, and I'm trying to get to chemistry. I still can't get the stupid dream out of my head, which is not like me since, as I say, I always dream weird stuff, and normally, it doesn't particularly bother me. But right now it's like I've hit a mental repeat button or something, and the images just won't leave me alone—the girl in the white dress and the old woman with the metal teeth. That jaw unhinging and trying to swallow me whole...

Maybe that's why I have no patience for Mrs. Kaplan freaking over my belly area just because there's a miniscule gap between the bottom of my new J. Crew caramel-colored sweater and the top of my honestly-not-so-very-low jeans.

Or maybe it's because I just spent thirty minutes listening to Coach Wicker attempt to explain the political complexities of Colombia and the sugarcane-ethanol industry—which, let me say, he is totally incapable of doing—followed by another ten minutes of copying the gross national products of South American countries off the overhead, the charm of which wears thin after, oh, three-and-a-half seconds. Why the administration would allow someone to teach honors world history who mispronounces Bogotá and can't find Tierra del Fuego on a map because he thinks it's in Peru is a mystery to me.

"Skin," Mrs. Kaplan says again as I dodge out of range of her finger. "Pull that sweater down, dear."

"Okay," I tell her. I give the sweater a little tug, and when I realize she's still frowning at me, I tug at it again—and see, to my dismay, that the right side now hangs lower than the left.

"That's better." Kaplan smiles. "Thanks, dear."

I don't smile back, but at least she's no longer jabbing me in the navel, and I'm able to snake my way a little farther down the hallway.

The chemistry and physics labs sit in a row around the corner from the biology classrooms. Their positions used to be reversed until last spring when Kelly Owens tried to create her own death ray in AP physics, and the ensuing explosion caused the science folks to rethink classroom placement. Now, the labs are closer to the courtyard at the center of the building, allowing a hasty mass exit should someone try to blow up a classroom again.

"Hey, Michaelson!" The voice belongs to Adam Green, who's walked up next to me—he of the blond hair and brown eyes I used to find absurdly attractive until I realized that his conversational skills were a little less honed than his ability to unhook my bra with one hand while still holding his bottle of Corona with the other. Not that I didn't appreciate the dexterity or anything—just that he never seemed to want to do anything else, and after a while, the novelty had worn thin.

"Do you know your sweater's a little crooked?" He grins at me so I know he's just seen my one-on-one with Kaplan.

"Funny," I tell him. "You are so hilarious."

"Knew you missed me," he says. He flashes me another grin.

"Not that much," I tell him. "But thanks for the info about the sweater."

"You coming to the game Friday?" he asks. Adam is nothing if not persistent. He also plays cornerback on the Kennedy High football team. We've had a mixed season so far, but Adam's been playing well, which I have to give him credit for, even though last week, he made sure to put the moves on Brittany Selby—the cheerleader fly girl the other ones fling into the air when they do those basket tosses—in front of me while we were all standing around right after the game.

"Maybe," I say. "Not sure yet."

"They're doing that tribute thing," he says then.

"Like I said," I tell him as my stomach does a little clenching number that I'm not particularly happy about. "I'm not sure yet. I'll let you know. But you do good out there, okay?"

I realize I do mean that last part. As for the rest of it, I'm a little less certain. Once a year, the Kennedy High Warriors do a pre-game salute to the best of the past players. We used to do it at Homecoming, but added to crowning the king and queen and the special band performance, halftime got too long. So someone decided to move it earlier in the season.

All of which would be neither here nor there except for one thing—my brother David had played football. He was the top varsity receiver his sophomore year, when both Adam and I had still been in eighth grade. Things were a little less glorious his junior year, of course, since that's when the cancer was diagnosed, and things kind of went downhill after that. But he'd been this absolutely phenomenal player—the kind who probably goes on to get college scholarships and maybe even has a chance at going pro, if he wants to.

Unless, of course, he dies before he even takes his SATs.

I'd seen the tribute invitation on the kitchen counter a few weeks ago. Neither of my parents had mentioned it beyond that. Two years might be a long time for some things. But for this, for them, it was more like two seconds.

Adam nods, and we kind of look at each other for a few moments while all this goes through my mind and some of it possibly goes through his.

"I'm gonna be late," I say eventually, and even though it's true, it sounds sort of lame. But honestly, what else is there to say?

There's a break in the crowd, so I make a run for it. I've hooked my backpack over just one shoulder in my rush to leave Coach Wicker's class, and it's starting to slide off, so I yank it a little higher. But then something sort of catches on my already crooked sweater, and I turn my head to see what it is as I round the corner to chemistry.

So I don't notice the tall, leather-jacketed boy until I've smacked into him hard enough to cause my backpack to crash to the floor, smashing a couple of my toes in the process.

I mutter a couple of words that, were she still in earshot, Mrs. Kaplan would find just as objectionable as the length of

28

my sweater. All I want to do is get to chemistry, and this idiot is blocking my way.

Only then I look up at his face. And realize it's him.

The guy from the ballet. The one Tess calls Mr. Stealthy.

My toes—the same ones I'm going to have to shove into pointe shoes this afternoon—are screaming, but he's standing there with that same annoyingly perfect posture. And staring at me with those sky blue eyes.

Lots of things happen here at good old Kennedy High. But having my blue-eyed—and, okay, lean and definitely packing some serious muscle under that leather jacket—stalker appear out of thin air was not something I expected.

We eyeball each other for a few seconds. And then a few more. He shoves his hand through that slightly shaggy, chestnut hair, like maybe he's a little shy or nervous or possibly just aware that he's kind of freaking me out with all the staring.

"I—uh, I saw you the other day," I say finally. Maybe Mr. Stealthy is actually mute or overdosing on lithium or something. "At the ballet," I finish lamely when he continues to say nothing. "You know, *Swan Lake?* I'm in pointe class this year, and we have to go to at least one ballet each semester so that we can…"

I dry up. There's no point in babbling if he's only going to stare. Even if maybe Tess was right and he *is* sort of hot. But then I remember Adam and remind myself that guys who can't carry on conversations usually try to express themselves in other ways that eventually get boring and repetitious.

"I'm Anne," I tell him. I have no idea why I'm telling him, except that it's been an odd couple of days with the dreams and all, and maybe my defense system isn't what it used to be.

"Anne Michaelson. And you are—?" I flash him a smile and hope it will finally encourage him.

Amazingly, it does.

"Ethan," he says. "Ethan Kozninsky." He smiles back and opens his mouth as if to start another sentence, except the warning bell bleats and cuts him off just as things are finally starting to get somewhere.

I bend down to retrieve my fallen backpack. But Ethan bends down too, and we sort of smack into each other again. And his arm brushes—hard—against mine as we both grab the backpack at the same time.

We both jolt backward. A rush of something that feels like energy courses through my arm, flashes upward until I feel it in my face like a fever. Ethan holds my gaze with those blue eyes. And then he smiles.

"Some static," he says mildly.

"Static?" I grab the pack from him. Pain still spikes through my arm so intensely that for a few seconds, it's hard to collect my thoughts. "That was more than static. I don't know what it was, but it was way more—"

The bell rings again. A few feet in front of us, Mrs. Spears's door is still open. If I sneak in now, I can escape getting another tardy.

"Anne," Ethan says. And then he pauses.

"I've gotta go," I tell him. I make a dash for the room. But something makes me stop just as I've got one foot in the door. I turn around.

And realize that once again, Mr. Stealthy is gone.

TUESDAY, 11:00 AM

ETHAN

"D UDE." A GIRL WITH A RING THROUGH HER EYEBROW AND a small stud right at the top of her lip steps out of the bathroom as I head down the hallway, now mostly empty. "Can I bum one of those? I'm all out."

It's only then that I look down and realize I've yanked the pack of Marlboros out of my pocket.

"Uh, sure," I tell her.

Clearly, I haven't grown any more articulate in the last thirty seconds.

Or any brighter, as she continues to stand there until it occurs to me that I need to pull a cigarette or two out of the pack and hand them over since that's what I've offered.

"Thanks, dude," she says, and then I hustle myself out of the building before I make an even bigger mess of things than I already have.

I'm still dying for a cigarette, but as I've finally remembered that I'm supposed to be an eighteen-year-old senior standing on the sidewalk outside his public high school, that's pretty much out of the question. So is the dying, for that matter, but that's quite another story—one to add to things I'll eventually impart to Anne. Once, that is, I figure out a way to stop actually acting like the tongue-tied schoolboy I seem to be.

So I have to wait until I'm well out of sight and headed down the street to where I've parked my car before I fish the Marlboros back out of my jacket pocket, light one up, and take a few deep drags.

I realize that I could smoke the entire pack and still be what Anne would call me if she knew the word.

Zalupa. As in, Russian for dickhead. As in, the guy who waits and searches for decades for this specific girl and then when he finds her, stands there like an idiot and just stares. As in, the guy who is me.

Ethan Kozninsky. *Zalupa.*

Maybe the words froze in my throat because suddenly they were too big, too monumental, too important to say. Or maybe it was because, in truth, there is no way to prepare her for a destiny about which she knows nothing—and a task I'm fairly certain she will reject as impossible or crazy or both.

Maybe I've always been the wrong one to tell her, but it's far, far too late to do anything about that. I can only keep walking to the car that I've parked a fair distance from the school because it's the Mercedes sedan I've always favored, and I figured it would stick out in the student parking lot. Only I've clearly underestimated the conspicuous consumption of the North Shore Chicago suburbs and have realized with one glance around the lot that the Mercedes is actually a lot less flashy than I thought.

Now it's occurring to me that smashing her to the floor in between classes in order to inform her that she is the girl who alone has the power to save the Grand Duchess Anastasia

Romanov from the hands of the witch Baba Yaga is just possibly not the best plan I've ever had.

Like I keep saying: *zalupa.*

I slip the Mercedes key out of my pocket as I cross the tree-lined street, flick the remains of the Marlboro to the pavement, and click the remote to open the door. Then I strip off my jacket, toss it in the back seat, and lean against the car while I roll up my sleeve.

My breath hitches a little as I see it.

The mark—round and red—sits on my forearm, just where it brushed against Anne. It throbs as I run my fingers over it, the pain radiating up my arm. But it is there, this physical marking that connects her to me—the sign for which we have all been waiting for so very long.

Ever since that day in 1918, when I truly was the person I still appear to be. Since the time even before that, when Brother Viktor pulled me aside in the small stone chapel and told me what was coming.

"There will be blood, Brother," Viktor had said. "Blood and suffering and destruction. The Romanovs are on the brink of destruction."

His words did not surprise me. The troubles in Russia had been brewing for a long while. The scandal with that crazy bastard they called Rasputin—who died of poison or bullets or drowning or maybe even the darkest of magic, depending on whom you chose to believe. The obsessions of the tsarina and the weakness of the tsar. All of them had led to this moment.

But what he had said next—well, that was a different story.

I did not have to understand, he said. I simply had to do what I was told. The Romanovs must survive. They were believers, like us. That is why the Brotherhood existed. To protect them from those who wished them destroyed.

Still, what he had proposed shocked me. I had seen many things in the years I'd spent in the Brotherhood, learned many spells. But always there had been one rule: the natural order of life could not—must not—be disrupted.

Until now.

When I was a child, my sister Masha and I had loved the old Russian folktales—tales of the gigantic witch, Baba Yaga, who would eat us if we strayed too far from home. Of the pure and innocent Vasilisa, who traveled through the forest to the witch's hut and who alone knew how to outwit the hag. But until that day, they had just been stories. Nothing more.

Only I was wrong.

And I think now as I roll down my sleeve, climb into the Mercedes, and turn the key in the ignition that perhaps there's another reason for why I behaved so ridiculously with Anne. Because how do you tell someone that a fairy tale is real? That Viktor found magic old enough and powerful enough to hold back death? That Baba Yaga, the witch from those childhood stories I loved, truly existed? Our magic had compelled her to save a Romanov. And until Anne, like Vasilisa the Brave, could find a way to reach Baba Yaga's hut, that same Romanov would remain trapped.

In truth—and it is occurring to me that this type of truth is not something I've explored for a while—I must admit that there is more to this tale—a tale that is mine and real, not something from a child's storybook.

How will I tell Anne that I should have wondered more at what Viktor told me? That I should have questioned, even as I was afraid? But I was young, and I did not know the things I do now. I had little idea about history and still less about destiny. Even now, I'm not sure that I know enough.

I only know that back then, I was willing to pledge my life. Anastasia Romanov is not the only one who is trapped.

But all that seems about to change. I've found the girl who can reverse what happened that July day so many years ago—the day the Romanovs fell in a rain of bullets and blood. The day I watched as the air stirred and darkened and Baba Yaga's enormous hands—the hands I believed were just part of a child's fairy tale—reached down and closed around the tsar's youngest daughter, Anastasia, and swept her away. The day the world believed she died.

Through my sleeve, I touch the mark on my arm once more. I think again of Anastasia, held captive for so long. *We will come for you,* I tell her, even though I know she cannot hear me. *Anne and I. We will be there soon.*

But only if I can stop being such a *zalupa.*

TUESDAY, 11:55 AM

ANNE

WHAT'S WITH YOUR SWEATER?" TESS ASKS ME, THEN takes a swig of her bottle of green tea. "Do you know it's crooked?"

I just shake my head. "I so don't want to talk about it," I say. "Although it's been a big conversation starter, let me tell you."

Tess squinches up her forehead, shoves a stray strand of blond hair behind her ear, and, when I don't choose to say anything further about the sweater, grabs the plastic fork that's sitting next to her and digs into her salad.

She's got the fork to her mouth when she looks at me again.

"You okay?" she asks. "Honestly, Annie, you're kind of pale. You feeling sick or something? Maybe it's the smell of this cheese." She pokes her fork at the hunks of feta she's extracted from her salad before my arrival. Tess loves to eat, but she's notoriously picky about what crosses her lips. "'Cause it is seriously stinky."

"Not sure," I tell her as I flop down into a chair, unzip my backpack, and pull out my lunch sack. "About me, I mean. Not the cheese."

An hour of chemistry has come and gone, and now it's lunchtime. I've managed to make my way to the cafeteria, where everyone else seems to be ticking along just like always. Tess has picked all the feta cheese out of the Greek salad her mother has packed for her because it's Tuesday and Tess's mother—who lived in Athens her junior year at Brown because she was a Classics major—makes Greek salads on Tuesday. Our friend Sarah, who's sitting across from me, is alternately texting her boyfriend and sipping a strawberry smoothie.

I, on the other hand, am a mess.

My arm no longer aches, but I'm pretty sure the only other time I've ever felt a buzz like the one that shot up my arm when I bumped into Ethan occurred when I was three and David convinced me to stick a My Little Pony barrette into a light socket.

Only that time wasn't accompanied by a full Technicolor flashback of the girl and the creepy metal-teeth lady from my recurring dream. Or a feeling that everything was about to somehow shift in some way that I wasn't sure was good and I wasn't going to be able to stop it when it came.

Before my brother got sick, whenever something would go wrong, my mother would always tell us, "It will be okay." No matter what the problem was—the time in Little League baseball that David struck out five games in a row; my unrequited crush on Jared Pierce in the fifth grade; the time I came down with the flu and couldn't go on the seventh-grade trip to Washington, D.C.—she'd smooth her hand over my hair or rub David's back and say, "It will be okay."

And honestly, it seemed that it always was.

Until David got cancer, that is, and nothing was okay. Then I understood that she'd never really been sure—just hopeful—which is really not the same thing at all.

So now I don't know what to think about what I'm feeling, and I'm suddenly missing my brother with an intensity that actually has tears stinging the backs of my eyes, even though the last thing I plan on doing right now is crying. David, I figure, would know just what to do about this Ethan guy, because that's what older brothers are for. Like I'm certain he'd have pounded the crap out of Adam for plying me with three Jell-O shooters at Emma Hartwell's party last June and then hoping I'd let him take my shirt off which—vodka or no vodka—I *so* wasn't about to let happen.

Although I'm wondering if even David would know how to solve the mystery of a guy who keeps appearing and disappearing and whose touch seems to have the zapping equivalent of a stun gun or something.

"Feta?" Tess has forked up one of the hunks and is sort of waving it in front my nose and then in front of Sarah's.

"Gross," I tell her, but Sarah grabs the hunk of cheese off the fork and tosses it in the garbage can a few feet away.

"Enough with the stupid cheese," Sarah says. She flips her cell closed and stuffs it into the pocket of her jeans. "You are so freakin' compulsive sometimes."

"I just like what I like," Tess tells her, grinning, and all at once, everything feels normal again.

"You are *so* not going to believe who I saw before chemistry," I say as I finally dig my turkey sandwich, apple slices, and bottle of water out of my lunch sack.

"Adam?" Sarah guesses. "'Cause actually, I saw you talking to him while I was headed to physics."

"Well, yeah," I tell them. "I did see him. But it's not him."

"Then who?" Tess asks around a mouthful of salad. She pokes her fork into the plastic container, spears up another tiny crumb of feta, and holds it in front of my face.

"Do you have any attention span?" I swat her hand away. "He's here. Ballet guy. I bumped into him—literally, I might add—right there in front of Mrs. Spears's room. I mean like I crashed into him so hard that I dropped my backpack on my foot. And then we both bent down to pick it up and—"

"Stealthy hot guy?" Tess turns to Sarah. "Seriously hot. Wicked—oops, sorry, I know I promised—hot. He's got this hair and these blue eyes that—well, you just have to see him." She flips back to me. "He's here? At Kennedy? Is he, like, a student? You'd think we'd have noticed or something. What did he say? Did he remember you?"

"What's his name?" Sarah manages to squeeze in the question before Tess can ramble on again.

"Ethan," I say. "He said he was Ethan Kozninsky. But other than that, he didn't say anything. Which I guess is sort of weird, but I don't think I really gave him any time, because the bell was ringing, and besides, when he bumped into me, it was like—"

"Like what?" Tess interrupts again. "Like you leaped on him right there in the hallway and performed your own special little love ballet?" She grins her evil Tess grin and forks up another bite of salad.

"You are seriously so annoying." I chug some of my water, then break off a bite of the turkey on whole wheat and pop it into my mouth.

"Oh that's right," Tess says. "I forgot." She turns back to Sarah. "Our friend Anne here thinks he's a loser because he has über good posture. So," she directs this part to me, "was he standing up really straight today?"

"Ha, ha," I say. I pick off another bite of sandwich—and realize as I chew that, posture aside, I have my own series of unanswered questions about Ethan.

Why was he suddenly here as though he'd dropped out of the sky? Why had he looked at me that way, as if I was the long-lost cousin he'd been looking for or I'd won some super-secret lottery or something? And why was he watching us at the ballet the other day?

Lots of questions, but no answers—especially regarding the electrical buzz, which, because it just sounds so ridiculous, I decide to keep to myself.

I chew another few bites of sandwich. Normally, I'm raven-ous, but I guess today is anything but normal.

"I love this," Sarah says. "I mean, when does something like this ever happen? You see a guy, and suddenly, poof! He's going to your school. It's like a fairy tale or something."

And then, because I've gotten to lunch late and taken up most of it wondering about mystery-guy Ethan, the bell rings.

"I've gotta bolt." Tess tosses the remains of her salad into the garbage. "I've been late to pre-calc five times already, and she is so going to write me up if I'm late again. So save it and tell me at dance this afternoon. And if there aren't enough good details, you can make some up before then."

That said, Tess heads off toward the stairs and Sarah heads off to her sculpture class, because not only is she a dancer but she can create these amazing clay pieces that look like real people.

As for me, I pack up my stuff and start the trek to English class. Then just as I hit the hallway right outside the cafeteria, the buzzing tingle shoots back up my arm like a flame. My hands go icy, the world feels like it's spinning, and I think I might faint. For a few seconds, I have the unmistakable feeling that I'm being watched.

Find her, says a small voice that seems to come from nowhere and everywhere at the same time. *Come for her.* In front of me, something flickers—a quick flash of light that's gone almost as it catches my eye.

The world stands still again. The warning bell rings, people zoom around me on their way to class, and life at Kennedy High trudges on as always.

This is becoming so weird it's not even funny. Not even a little.

But when I look around me—because some part of me that's not freaking out wonders if he has something to do with it—my new pal, Ethan, is nowhere to be found.

My dearest Olga, Tatiana, and of course, my room-mate Maria—

I have begun this journal with our darling Alexei, but it is to you three sisters that I have always told the longings of my heart, and it is to you that I tell the next piece of my tale. For Alexei, my story was about blood, and although blood runs through everything I have to say, it is not that which I will share with you, my sweet, sweet sisters.

I think of you so often, and I wonder if you think of me. Do you remember how headstrong I was? How important it was that I win at card games or my tennis matches, and how we rode our bicycles and raced as fast as we could, daring each other to go faster but not to fall? How I painted silly portraits of each of you and told jokes to make you laugh?

Do you remember, sisters, the life we shared? Our rooms, so filled with color and pictures and all of our little treasures, like the beaded necklaces that Mr. Fabergé so kindly helped us create? Our routines and schedules that were so very important to Papa? Those cold baths we hated that he assured us would build our characters? The dances and the teas and the time when we played charades and I pretended to be Father Grigory, scandalizing the three of you and perhaps even myself, if I am to tell the truth, which I am desperately attempting to do?

But I need to tell you what you do not know. Yes, my darlings, your Anastasia has kept some things from you. I suppose all women have their secrets, and in that sense, I am no exception. Neither, I would imagine, is each of you. Or our dear mother, for that matter. But I have come to believe that some of my secrets are deeper than you might have suspected. And if the entry to Alexei began the tale of a boy who was the other son, then this entry to you continues with the story of that boy grown to manhood.

It is not a love story. Not exactly. Do you remember all the boys you said you loved, Maria? We were always teasing you about your many crushes, weren't we? But I think you might have been surprised to know that I had one of my own, although not in the romantic sense of the word.

So let me say this. He didn't visit often—not after that first time I met him when I was still too young to understand. And as this seems to be a tale within a tale within yet another story, let me tell you another secret first. One that he told me later and made me swear I would never divulge. As our secrets now are just dust, I suppose my promise is of little consequence.

Our father's father, who died the year before Olga was born, did not want Papa to marry Mama. Yes, it is very true. I swear it on my life, such as my life is these days—not what I was, but not what you are either, my dear sisters. To our grandfather, marriage was not something one did for love. Marriage was for power, for alliances, for politics. He wanted Papa to marry someone of French royalty so Russia could strengthen its alliances with France. He did not want Papa to love our mother.

But love, like life and destiny, is a funny thing. Papa loved Mama anyway. Even though she was a Protestant and not Orthodox, and even though she did not know much Russian. He wanted desperately to marry her. And, as you know, soon after our grandfather died, he did, and our family came into being.

But our papa was, I realize now, not always the strongest of men. Certainly, he did not anticipate what was to come in our beloved Russia. But he also did not believe that his father would give in. And so there was a time—before he married Mama—when our papa let himself love someone else. Now, there were rumors that Papa's girlfriend before Mama was a dancer in the Imperial Ballet named Mathilde. And indeed, I think he did court this woman for a time. Maybe he even loved her.

But there was another. I do not know her name or what she looked like, although I would imagine that she had the dark hair and even darker eyes of her son. Her son, who had Papa's chin and Papa's posture and even, I think now, Papa's faith in the impossible— but never Papa's heart.

I know it is not proper for young ladies to speak of such matters. But here is what I know. Unvarnished and plain as the wooden floor beneath me as I write this.

Although Papa waited and waited for a son through the births of each of his four daughters—you, Olga, and then Tatiana, and then Maria, and finally me—the truth is, he already had one. Two years before Papa married Mama, our secret brother was born. It is he I first saw that day in the park when I was five. And it was he who spoke to me again the year I turned ten.

I was walking by Papa's study that day, right after Easter, when I saw him. Right after the Fabergés had made that lovely, new decorative egg for us with all our pictures on it. Alexei was ill again, the three of you were at various lessons, and I was supposed to be practicing the piano, but I was restless that day, and so I had gone wandering.

At first, I thought he did not even see me, because the look on his face was so sad, so serious, that I remember wondering if he was seeing anything at all. But I knew him immediately, even though five years had passed. That handsome, angular face. Those dark eyes that seemed to hold so many secrets.

"Anastasia," he said to me, just as I was certain we would pass without speaking. "You have become quite a young lady."

I smiled at him, not sure of what—if anything—I should say next. And it was then that I noticed his clothing: his long brown robe, and the small, wooden cross that hung on a leather string around his neck.

"I am of the Brotherhood now," he told me. He gestured to what he was wearing, and for the first time, he smiled.

"Like Father Grigory?" I asked him, assuming he would know I was referring to Rasputin.

He made a face at that, which surprised me, even though, as you know, I was never fond of Father

Grigory and always felt uncomfortable when he was with us. Like the face you made, Tatiana, when my spaniel, Jimmy, did his business on the floor of your room.

"Not like that, exactly," he told me. "What I am now is much, much more. That is why I have come back to see your father. That is what I have told him."

"I am sure he was pleased for you," I said.

I saw something angry glimmer in those dark, sad eyes of his. "Perhaps," he said. "Perhaps not. It is hard to say." He thrust his hands into the pockets of his robe as though he wasn't sure what else to do with them. And then he smiled at me again.

"I know a young man whom you would like," he said abruptly. "But he is not for you. And besides, he is a serious sort. And he is certainly not someone your father would approve of." He smiled again, but the smile did not reach his eyes. "But then, Anastasia, your father does not approve of me either. If he did, perhaps a fine portrait of me would grace that lovely Fabergé egg sitting in his study."

He said your and not our, but I think I understood anyway.

"I will tell Papa that he needs to do so," I said, feeling suddenly very bold.

He laughed and said to me, "So. You are Anastasia the Brave, are you not?"

"Yes," I told him, and I laughed too because I knew what he meant. It was, after all, one of our mother's favorite stories to read to us. "Yes," I said again. "Like Vasilisa. I will go into the forest of my father's study and tell him that you are very nice. And if there are any witches in there like Baba Yaga, I will beat them over the head until they are gone."

Oh, sisters, how clever I thought I was being. But he looked at me very oddly. Like he was seeing me, but also seeing something else. "Be careful, little girl," he said. "I have met Baba Yaga. And she is not particularly nice. You would not want to get eaten. Although I do thank you for your kind wishes on my behalf."

And then, sisters, he walked away without another word.

There is yet more to come in this tale, but as I have decided, each piece belongs to one of you, and I must tell it in the order in which it should be told.

Until then, be happy sisters, wherever you are. Remember that we are OTMA: Olga, Tatiana, Maria, and your loving,

Anastasia

TUESDAY, 4:35 PM

ANNE

WHAT YOU NEED," MY MOTHER TELLS ME, GRINNING, "IS THE tiara." She lifts the little silver-and-rhinestone crown from the display case and settles it on my head. I'm already wearing the matching rhinestone bracelet, but as you can never have enough tacky bling, I let her have her way.

We're standing in the Jewel Box, the vintage and estate jewelry shop my mother helps manage. It's a small store just a few blocks from Miss Amy's Studio, where I'm headed for my five o'clock class.

"I am so the princess," I say as I peer at myself in the little mirror standing on the counter. The bracelet is heavy and really kind of ugly, with dozens of rhinestones alternated with marcasite to up the sparkle level. But I like the tiara, because honestly, what girl doesn't have royal aspirations?

And what I really like even better is that every piece in this shop has a story, and everything used to belong to someone else. I guess some people might find that kind of icky—like Tess, for example, who last time she was here with me picked up a pair of intricate, coral clip earrings and commented, "I can just see these on some fat old lady with boobs that look like a shelf"—but I don't mind at all.

I like knowing that there's a story behind this bracelet and tiara and that they used to touch someone else's skin. Maybe even though I think the bracelet is the definition of hideous, some lady somewhere thought it was really pretty—or maybe she didn't, but she wore it once in a while because her husband or lover or whoever had thought it made her look beautiful. All of which, in my opinion, is way more romantic than Adam telling me that my new, pink, Gap scoop-neck T-shirt would look better if he could take it off me.

In any case, my mother and I are alone in the store, because the owner, Mrs. Amelia Benson, is off this afternoon, and currently, no customers are in sight. Mom is cataloging new pieces, and I'm arranging the displays, only the tiara and bracelet were too over the top to pass up, so I convinced her to let me try them on. I stopped in on impulse—something I clearly don't do enough, judging by the level of surprise on my mother's face when I arrived about ten minutes ago. But my day has been just so crazy that I found myself heading over here without even thinking.

Not, of course, that I plan on telling my mother about the whole Ethan thing or the pain in my arm that's still lingering just under the skin like a nagging toothache, or even about last night's dream, for that matter. And I'm certainly not planning on telling her about the voice that echoed in my ears while the whole world started spinning just outside the cafeteria, because beyond the obvious that maybe I just imagined the whole thing, who in her right mind tells her mother that she's hearing voices?

Besides, that's the way it works with us these days. Since David. I don't worry her, and she doesn't push for information.

But it's sort of soothing to just stand here helping her while she fiddles with the jewelry, and I try on tiaras, and she gives directions to someone who called on the phone. "Yes, we're on Second Street. Two blocks from Main, next door to the Wrap Hut and across the street from Java Joe's."

"Where did these come from?" I unclasp the bracelet and then reluctantly lift the tiara off my definitely-not-so-princess-y head and lay them both gently back on the black velvet cloth in the display case where they belong. My mother loves the items' stories too, so I figure it's a good way to draw out this visit a little longer since, ballet or no ballet, I really just don't want to leave.

"Estate sale up in Lake Forest," my mother says. "Kind of sad, really. This woman, Owena McChesney, lived all over the world, collected all sorts of stuff—art, sculpture, jewelry." She smiles as I roll my eyes back at the bling-ilicious bracelet and tiara. "Okay, not all of it is your taste. Or mine. But there's some pretty cool stuff. And now her kids are just basically selling it all off."

There's a small pause, during which I'm absolutely sure that both of us are pondering the knowledge that David's room is exactly as he left it two years ago. Nothing's been moved even an inch, except to dust it. If he'd been a girl with a tiara, it would be right where he—okay, she—had left it.

But as there is nothing either of us can do about that, my mother collects herself and says, "No, really, Anne. There are these Russian boxes she had that Amelia purchased. Lacquer boxes, they're called. We're going to set up a display of them in the front window, I think. Here, I'll show you."

My mother flits into the back room and emerges about thirty seconds later with a small box. "It's Russian folk art," she says and slips the small, rectangular, black box into my hand. "Usually they depict fairy tales or folktales. Isn't it beautiful?"

Unlike the rhinestone bracelet, it really is. It's a little bigger than my palm and very smooth. On the cover, there's a painting. The colors are vivid—all bright reds, greens, and golds. A young girl in a long dress stands in the middle of a thick forest. She's got long, black hair wrapped in a scarf she's got tied under her chin. In one hand, she's carrying a torch of some sort. In the other, she's holding a tiny doll dressed in a similar outfit. Behind her ride three horsemen. The horses' legs are painted to give the impression that they're in motion, moving swiftly through the forest. Each one is a different color, both horse and horseman matching—one white, one red, one black.

"So which story is this?" I ask her. "Do you know?"

She nods. "It's called 'Vasilisa the Brave,'" she tells me. "About a young girl whose wicked stepmother sends her through the forest to get light from a witch. The horsemen are the witch's servants, I think. Each one is a color of a different time of day—red for sunrise, white for morning, black for night."

Gooseflesh prickles my arms at the word *witch*. In my head, I see the old woman with the metal teeth. That jaw unhinging to swallow me whole.

I shake off the image. "Wicked stepmother, huh? Kind of like Cinderella?" I think of Tess for a second because of the word *wicked* while I peer again at the pretty girl on the box. Then I notice something else.

"What's that?" I point to the small hut behind some of the trees.

Mom shrugs. "I never noticed it before. I guess it must be the witch's house." She reaches out to take the box from me. Then, as almost an afterthought, she says, "It opens, you know. The inside is pretty too."

I place my thumb on the front of the box and push, but the lid stays firmly closed. I push again. Clearly, this is the piece that's supposed to lift up, but it doesn't. From the back of the store, I hear the faint sound of a Caribbean-sounding ringtone.

"You know," I say to my mother. "If you keep your cell phone in your pocket, you don't have to run to your purse every time it rings."

"Just watch the front for me."

"Will do," I tell her. "If someone comes in, I'm going to pawn off that god-awful bracelet on her."

My mother makes a face, then hustles to the back to answer her cell.

I poke the box one more time with my thumb. The lid gives a sucking sound, as though it's been glued shut or something. I push again. The top lifts up, revealing a glossy, red interior. Painted in the center is a tiny gold key. I trace it with my finger, feel how it's raised slightly from the rest of the box.

I glance at the wall clock. It's almost five. I really need to dash.

"I've got to run," I say loudly enough that Mom can hear me. I close the lid and plop the box onto the counter.

And then my breath catches in my throat.

Because the hut on the box's front cover—the one I swear had been barely visible behind the thick grove of trees in the painting—is now resting in the clearing.

Even for the weirdness of today, this is absolutely impossible. I blink and rub my eyes, afraid to look down. But I can't

53

help myself. I look again. The hut is back behind the trees, just where it had started.

"Are you okay?" Mom walks back to me. She's looking at me closely, which is never a good thing.

"Fine," I lie. "Just fine. I, uh—fine. I just—I really have to go. I'm late." It is almost exactly what I told Ethan right before chemistry—right after the lightning bolt or whatever it was jolted into me.

"Your father and I have that fund-raiser dinner, tonight, remember?" My mother presses a quick kiss to my forehead. "So I'll leave dinner for you."

I nod at her, which is about all I can manage, words having pretty much dried up in my throat. Then I grab my ballet bag and rush from the Jewel Box and across the street so I can head down the block to Miss Amy's.

I don't look back at the lacquer box. If the hut on the cover makes another move, I just don't want to know.

Nor am I in the mood to realize, as I dash by Java Joe's, that my blue-eyed friend, Ethan Kozninsky, is sitting at a table at the window. Or that although he turns his face when I see him, he's clearly been watching me.

I hesitate for only a second and then let my feet make the decision for the rest of me.

"Hey," I say once I'm inside Java Joe's and standing next to the table where Ethan's sitting.

"Uh, hey." He tilts his head and looks up at me as though he's seeing me for the first time.

"So," I say, "are you following me?"

The question clearly stumps him. He shoves his long fingers through that thick, brown hair.

"No," he says finally. "Um, no. I'm, uh—waiting for my study group."

Other than his cup of coffee, I see nothing else on the table. No backpack at his feet.

He shoves his hand through his hair some more. I should walk out of here and not look back. I should yell, "Stranger!" loudly and point at him like they told us to do in elementary school if we thought someone was trying to kidnap us. But I don't do any of that. The look in those blue eyes—part surprise, part amusement, part something I can't identify—holds me there.

Plus, I'm still sort of collecting my freaked-out self after the lacquer-box incident.

I glance at the clock over the coffee bar. I'm officially late for ballet.

"Enjoying your latte?" I ask him. I'm unnerved and kind of pissed, and also feeling like an idiot right now.

"I—sure," he says. "Are you getting some? Please, sit. I'll get it for you. I know you think I've been rude. Here, really. Sit down. Join me." These are the most words I've heard him string together.

He reaches up and places one hand lightly on mine.

The tingling sensation flickers up my arm again.

My mouth dries up so the words sort of stick to my tongue as I force them out. "No," I manage to say. "Absolutely not."

And before he can say another word, I bolt from Java Joe's.

TUESDAY, 6:05 PM

ANNE

So spill." Tess mops her face, then shoves the towel into her oversized, maroon gym bag. We're sitting together on the wooden bench in the changing room at Miss Amy's. It's been a beast of a class, and we're both fairly rank at the moment, but there's no shower here, so all we can do is towel off the surface layer of sweat and make the best of it.

"Spill what?" I rub my aching feet and wonder idly if I can guilt Mom into doing the mother-daughter spa pedicure thing this weekend. My toes look like they've been through a war. And lost.

"Whatever's up with you, that's what. You are seriously knotted up about something. You have been for a couple of days now." Tess pushes a few sweat-soaked strands of blond hair away from her forehead and slings one long leg over the bench so she can face me. "And don't give me that innocent, 'Who, me?' look. I've known you since we were practically in diapers."

I finish wrapping my ballet slippers and tuck them into my bag. I'm not even sure where to begin. "I'd tell you if I knew," I say. Even as it exits my mouth, it sounds utterly lame. "Really, I would."

She wrinkles her nose. "Liar," she says, but she doesn't push me for more. Instead, she zips up her bag, shrugs into her denim jacket, and stands up. "C'mon, my dad is probably waiting in the car."

Like me, Tess still has just a learner's permit, which means that unless hell freezes over, neither of us can drive without an adult in the car—which also means we have to walk everywhere or bum rides or wait for a parent to pick us up.

I gather my gear, shove my arms through the sleeves of my navy blue hoodie—the one with the Miss Amy's logo and the slogan, "Ballerinas do it better," on the back—and follow her to the front of the studio and then out into the night air. We both look around. Tess's dad is nowhere in sight.

"Figures," she mutters and rummages in the pocket of her jacket for her cell phone. She presses three on the speed dial and taps her foot impatiently.

"Where are you?" she asks when her dad answers. I watch as she nods her head to whatever he's saying on the other end.

"Stuck in traffic." Tess flips the phone closed and shoves it back into her pocket. "He says he should be here in about five minutes."

"Still better than walking," I say. Brutal ballet class or not, I'm still so tense from everything that keeps colliding with me lately that I find myself standing there contemplating squeezing in a run after dinner. Probably impossible since I've got an essay to finish for English, approximately a zillion pre-calc problems to solve, and a large number of Latin verbs to commit to memory for tomorrow's test.

"Well," Tess says now, interrupting my less-than-thrilling mental rundown of the drudgery known as homework, "now that we have a few extra minutes, I say we spend it getting to the bottom of whatever's got your panties in a bunch."

So what do I tell her? That ever since I bumped into Ethan this morning—ever since we saw him at *Swan Lake*, actually—I've felt like all my nerve endings are standing at attention? Like I'm a gazelle on one of those Animal Planet shows—the one that senses something is about to attack but doesn't know where?

Down the street, I can see a crowd in front of Java Joe's. I wonder if Ethan's still there, and why he seems to keep popping up everywhere I am. The usual stream of SUVs and Volvo sedans whiz by us, along with a few hybrids.

"Ethan," Tess says loudly enough to make me jump. "It's mystery hot guy, isn't it? Oh. My. God. Anne. I can't believe that he's got you all wired. I mean, he's cute and all, but geez, it's not like you to get so crazy over some guy you've known for all of three seconds. What are you now? Me?"

"I know—" I begin, but she cuts me off.

"Ha! I'm right. It *is* him, isn't it? Well, we need to take care of this right now. We simply can't have you moping around anymore, looking like you've lost your best friend—which is me, by the way. Remember me, your BFF, the one who knows all your nasty little secrets? Or at least who did till now? Where does he live? We've got time. We'll tell my dad to drop us off. Tell him we've got a study group we forgot about. We can stalk old Ethan. We can peek in his windows. Ooh, we can see him naked, and—"

"Enough." I put my hand over her mouth for emphasis and try my hardest not to laugh. "Enough." Any more of this, and we'll end up lurking in Ethan's bushes—which is sort of funny, if you think about it, stalking the stalker and all—but still not exactly what I had planned for the rest of tonight's entertainment.

"Party pooper," Tess says. "Remember, my dear Anne," she makes a grand gesture with her arms, then executes a full ballerina curtsey in front of me and an elderly woman in a head scarf walking by us, "love has no schedule. And neither," she wiggles her tongue at me, "does lust."

I just shake my head. I see what looks like her dad's Avalon coming up the street. And then I realize that the woman in the head scarf has stopped alongside us.

She's so old. That's the first thing that pops into my head when I look at her. Impossibly old looking. Her skin is brown and wrinkled, her hands veined and broad. And suddenly my pulse kicks up hard and fast, like it's sprinting through me. Her gaze fixes on mine. My skin flushes—a burning prickle that rushes its way up my arms, my throat, my face.

"Anne?" Tess sounds like she's a million miles away.

I'm falling, I think, into those two dark eyes that won't leave mine—eyes dark like pools of oil, a tiny skull in the center of each.

She smiles. Her metal teeth gleam in the twilight.

All I want to do is run. But I can't even move, can't even scream. My heart slaps against my ribs so hard that I think they might break.

"You're the one." Her voice echoes around me, inside me. "You feel us. You know we're there. Now, come to us."

Unable to even swallow, I close my eyes. The world spins dangerously around me, turning and turning.

"Anne." I hear Tess again at my side.

I open my eyes.

The woman is gone.

"You okay?" Tess tilts her head a little and peers at me. "You sort of faded away for a second."

"Did you see? Did you see her?" My voice is tiny and thin, like it's afraid to come out.

"See who? And why are you so pale? Here." She rummages in her bag and hands me a bottle of water. "I think your electrolytes are screwed up or something."

I realize that she hasn't seen a thing, hasn't felt the world turn into one giant carnival ride.

Tess places a hand on my shoulder and looks me in the eyes. The connection feels good, solid. Maybe I really am just tired—just imagining that I saw the crazy, metal-tooth witch lady from my dream here on Central Avenue, staring at me with her skull eyes.

Mr. Edwards pulls up to the curb in his maroon Avalon.

"Whatever it is, Anne," Tess says, one hand on the car door, the look on her face no longer joking, "don't you dare go turning yourself inside out about it. You watched me do that over the summer and you know it wasn't pretty."

She means her summer romance with Neal Patterson, the guy she'd decided was special enough to let divest her of her virginity, and who, according to Tess had sworn he was also a novice to such activities. Except it turned out that he'd used that line on at least three other girls—which, let me say, did not sit particularly well with Tess. "Thank God I made him wear a condom," she'd said of the experience, "especially since the whole thing was over so fast, I barely figured out what he was doing down there in the first place."

"Don't worry," I whisper as she slides into the front seat of the car. "It's not like that. It's just—" I stop in mid-sentence. My heart jolts into my throat again. I wait for the world to start spinning, but nothing happens. No lady. No voices. And for once, no Ethan.

"What is it?" Tess asks from inside the car.

"Nothing. I guess I'm just jumpy tonight."

I climb into the back seat. I take one more look out the back window as we pull away from the curb. A dark sedan that might be a Mercedes is turning the corner about a block behind us. I watch it until it disappears.

"Hi, Anne," Mr. Edwards says from the front seat. "Are we going to pick you up tomorrow morning, as usual?"

"Sure thing," I tell him. Then I sit back, pretend everything is normal, and listen as Tess and her father banter back and forth about nothing much in particular.

"Thanks, Mr. E.," I say when we get to my house a little while later. "See you tomorrow." I slide over to the door and grab my bag. Tess reaches over and gives my free hand one more squeeze. I look at her, and she smiles.

"Be careful, Annie Bananie," she says, using the name she used to call me when we were eight.

"Will do," I assure her, although I'm not sure why she's said it. Do I really have something to be careful about?

They drive off down the block, and I let myself into the empty house. Our tabby cat, Buster, races in from wherever he's been hiding and meows hopefully, rubbing himself around my legs.

"In a minute, Buster," I say to him. "Just let me put my bag down, and I'll feed you." I reach down and scratch his ears. He allows me a few seconds of petting him and then slips away and pads toward the kitchen. I follow.

There's a note on the fridge from my mother, detailing, in her slightly compulsive way, what's available for dinner and how I should go about preparing it. *The leftover spaghetti is in the blue Tupperware on the second shelf of the fridge.* As though I'd be completely flummoxed if the note simply said, *Spaghetti in fridge.*

I pour some Purina in Buster's dish and then snap on the kitchen television to keep me company as I—phew!—manage the task of heating up leftover pasta in the microwave.

A few minutes later, I'm sitting at the kitchen table, scooping the now reheated pasta primavera onto a plate. On the television, E! is showing part three of a special series about celebrity weddings—just the type of mindless distraction I need. Then, as I reach for my fork, I glance idly at my hand—and notice that it seems to be glowing. Yes, glowing—a distinctive, blue and white aura type of glowing. My fork clatters to the table, startling Buster, who runs from his food bowl, an angry look on his little cat face.

I squeeze my eyes shut. When I open them, my hand is—well, just a hand again.

So I sit there while the E! reporter gushes over Angela Kurasowa, baker to the stars, and Buster edges cautiously back to his dinner, and my pasta cools and congeals on my plate. Either this is indeed the strangest day ever, or I'm losing my mind.

Maybe a little of both.

The Forest, Midnight

Anastasia

A T NIGHT, NEXT TO ME, MY *matroyshka* DOLL WHISPERS. I am not Vasilisa, and this is no fairy tale, but still she talks, which is a secret that not even Auntie knows. She is the nesting doll my mother gave me—my mother, who believed, even until the end, that there was more to this world than we could see, although I think those thoughts were part of what destroyed us. Because in looking so intently at what might be, my mother did not always see what truly was.

Like the parts of the *matroyshka* doll herself, the truth is sometimes hidden. Layered so deeply, each piece inside the other, that it's often impossible to see. Even so, I do not question the idea of the doll's speaking. I simply listen.

Be sure to sweeten Auntie's tea the way she likes it, she tells me. *Three sugar cubes should be just right.* Or, *Be kind to Auntie's black cat. Feed it tidbits from your plate when Auntie is not looking.* Or what she tells me tonight, just as I am about to drift off to sleep, hoping the dreams will not come again.

Listen carefully, Anastasia, she tells me, even though her red painted lips do not move. *You must not sleep tonight. You must stay awake and watch Baba Yaga. Promise me, Anastasia. It is important that you know what she does. That you see what she sees.*

Ever so slightly, I turn my head. Across the room in her rocking chair, Auntie stares into the fire, humming some wordless tune I do not know.

I nod. "Yes," I whisper. "Yes, I will." Then, gently, I slide my *matroyshka* under the red and blue quilt. Tuck her away where Auntie will not see. And with half-closed eyes, I watch, and I wait.

The fire burns lower, its embers glowing red in the hearth. Auntie rocks in her chair, hums that same wordless tune. The room is warm, close. I think for a moment that I might drift off to sleep. And then the rocking stops.

Auntie reaches with both hands into the front pocket of the apron she wears over her dress. Her huge, wrinkled, brown hands—the same hands that hold the mugs of sweet tea I bring her. And from inside that pocket, she brings forth a skull.

In the life I used to have, I might have gasped. Certainly my stomach still clenches, and my skin feels flushed with the panic that never really leaves, just recedes from the surface and lets me seem braver than I am. Although in my old life, I would have screamed or run, I do none of those things. Instead, I watch.

She holds the skull, its surface smooth, bone bleached and pale like the twelve skulls that surround this hut. Skulls that stand on wooden spikes in even intervals and remind me, even when I try to pretend that this place is now my home, that I am somewhere I do not want to be.

The skull floats into the fire, the flickering flames dancing in and out of its empty eye sockets.

"*Ya khachu videt!*" Auntie calls to it.

Three times she repeats it. "*Ya khachu videt.*" I want.

I think for a moment of my mother—how she scolded my sister Olga just before Christmas the year I turned thirteen. The year Olga desperately wanted a pair of diamond earbobs. "Do not say that you *want* something," she told Olga. "Polite young ladies say, 'I'd like,' not 'I want.'" And I almost laugh aloud as I imagine my mother standing here, scolding Baba Yaga the way she once reprimanded Olga.

Only then I remember. My mother is dead.

Inside the skull, the flames glow red, then yellow, then blue. Stronger and stronger, they have now become a single ball of fire that swirls and opens. *Ya khachu videt.* I want.

And then, inside the flames, I see him. The man with blue eyes who was there the day I disappeared. The man who was not the one I expected. Not at all. The one whose blue eyes, ever watchful, ever serious, filled with tears as my family died, one by one.

What did he know as he stood there? What had he been told? Did he know the lies I had been fed? Or was he betrayed as well?

"The time is coming," Auntie says. "Soon."

Ya khachu videt. I want. But what I want, I am not certain.

WEDNESDAY, 2:00 AM

ANNE

IT'S THE MIDDLE OF THE NIGHT, AND MY PARENTS ARE SLEEP-ING. I, however, am huddled in my brother David's bed, clutching so tightly at his navy blue comforter—the one that still smells faintly of boy sweat and Lucky cologne—that I think the feeling is going to leave my fingers. I'd curled up here a couple of hours ago, chasing sleep. Sometimes, this helps. Neither Mom nor Dad has had the heart to change this room yet, even after almost two years—as though changing it might erase David even more than he's already been erased. In fact, for a while they didn't even turn off his cell-phone service—not until they got the bill and realized I was calling his phone two or three times a day just to hear his voice when it flipped over to voice mail.

But right now, I'm not sleeping. Far from it. Oh, I was. But now I'm sitting bolt upright, willing my pulse to settle and failing miserably.

She's invaded my dreams again: the girl with the long, brown hair and the white dress spattered with blood. Around her, like last time, people were dying. A family, I realize now. Probably her family—a man and a woman, who I assume were her parents, and some other girls and a boy. Even a couple of dogs. All of them executed. All of them bleeding and screaming and dying.

I still couldn't understand what they were saying, only this time, I did pick out a name. *Anastasia.* The woman I guess was her mother screamed it as she tried to reach for her. *Anastasia.* Over and over as those same two giant, wrinkly brown hands came down from that black cloud that appeared out of nowhere and grabbed her—carried her off as her mother fell to the floor.

But that's not what has me sitting here, certain that I'm not going to fall back asleep anytime soon.

This time, there was one other person in the room. He was standing behind a pillar, clothed in a brown robe. A wooden cross hung from his neck, and his brown hair was long and disheveled. When he lifted his head and stared straight at me, his deep blue eyes burning with anger, fear, and tears, I didn't have to listen for someone to call his name.

I already knew it. *Ethan.*

WEDNESDAY, 2:05 AM

ETHAN

I AWAKE WITH A JOLT, THE MARK ON MY ARM BURNING. IT'S ALL happening faster than I ever imagined it would. Finding Anne has set it all in motion. The mark. The lacquer box that her mother believes came to her through a simple sale, which was, in truth, not simple at all. The hut that moved in ways that only the right girl—the girl who is Anne—could see. The dreams we've both had now of that day in 1918. The moment that Anne's sleeping self looked up and saw me looking back.

All this is good. It is what I have worked toward for so many years. She is the one. I am absolutely certain.

Only there is one problem. She is absolutely nothing like what I imagined.

And I—well, I am behaving nothing like I imagined either. And as I am no longer the inexperienced boy who once crouched in that filthy basement and watched the Romanovs die, said the words that Brother Viktor taught him so that Baba Yaga would come for Anastasia and at least one life would be saved, I would expect things to work differently.

But they're not.

Because, as I've been saying, I'm a *zalupa*. In more than one lifetime, by the way, if my fashion sense and regrettable hairstyle from the dream I've just had are any indication.

Also, because this girl is the most frustrating female I have met in a very long while. For me, that's considerable—long-term relationships are out of the question since I am—well, much more long-term than most.

Even so, I had thought that over the years, I'd figured out some things about women. It is clear now that I was very wrong about that.

"Absolutely not," she told me this evening when I asked her to sit down with me at the coffee shop. "No. Absolutely not." This, of course, after she had asked me if I was following her.

Of course I am following her. I have to follow her. It just hadn't occurred to me that I was so clumsy at it that she'd have noticed.

Still, the time is here, and Anne's power—the power she does not yet know she has—is growing. So I fumble for my cell phone on the table next to my bed and punch in the proper numbers.

I wait as it rings.

WEDNESDAY, 2:30 AM

ANNE

I PULL DAVID'S COMFORTER TIGHTER AROUND ME AND WAIT FOR my laptop to power up. I'm back in my own room now, sitting on my own bed, and my pulse has settled back down to something resembling normal, but I've taken the comforter with me. The weird dreams have come along too. And so, it seems, has Buster, who pads in, looking sleepy, and curls up at my feet. The vibration of his purr tickles my legs.

I guess if I'm going to dream about a witch, I might as well do it with my cat keeping me company.

As for the girl—well, at least now I know her name. Anastasia. I don't have a clue why she's haunting my dreams or why an oddly dressed Ethan just appeared in the middle of the last one, but at least I know who she is.

I log on to the server. I'm pretty certain the Internet is not going to unearth any information on my new mystery buddy, but I Google *Ethan Kozninsky* just to be sure. Nothing.

So I type in the name *Anastasia*—or actually, *Anastasia Romanov.* I'm not an expert or anything, but I know a little.

As long as I can remember, my mother's had this—well, *thing* about Russia. And not just Russian lacquer boxes like the one at the Jewel Box. (Although I'm sure her affection for it would dim a bit if she saw the house on the cover move like I did.) Over the years, she's gone through her Russian cooking phase, which ended after a disastrous episode with borscht; her Russian music phase, which I think is why she originally signed me up for ballet; and more recently, her Russian history and literature phase.

The summer before I turned thirteen, she plowed her way through *War and Peace* and *Anna Karenina*. And during one of her "Let's improve Anne's cultural background" missions, she'd presented me with a copy of *The History of Nicholas and Alexandra*.

But that summer I was more interested in whether or not David's football friends thought I looked cute in my turquoise and white, two-piece swimsuit than in reading about some horribly doomed family from back in the horse-and-carriage days. So I flipped a few pages, looked at the chapter headings, and moved on. I remember some of it: last of the Russian royal families, creepy religious advisor, daughter named Anastasia, tragic ending. Had I known that a few years later, I'd be reliving their assassinations, I might have paid better attention.

I press enter. Within seconds, I'm scrolling through website after website proposing that somehow Anastasia didn't die with the rest of her family. What is this girl? The Russian Elvis?

Not surprisingly, no one seems to be proposing that, instead of getting splattered on the floor with everyone else, she was somehow carried away by a giant pair of ugly hands.

At my feet, Buster yawns, punctuated by a little half-meow, then curls up tighter and continues to purr.

I take a breath, click on another entry, and continue reading.

WEDNESDAY, 2:30 AM

ETHAN

I HAVE FOUND HER, BROTHER." THE WORDS TUMBLE FROM ME as soon as Viktor answers my call, his voice heavy and tired even though it is the middle of the day in St. Petersburg.

"The signs, Etanovich?" he says after a brief silence. "They are there?"

"The signs are right, Viktor. There is no mistaking it. I have found her. Anne. Her name is Anne." I take a breath, shove my emotions—more raw than I had realized—back below the surface. "She is here, Viktor. Right outside Chicago."

For a moment, Viktor stays silent again.

"Chicago?" he says then, and something I can't quite identify edges into his tone. "You are in Chicago? I had no idea, Brother. It was not in the report I received from our contacts. I know we have not spoken, but I thought—I had understood you were still in Paris, Ethan."

He has shifted to my Americanized name. And there is still something in his tone that I know I should attend to, but my story continues to pour from me. "Paris was this summer, Brother. A Slavic languages professor I had met in Budapest was there. He helped me gain access to some documents that—"

"Documents?" Viktor interrupts. "What documents? You have told me nothing of this, Brother." And something I *can* identify edges into his voice—anger.

This time, it's my turn to stay silent. His attitude of superiority is nothing new. It's how our relationship began and—despite the many years that have passed—how it continues. Still, an uneasiness—the same tiny shiver of concern I'd felt a few seconds ago—slips its way up my spine and burrows in. There is indeed something else there, just below the surface.

Even so, what I do next takes me by surprise. I lie.

"The papers were nothing, Viktor," I tell him. "The man was a fraud. I stayed in Paris a few more weeks and then headed to the States."

He clears his throat, seems to consider what I've said. "A fraud, eh? It has happened before, Brother. Remember Rome? No matter. But tell me, how did you end up in Chicago? How did you find her?" His tone is lighter now, but the sense of distraction remains.

"Just luck, Brother," I lie again. "Just luck. I had not been to Chicago for a long time. At the ballet, I saw this girl. I—I felt something, and so I followed her, and now, now that I have met her, I know. The spark was there, Viktor. She is the one." Although I have begun my answer in a lie, it ends in truth.

"If this is so, Etanovich," Viktor says, "then you know what you must do. We have waited a long time, Brother—a very long time. Be certain you are correct. When you are, I will be waiting."

"Yes, Brother," I say—and realize I am talking to dead air.

ANNE

Two hours of research later, the Romanov family stares at me from the photo on the monitor.

Tsar Nicholas, his wife Alexandra, and their children—Olga, the eldest daughter, followed by Tatiana, Maria, Anastasia, and the son Alexis, who they called Alexei. I wonder, as I rub my hand across my eyes, if any of them had a clue what their fate was going to be.

For old-time people, they're all rather attractive. Sometimes in those older photographs, people look kind of wild-eyed, probably because they had to sit still so long for the whole flash thing to happen. It's like the time my Grandpa Sam tried to take a picture of me with his new digital camera: by the time he figured out what button to press—"Is it this one, Anne? This one?"—I looked sort of bored and cockeyed.

There's one person, though, whose picture definitely looks totally crazed and I don't think it's from having to sit too long for a bunch of flashbulbs to go off. That's Father Grigory, also known as Rasputin.

Besides being the poster child for ick, what with the long, greasy hair, squinty eyes, and the whole Hogwarts robe thing, the guy was beyond certifiable, which leaves me clueless as to why the tsarina took his advice so seriously. But she certainly let him do quite the brainwashing job on her and Tsar Nicholas—at least until a bunch of people, including some Romanov relative named Felix Yussupov decided he was not only nuts, but also dangerous. They invited him to a party, fed him enough poisoned cake and wine to kill an elephant, then shot him a bunch of times. Ungracious guest that he was, he refused to die. So they dumped him in the river, where, finally, he drowned.

He might have been crazier than a loon, but he was one powerful whack job, that's for sure. If you believe some of the wilder sources, he wasn't just a priest of some sort, but also this kind of evil magician.

Which, of course, might explain his refusal to die.

I reach down and gently shove Buster off my feet, where he's successfully managed to cut off much of my circulation, and I wiggle my toes to bring back some of the feeling. He blinks at me a few times, then stands up, leaps off my bed, and stalks away. I return my attention to the computer and scroll down from the family picture to one of just Anastasia.

Anastasia. The doomed Russian princess who I've finally realized is the one who's been lurking in my dreams for the past few years.

She looks back at me from her photo—this truly pretty girl with long, curled hair and thoughtful eyes—and I wonder. Did the bullets just bounce off the jewels she had sewn in her clothes, allowing her to escape when the guards got freaked out because it looked like magic? Did someone help her? Or did a giant pair of hands truly swoop out of a thundercloud in the ceiling and carry her away while Ethan, or someone who looked like Ethan, said some prayers in the corner of the room?

Because that's the part I still don't get. Why would I dream that Ethan was there? I'm sure it's just one of those things. Like how last week Tess dreamed she went bowling with Neal Patterson, and then out of the blue, his head popped off, and she used it to roll a strike.

I yawn. It's almost five. I turn off the laptop, close my eyes, and lean back against my pillows. Outside I hear a car coming down the street and the not-so-gentle thump of our morning newspaper hitting the driveway.

I'm dozing off when the pain hits. It jolts through my right forearm—the same arm that brushed against Ethan yester-day—with a force that makes me gasp.

I turn my arm over and look. There's a circular red spot, as big as a quarter, glowing like a little sun. I rub at it, but like everything else that's been happening to me lately, it refuses to go away.

WEDNESDAY, 6:25 A.M.

ANNE

HAVE A GOOD DAY, HONEY." MY FATHER—WHO I HEARD get up to run when I finally dragged myself and my aching arm into the shower—has to catch the 6:50 train into the city, where he's partner at Enright, Vogel, and Michaelson. The last name, of course, is his—Steven Michaelson, Attorney at Law.

My dad used to be this obnoxiously cheerful morning person, singing, laughing, and telling jokes when the rest of us could barely pry our eyes open. But these days it's like the fizz has gone out of him. He still gets up absurdly early to run, and sometimes adds a run at the end of the day too, but it's more of a routine than anything else—as if he's thinking, *If I just keep getting up and running, one morning I'll enjoy it again.*

"Love you, Dad," I tell him. "See you tonight."

He throws me a kiss, shouts, "I'm headed out, Laura," to my mother, and disappears down the stairs.

I've managed to pull on the pair of jeans I wore yesterday, along with the University of Illinois sweatshirt that was draped over my desk chair, and gather my hair into a ponytail. Not exactly high fashion standards, but with the almost-all-nighter, the paranormal antics, and the mark on my arm that's faded some but still visible if I roll up my sleeve, it's the best I can do.

I swipe on a little lip gloss—although I'm sensing that even the Benefit people can't help me much at this point—and head downstairs to the kitchen, where I shove a filter into the coffee maker, scoop a sufficient amount of grounds out of the coffee can, fill up the water, and press the on button. It's going to take a boatload of caffeine to get me through the day.

Then I feed Buster, who crunches loudly as he bolts down the Purina, pour myself a bowl of cornflakes and milk, slice up half a banana—to be eaten plain, not in the cereal where it will get all mushy—and sit down at the table. I may be freaked out and exhausted, but like Tess, I like what I like, and I figure sticking to the routine right now can't hurt.

I'm chewing on a slice of banana when my mother clatters into the kitchen dressed in black pants, a silky, turquoise T-shirt, a black blazer, and black boots.

"Chamber of Commerce breakfast this morning," she says, and then unceremoniously plops the Russian lacquer box from yesterday on the table next to my bowl of cornflakes.

I try not to gag. The piece of banana now tastes like half-chewed sawdust.

"You seemed to like it so much," my mother says as she rummages in the cabinet for a mug and pours herself a cup of the coffee that's finished brewing. "So after you left I bought it for you."

"Thanks," I say. I give her what I hope is a sufficiently enthusiastic smile—one that says, *Gee, thanks so much for the wacky enchanted box from Russia.*

"You're welcome, sweetie." She leaves her mug on the counter, walks over, and bends down to hug me. I reach up and put my arms around her. Tess had said my mother looked less fragile, but I'm not feeling it right now. What I'm feeling under the bulk of her clothes is a thin frame that's gotten even thinner, which doesn't surprise me, since she spends most meals pushing her food around on her plate, trying to reconfigure it so Dad or I won't mention that she's really only taken a bite or two. Just the ongoing fallout of our family of four turning into a family of three.

"You want some coffee?" she asks me as she returns for her cup.

I nod. She grabs another mug, fills it, and brings it to me.

"How was the fund-raiser last night?" I ask her as I push the lacquer box away from me—subtly, I hope—in case it decides to start putting on a show again.

"The usual." She takes a sip of her coffee. "Speeches, stuffed chicken breast, and a silent auction. But we did raise a lot of money."

My parents have recently joined the board of the local chapter of the American Cancer Society, something they initially had some rather loud fights about. Dad had said it made him feel better to do something positive to aid research. Mom had said she wasn't going to use her dead son's memory to get someone to write a bigger check. I had closed my door and turned the sound up on my iPod. But eventually, my mother acquiesced, and thus, last night's banquet.

I nod my head, eat a spoonful of cereal, and then wash it down with a generous sip of my coffee. I've got the spoon halfway to my mouth for another bite when I realize my mother is staring at me.

"Are you okay? Your dad said you were already in the shower when he got up to run." This is typical of my mother's interrogation style: prime me with a gift and coffee, then go in for the kill.

I surprise myself by starting to answer. "Mom," I say. "Do you…did you ever…?" I swish around my tired brain for the right words. If I don't hurry this up, though, she's going to think it's about sex or alcohol.

Of all the things I can think of to be worried about, there's only one that seems safe enough to ask her. "Have you ever dreamed something over and over? Like this dream loop you just can't get out of?"

"Only once," she says, her response so abrupt it startles me. "When I was about your age, actually."

She pauses.

"I used to dream I was Anastasia Romanov," she says. "You remember your history, right? What happened to her and her family?"

I nod. I taste the acid backwash of coffee on my tongue. For a moment, it's so quiet between the two of us that I can hear the clock above the stove ticking.

"I never remembered much when I woke up." She takes a sip of her coffee. "Just that I'd been her when she died and that it was horrible. I'd wake up feeling hollowed out—like an open wound." Her eyes sort of drift as she tells me this. I can see she's thinking about more than just poor Anastasia.

"Must sound crazy," she says when I stay silent.

"Not really," I manage.

She runs a hand through her hair, which is auburn like mine, only with a little more brown. Her gaze refocuses on me. "I guess that's what started my Russia obsession. I figured if I was going to dream about it, I might as well know about it." She smiles. "Hey," she says, and I can tell from the look on her face that she knows we're both thinking about David now and that she's going to say something to change the subject. "Maybe I should try that borscht recipe again. I think I've figured out what I did wrong."

"Please don't," I say. "Anything but that."

"So what did you dream?" my mother asks.

I open my mouth to reply. A horn honks outside. I glance out the window. Tess and her dad are here to pick me up.

"Nothing I can really remember," I tell my mother. "Love you." I'm out the door before she can say what I know she's going to—or at least what she should—which is that I'm not telling her the truth.

"You look tired," Tess's dad says, glancing at me in the rearview mirror when I slide into my spot in the back seat.

He doesn't know the half of it.

WEDNESDAY, 10:15 AM

ANNE

C AN YOU BELIEVE HE'S WITH HER?" TESS WHISPERS. "She's wicked nasty. I bet they're doing it like monkeys every chance they get." Her eyes narrow to a rather evil squint. "And no," she adds, "I'm not taking back the wicked."

I narrow my eyes right back at her but let it go.

We're sitting at a table in a corner of the library halfway between fiction and biography, courtesy of both Coach Wicker and the speech teacher, Ms. Tallie Bozeman, who also directs the Pom Pom squad and whose claim to fame is being able to stand on her head for prolonged periods of time. They've both brought their classes here for research, although given the flirtatious body language they're giving off over by the copy machine, perhaps other factors were involved.

But they're not who Tess is focused on, which is just fine with me, since even the vague thought of two of my teachers having sex is a disturbing mental image I'd rather not have lingering in my brain. Instead, Tess is in full obsession mode over Neal Patterson, who's cozied up in the back of the room, putting the moves on senior Kate Harris.

"Even if he's screwing her brains out," I say to Tess, still keeping my voice low, "you're done with him, remember? And besides, this is Kate Harris we're talking about—the same Kate Harris who did it with the entire starting lineup of the baseball team last spring."

"It wasn't the entire starting lineup," Tess corrects me. "Just the infield."

"Whatever. This is the guy who slept with you and then wouldn't return your phone calls. Why on earth would you care what—or who—he does?"

"Because," Tess says, and I can hear the misery in her voice, "what does that say about me? Is that why he went out with me? 'Cause he thought I was easy? Is that the vibe I give off?"

We've been through this discussion, and various versions of it, many times since August, when the cheating scumbag known as Neal broke Tess's heart. He told her he was one thing and turned out to be another, and then she had to dump his sorry ass, and I guess there's still a piece of her that just can't let that go.

A piece of me too, I suppose, since Tess is my best friend and I hate it that some guy could hurt her like that. "No," I tell her. "You're perfect. He's the jerk, remember? Not you."

She nods, but I'm not sure she's convinced. Tess puts on a good show most of the time, but even she has her moments, and this is definitely one of them.

A wave of exhaustion rolls over me. I've come no closer to figuring out what's going on with me. The mark on my arm is still aching dully, and what little energy I'd had left has now been diverted to Tess's current crisis. And Ethan Kozninsky—he of the blue eyes and stalker tendencies—has yet to make an appearance.

"I'm going to get on the computer now," I tell Tess. "I've got to find three articles about the current elections in Chile.

Just don't look over there anymore. Don't you have something you're supposed to be doing?"

She rolls her eyes. "Nothing I can't do in three minutes on my own computer once I get home."

I know if I walk away and leave her to her own devices that she'll do something—like smack Neal's head with the bust of William Shakespeare resting on top of the reference shelf—that we'll both regret later. So I grab her by the arm and pull her out of her chair.

"C'mon." I push her toward the bank of computers, shove her into an empty seat in the last row, and flop down next to her. "I can get my work done and you can—I don't know, check your email or something."

"You know," Tess whispers, "maybe this whole Neal thing happened for a reason. My Aunt Margie says there are no co-incidences. She says…"

Tess rambles a bit more, but I've stopped listening. *No coincidences.*

How could it not have occurred to me?

"I need to look at something," I say to Tess. My heart gives a little skitter inside me. "Just give me a minute."

I log on to my computer and type in the words *Vasilisa the Brave*, the name of the fairy tale my mother had mentioned. I skim through the first few entries, read the basic story which someone's posted on one of them, look at the drawings of Vasilisa and the witch she has to find.

A violent shiver arcs its way from my toes to my scalp. Because that witch whose hut Vasilisa is headed for on the cover of the lacquer box? She's a close match for the hideous old woman in my dream—the one who paid me a visit in front of Miss Amy's.

I pull up a couple more images and read another version of the story, but they're all the same. The witch is huge with enormous hands, a long nose, and iron teeth. In every picture, she's inside this little hut that stands on chicken legs, and outside are all these spikes with skulls on them. And she's got a name: Baba Yaga.

"Yech." Tess elbows me aside so she can peer at my monitor more closely. "Who's that?" She points at the illustration of Baba Yaga on the screen.

"She's called Baba Yaga. She's a witch in Russian folklore. I've—well, I—"

"We should fix Neal up with her," Tess interrupts, clearly not ready to leave the "Neal sucks" topic anytime soon. "Maybe she could chomp him in two with that metal grill."

"Tess," I say. I put my arm on hers. My heart is now hammering in my chest. I haven't been able to get the words out, but now I feel desperate to tell her. "Stop. I need you to listen. Things have been happening to me. I've been seeing things and hearing things, and that guy, Ethan, he's been—"

"Whoa." Tess looks at me sharply. "Slow down. Ethan? Hot guy? What's he done? And what's it have to do with her?" She gestures to Baba Yaga.

Now that she's listening, I barely know where to begin. "She's on the cover of this decorative box—lacquer boxes, they're called—that my mom gave me from her store. Well, not the witch, but her hut. And a girl named Vasilisa. She's on the cover too. It's a Russian fairy tale. Vasilisa's wicked stepmother sends her to get light from Baba Yaga's hut. And so she travels through the forest with just her doll for company. The doll talks to her and helps her so she can get to Baba Yaga's and escape. 'Cause most kids who go to Baba Yaga's end up getting eaten. But not Vasilisa. She's too smart to get caught."

"And what's with the poultry motif?" She points at the chicken legs on which the hut is standing.

"I don't know yet," I tell her. "I think it may be—"

"It's so she can move the hut from place to place," says a deep and familiar voice behind us. "So she can elude her enemies. Have a world without set boundaries until she chooses to set them."

The mark on my arm gives a sudden, intense throb of pain. Tess and I whip around.

Ethan is standing behind us. He's got on the same brown leather jacket he was wearing yesterday. He's looking at me with those blue eyes that Tess keeps telling me are so attractive.

"Who the hell are you?" I ask him.

"Ethan," he says.

"Yeah, I got that part," I tell him.

I don't know whether it's stray traces of righteous indignation at Neal and his crappy behavior toward my best friend, or lack of sleep, or just plain old fear at all the weirdness that has barreled its way into my life. Maybe it's a combination of all of those things. But now I'm angry. And I'm really certain that whatever is happening to me, Ethan is connected.

"I'm asking you again," I say. My voice is louder than I'd like it to be, but I have no patience to control it. "Who are you? First we see you at the ballet. But you disappear before intermission. Then I bump into you yesterday—and you know, right now, I'm not even sure that it was my fault—and since then, everything in my world has gotten totally weird."

"It has?" Tess asks. I've almost forgotten that she's still sitting next to me.

I ignore her and go on. It's like there's a flood of words that has to flow out of me, and I can't do a damn thing to stop it. "I've had these dreams that no sane person would ever have. And guess what? You've been in them. And my hand—I almost forgot about my hand. Last night, my hand starting glowing."

"Seriously?" Tess is looking at me like I've gone totally crazy, which is about how I feel right now. "You didn't tell me this. Why didn't you tell me this? Are you saying that—"

"Not now," I tell her. I turn back to Ethan.

"You know that, don't you?" Although I know it's true when I speak, I'm still shocked when he nods his head yes.

"I can explain," he says. "If you'll just come with me, I'll explain—"

"Come with you?" I can hear my voice getting shriller by the second. "Come with you where? Back to 1918 Russia and the Romanov assassination? To some witch's hut in the forest, where she can chew me up and spit out my bones? To wherever—"

Oh my God. This absolutely cannot be happening. I stop and turn back to look at the screen. Her hands. Baba Yaga's enormous hands.

I look over my shoulder at Ethan. "It's her." I jab my finger at Baba Yaga's picture on the screen. "It was her hands that came out of that cloud and swept up Anastasia."

"Yes," he says evenly. He steps a little closer. "I need to explain. And you need to calm down. We're drawing a crowd here."

It's the longest string of words I've let him get out. And he's right. Coach Wicker has stopped flirting with Ms. Bozeman and is looking at us, clearly trying to decide if it's worth coming over. Even Neal and Kate have come up for air.

The mark on my arm gives me another intense jab of pain. I place my hand over it. Ethan places his hand over mine. The look on his face is fierce and focused, but his touch is surprisingly gentle. I can feel the warmth of his palm against the top of my hand.

"It'll be okay," he says softly. "You just need to trust me."

"It was just a dream, right?" My cereal and banana threaten to reappear.

"No, Anne, you know it wasn't just a dream."

"What wasn't just a dream?" Tess is looking from me to Ethan and back again. "Have you two taken a whole lot of drugs or something? What the hell are you talking about?"

"And the hut that moved on the box?"

"You saw what you think you did." Ethan's hand is still pressed firmly over mine. His gaze is boring into me.

"That's impossible," I tell him. "Things like that just don't happen. Objects in pictures don't just move on their own. Giant hands don't swoop down out of the air and grab people."

I yank my arm away. "C'mon," I say to Tess. "We need to get our stuff. The bell is going to ring." I half-drag her back to the table to get our backpacks. She keeps turning around to look at Ethan, who follows behind us.

"What's going on?" she says to me. "I don't understand. Were you two talking about the lacquer box your mom gave you? What's that got to do with the Romanov assassination?"

"Nothing," I hiss at her as the bell bleats overhead. "Just ignore him." I hustle Tess out of the library with Ethan behind us. "Listen," I say, whipping around to face him. "You need to leave me alone. Whatever it is you think you need to tell me—well, don't. Keep it to yourself. Whoever it is you think I am—your long-lost cousin or true love or date with destiny or whatever—it's not me. So get lost."

"I wish it were that simple," he says. "Anne, I—"

"What's going on here, Anne?" Coach Wicker strides over, having chosen this particular moment to pay attention to something other than football or hitting on Ms. Bozeman. "And you." He turns to Ethan. "Where do you belong, young man? I'm sure there's somewhere you need to be that's not here bothering these young ladies."

I've got an out here if I want to take it. All I need to do is tell Coach Wicker that Ethan is acting like a deranged lunatic and the academic cavalry—or at least the grossly overweight campus police officer—will come to my rescue. Whatever happens next, or whatever it is that Ethan wants me to know or understand or do, will no longer be my problem. I'll head on to chemistry like I did yesterday, and I'll balance some equations or cook something in a test tube, and then I'll eat lunch with Tess and maybe Sarah.

But that's not what I say or do at all.

Because when I look over at Ethan—who's standing there watching me with those ridiculously blue eyes—something inside me shifts. I don't know if it's his eyes or the sound of his voice. I'm no less angry and no less scared. But all at once, I simply believe him.

I stand very still, not at all sure what I'm supposed to do.

Next to me, Tess looks confused. Around me, students are racing to their classes, talking, laughing, and going about their days like always. But my entire universe has reduced itself to this moment.

"Anne, please," Ethan says. "Please."

And just like that, I take a breath and make my choice.

"It's okay, Coach," I say. "Just a friendly little argument. It's over now."

To his credit, Coach Wicker doesn't seem to buy this. "You're sure?" He looks at me closely. "What were you two arguing about?" He directs this last part to Ethan. Personally, I can hardly wait to hear his answer.

Ethan opens his mouth, but Tess speaks first. I've leaped into the fire, and it seems she's leaped in after me.

"It's my fault, Mr. Wicker," she says. "I bet Ethan ten bucks that Anne wouldn't go out with him. Told him that she's got better taste than that. And I was right. She just told him to piss—uh, bug off."

I stand there staring at her like she's lost her mind. She raises one eyebrow and then holds out her hand to Ethan. "Pay up," she tells him.

He just sort of gawks at her for a few seconds, then digs in the pocket of his leather jacket and hands her a slightly crumpled ten-dollar bill. She folds it up and stuffs it in the back pocket of her jeans.

"All right," Coach Wicker says then. The fact that he's fallen for this little charade is not raising my opinion of his intellect. "All of you need to get to your next class. Now."

We do as we're told. Or at least we move around the corner and out of sight.

"Okay," Tess says to Ethan. Her voice is ice. "I saved your ass back there, but enough is enough. Now you really do need to shove off. She told you she didn't want to go with you."

"Is that what you want?" Ethan reaches over and pushes my

sweatshirt sleeve up, revealing the mark on my arm. "You really believe that this means nothing? That those dreams mean nothing? That none of this is happening? Are you really going to continue to delude yourself?"

"Okay, you've got five minutes to explain yourself," I tell him, and Tess gasps. I point to the outdoor courtyard, now completely empty since everyone but us has made it to class. "We'll go out there where it's quiet, and you'll explain. And then we'll see."

"You've got to be kidding, Anne," Tess says. "He's crazy. What the hell are you doing?"

She's right, of course. He is crazy. But so, it seems, am I.

"I'll be fine, Tess. You go to class. I'll see you at lunch. Go on. What can happen in the courtyard in broad daylight?"

"I don't like this," she says. But she doesn't stop me from following Ethan outside to the bench in the corner of the courtyard.

He'll explain himself, I think. *This is all just some bizarre coincidence or something.* I mean, it's just like I told Tess. What could happen in a courtyard in the middle of campus?

Of course, it's then that a strange buzzing sound fills my ears. The wind whips up, a black cloud appears out of nowhere, and a giant, wrinkled pair of hands dips down and tries to grab me.

"Run!" Ethan shouts. He yanks my hand.

There's no time to think. I let him pull me across the courtyard, back through the front lobby, and out the door to the street.

WEDNESDAY, 11:00 AM

ETHAN

BLACK CLOUDS ARE SWIRLING IN A MASS OVER THE COURTYARD. I don't let go of Anne's hand as we keep running, putting distance between us and the school. Between us and Baba Yaga. Or rather, between us and her hands.

"Look!" Anne has turned her head, looking back at the school. "It's still there. Ethan, it's still there."

"I know," I tell her. "Just keep moving." I point to a small park a block ahead of us. "Up there. Go there."

She's still keeping up with me as we reach the edge of the park with its couple of swings and benches.

"Stop," I say. "I need to—just stop. Here. It'll be okay." I feel her hesitate, but we both stop running and turn around.

Above us, the black mass of cloud grows larger.

I fumble through my memory for a spell, a protection—something, anything—to keep this thing from us. I stretch my arms out and utter what I can remember, but even as I'm doing so—and certainly long before my absurdly feeble efforts at this moment can affect anything—we both watch as the hands float back up into the sky and slip back into the clouds. Then, with an audible blip, the sky seems to open and swallow the whole thing.

Just like that, it's gone.

"Did you do that?" Anne's voice is edged with what seems to be a potent mixture of fear, relief, and anger. The anger, I would presume is fully directed at me, the person who has gotten her into this whole mess.

"I—uh, I don't think so. I started to do something, but then it was just gone. I think we're okay for now."

"Okay? You think we're *okay*? We are so far from okay, it's not freakin' funny!" She glares at me. "Is it going to come back? Are we safe? And was that what I think it was? The giant hands of a witch from some fairy tale? How is that possible? And once again, let me ask you, who the hell are you?"

Who am I? I'm the *zalupa* who thought he could handle all this. Who had been convinced up until this moment that he knew the exact sequence of events that was supposed to occur. Our magic had compelled Baba Yaga to take Anastasia and protect her. I'm one of the good guys. The one who, after all these years of searching, has found Anne so that we can finish this thing and free the grand duchess.

So why are we being attacked?

I look around us. The park is empty. "C'mon," I say to Anne. "Let's sit, and I'll try to explain." She nods and walks with me into the park, although I can see by her face that the last thing she'd like to do right now is sit and talk to me.

We settle ourselves on one of the wooden benches. For the moment, this park, with its swings and sandbox, its wide, wooden benches, seems safe.

"Look," I tell her. I shrug off my jacket and roll up my shirt-sleeve. Her eyes grow wide as she sees the mark on my arm that mirrors her own. She gasps, and then she reaches out to touch it.

"It sort of burns," she says, pulling her hand away. She reaches out again and once more runs her fingers over the mark. "I—I still don't understand," she says. "I need to get back to school. I can't just sit here in the park. I'm supposed to be in chemistry. I—"

"We're connected, you and me." I reach over gently and remove her hand from my arm. "It's—well, it's a bit of a story. It may take a while for you to understand all of it."

I'm feeling a little better about all this. She's calmer. I'm calmer. We're going to feel our way through this, and maybe everything will work out.

Then the expression on Anne's face shifts. "Understand what?" Her voice is pitched higher than I'd like it to be. And she's glaring again. "Why I dreamed that you were some turn-of-the-last-century guy with really bad hair who was there praying or something while the whole Romanov clan was getting murdered in a basement in Russia in 1918? That was just a dream right? Or do you want me to believe that you were really there when a giant pair of really ugly hands reached out the sky and took Anastasia away? The same hands which, let's not forget, just tried to kill us back there? Or maybe you want me to understand what my role in all this is? What are we now, two little supernatural mark-on-the-arm buddies who are supposed to spring Anastasia from Baba Yaga's hut?"

"Maybe," I say, "the explanation won't take so long after all."

She stands up from the bench, pulling on her backpack that she'd placed on the ground as we had sat down. "I'm right? I can't be right. I mean, if I'm right, then I shouldn't have just— You can't possibly have been there then and look exactly the same now. What would that make you, like a hundred years old or something?"

I smile at her. "Something like that. There's a bit more to it. If you'll sit back down, I'll—"

"You'll what? You know, I'm rethinking this. You just sit here and do whatever you need to, and I'm going to—"

"Shh." I hold my hand up and look beyond her to the street behind the park. "Just a second." A bad feeling washes over me. Really bad.

"What is it?"

I don't answer her. I'm too busy watching as a black limousine pulls up to the curb. One of its doors swings open, and it occurs to me that while I might be one of the good guys, I'm no longer sure about everyone else.

"Run!" I yell to Anne as she stares at me with a startled look on her face. I grab her hand and pull her behind me. "Run!"

She hesitates for only a second, then follows me. I can hear the thumping of her backpack as it slams into her while we sprint across the playground, leaving a wake of scattered gravel behind us.

I know I shouldn't slow down to look, but I can't help myself. Behind us, just as I'd expected, two men clad in black dusters are advancing on us at a swift pace.

We zigzag through the park, Anne's dancer's legs pumping to keep up with me, then sprint down the tree-lined street in the opposite direction of the school. I can see my car not too far down the block.

"Over there!" I shout as I half-guide, half-drag her the last few steps to the Mercedes. With my other hand, I search my jacket pocket for the remote. My fingers find it, and I press the top button. I yank open the passenger door and shove Anne inside. Then I race around the car to the other side.

One of the men is completely unfamiliar to me. But the other—the other is someone I haven't seen in a long while. And unfortunately, it doesn't look as if he's interested in having tea and getting reacquainted.

This time, when I reach my arms out, I don't fumble for the words. My brain clears of everything but the spell. I can feel the power surge through me as the magic does its work.

The air around me crackles, and I watch with a solid satisfaction as the thin blue flames fly from my fingertips and meet their mark. In front of me, the two men—the one I know and the one who is a stranger—kneel on the street, doubled over in pain. On the ground next to the stranger, a pistol lay, glowing a deep red.

I yank open the driver's door, climb in, turn the key in the ignition, and throw the car in gear. *This is not good,* I tell myself. *Not good at all.*

Next to me, Anne inches up from where she's been crouched on the floor and settles herself into the passenger seat. She glances briefly behind us, then at me.

"Oh my God," she says. "Oh my God. They were trying to kill us. Do you know them? Why were they—? And you? What did you just—I mean, are you—?"

"We need to get out of here first," I say. "I need to keep you safe. And you're not safe until we put some distance between us and them."

She nods and looks behind her another time.

As for me, I breathe in deeply, trying to slow my heart from slamming its way out of my chest. Then I steer the car around the corner and head west.

THE FOREST, LATE AFTERNOON

ANASTASIA

THE HANDS CRAWL SWIFTLY AND STEADILY ACROSS THE shining wooden floor. Auntie Yaga sits in her rocker, waiting. She holds out her arms, the sleeves of her brown dress empty and limp. She gestures to the hands, the ends of her sleeves flopping up and down as she does so.

Obediently, as I have seen them do many times before, the hands continue their passage. Up, up Baba Yaga's skirt they climb, up her legs, over her lap, and then, with a twisting motion, back into her sleeves. She smiles her hideous, gleaming smile. Her eyes glow deep and black, like two coals.

The house settles around us, its two hen's legs shuffling for a foothold amid dead leaves and piles of twigs and branches, curved and knotted like so many broken fingers.

"I let them compel me," Auntie Yaga says. "I let myself fall prey to their magic. Gave my power to men who dabbled in spells—men whose pride let them believe they could alter what no man should alter."

She stands, and with an odd grace, drifts across the room to me. My pulse skips a beat as she rests one of her hands—the same hands which have just returned to her from wherever they have traveled—on my head.

"But how could I do otherwise?" she says as she gently strokes my hair. "You are safe here. You are alive. And they are coming for you now, Anastasia. I did not believe he would keep his part of the bargain. But he has done what he set out to do. Ethan, they call him now. The one with the blue eyes. He has found the young woman who can take you back. Her name is Anne. Not that different from your own.

"I have seen her. Spoken to her. Tried to bring her to us now. Save her as I've saved you. But they ran from me. They do not understand the truth of what is happening. They do not see the danger."

We stand in silence for a moment. In the hearth, the fire crackles. I wait for Auntie to reach into her pocket. To remove the skull and bring forth the visions. But she does not.

"Look into my eyes, child," Auntie tells me. I bristle at being called a child. But to Auntie, seventeen is just that: a handful of years, inconsequential as dust.

I do as she tells me. Stare into those glowing black coals. In each pupil, a tiny skull appears. It is as though I am falling into her eyes, falling and falling until there is nothing but darkness. Her gaze consumes me.

"Watch," Baba Yaga tells me. "Learn."

In Auntie's eyes, a man sits at a table in what must be a restaurant, for there are many tables, each with a snowy white table cloth. He reaches into his jacket and removes a small, black device. He opens it, jabs at it with his fingers, and waits, tapping his other hand against the table. An impatient sound—the sound of a man who is used to getting his way. Then he speaks.

"You will stop him," he says. "Remember, he is holding something back. He has not told me everything. His betrayal is a surprise, Brother, but it is not something we—you—cannot handle. You are at an advantage. Ethan does not know I am here. He thinks I am still in St. Petersburg. Let us keep it that way."

He closes the device and slips it back in his jacket.

A waiter approaches and sets a plate in front of him. On it rests a cut of meat so thick, so large, it fills half the plate. The waiter steps back. I have seen this behavior before—the deference of servants to my father. Waiting to see if his meal is well cooked, his wine of the correct vintage, his every need met. My father was like the man I am watching—a man who looks at the world as if it owes him its bidding; who likes his fine surroundings, his comforts.

In that instant, I know what Auntie meant when she said they do not understand. For who could understand that this man—this man who I think is determined to stop the one Auntie says is now called Ethan—is not who he appears to be. That while he may enjoy the world of luxuries, they are not what he was born to. Not exactly. But they are what he has wanted for as long as I have known him.

Another waiter appears with wine, pours a taste in a goblet. Viktor sniffs, approves, then drinks with pleasure.

Viktor: the man I called my secret brother. The man who told me my family would be safe. The man I trusted.

"Enough," I say to Auntie. My voice breaks as I speak. It has been a very long time since I have cried.

But now I weep.

WEDNESDAY, 12:15 PM

ANNE

"DRINK." ETHAN PLACES THE STEAMING MUG OF TEA ON THE small wooden table in front of me. "It will help."

"I doubt it," I say, but I pick up the mug anyway and sniff. It's fragrant—like orange and some kind of spice—and when I take a sip, the tea is hot on my tongue.

"I've got honey," he says. "Maybe some sugar too. Let me look..."

"It's fine," I say. "It's fine."

We're in the kitchen of his loft in an older area on the far side of town. It's one of those places that used to be all factories and warehouses and is now slowly turning residential, *slowly* being the operative word here. I'm very clear on the fact that I'm alone in a loft with him in a basically isolated area, and that the only reason I've let him bring me here is because we were chased by a giant pair of hands, after which some guys started shooting at us, and he's assured me—oh, right—that we'll be safe.

Ethan's said more than once that he's going to explain, but so far what he's done is make me a cup of tea, which involved boiling water in a kettle, packing loose tea leaves in a metal-strainer thing, and then combining the two in an actual teapot before pouring it into my cup.

"Are you going to drink some too?"

"I—well—yes," he says, and it's clear he wasn't going to, but he walks over to the open shelves above the sink, pulls down another mug, and fills it with tea from the pot. Then, mug in hand, he sits down across from me.

"Is this how you always make it?" I ask. "I mean, this whole tea ritual?"

"It's not a ritual. It's tea. That's how it's made."

"Not in my house. We use a tea bag."

"Well," he says. And takes a swallow of tea.

He's performed another ritual since we arrived, but that didn't have anything to do with tea. It did, however, involve some more of the muttering and hand waving he seems to know so well. Warding is what he called it.

As in magic. As in something that, up until this morning, I really didn't believe existed.

As in, *Anne, I've warded the doors and windows, so we should be safe.*

Not that I'm feeling any great confidence about that at the moment. In fact, I'm doing my best not to freak out and just start screaming. The nine thousand *OMG where r u?* text messages from Tess on my cell phone aren't helping matters.

Neither is the fact that since the warding process, I haven't been able to get sufficient reception to text her again after my initial, *I'm ok. Talk 2 u later,* that I punched in when we got here. Now, I've given up on it, and my phone is tucked into my backpack, which is currently sitting on the floor at my feet.

We both take another few sips from our mugs. I glance around. I can see a bed over in a far corner, one of those armoire things where you can store clothes, a chest of drawers, a door that looks like it leads to a bathroom. A few other chairs. A laptop on a low table near a leather couch. Not really much else. If he lives here, he's been living pretty pared down.

"Okay," I say. I set my tea back on the table. My pulse is bumped up enough that I can feel it in my throat. "Talk. Tell me what all this means. Explain to me why I shouldn't just run from here screaming. Which, by the way, I'm not sure I won't do at some point anyway."

"It's a long story," he says. He takes another sip of his tea. "But the main thing is that you're—"

"No." I hold one hand up. "Not the part about me. Not yet. I—I need the whole story. I need to know who you are. Why you're here. Why I should possibly believe a word you're telling me."

"You need to believe because it's true," Ethan says.

"I'll be the judge of that. Start at the beginning. It's not like we're going back out there anytime soon."

He rests his thumb on his lip for a moment, like he's thinking that over. Studies me with those blue eyes of his.

This is all just crazy, I think. He's crazy. And I am too for ever listening to him. All this Anastasia stuff, and witches with removable hands, and huts that move on chicken legs. No one wakes up and suddenly gets swallowed by a fairy tale.

For a second, I think I really am going to scream, then try to find a way out of here—only Ethan finally begins.

"You must understand," he says, "that what I'm telling you happened a long, long time ago. That I am—well, you will see. It isn't a simple story in that way. But the beginning—well, it's not so complicated."

"Accepted," I say. "Now talk."

"I grew up in Russia," he says. "When I was ten, the Cossacks rode into our village. I had gone to the market for my mother. She was pregnant again, and my younger sister, Masha, was ill. It was harvest time, so my father was out in the fields.

"When I got home, I found them. Masha was dead, stabbed by Cossack swords. My mother lay on top of her, her belly sliced open."

Ethan sips again at his tea. His long fingers—the same fingers that wove the air as he performed the magic earlier—tighten around his mug.

"I was still on the floor holding them when my father ran in from the fields. I begged him not to go after the men who had done this. But he would not listen. How could he? His wife, his babies, were gone. I don't think he even really saw me as he turned and ran out the door."

He pauses. I can tell that he's seeing it again. That however long ago it was, there's probably never enough time to shut out that kind of hurt. And I get that. I might not understand all the rest of this. But that part, I get.

"When I caught up with him," Ethan says, and I can see the pain in his eyes as he remembers, "it was too late. He was stabbed from behind. The Cossack who killed him never even dismounted—just ran him through, pulled out this sword, and rode on. So there I was, orphaned at ten. In a few short hours, I had lost everything."

Ethan rakes his long fingers through his hair and looks at me. He takes another drink of tea.

"After that," he tells me, "I wandered from village to village. I lived with some cousins for a while, but when they could not even feed their own children, they closed their door to me. Winter was coming. I had the clothes on my back, a hunting knife that had been my father's, and the memories of my family's dead faces.

"And then," Ethan says, "I met Brother Viktor."

"Brother? Like a monk or whatever? You mean that's why you had that robe on in my dream? Is that what you are?" Tess, I figure, is going to be pretty disappointed. So much for her stealthy, hot-guy fantasies if Ethan is in some sort of weird religious order.

"Was," he says. "Then. And for a long time. I was a believer then. Now, I suppose it is much harder to say. But yes, Viktor was of the Brotherhood. And for a time, so was I."

Ethan stands then. He walks back to the counter, picks up a small, covered cup and a spoon, and carries them back to the table.

"I like it sweeter," he says, pointing to his tea. "In Russia, we liked sweet tea. My father used to put a cube of sugar between his teeth so it would sweeten each sip as he drank it."

I wait while he stirs in a couple of spoonfuls of sugar and shake my head no when he offers some to me. I know he's stalling. But I also know how it is to have a story you just don't like to tell.

"Viktor was older," Ethan says then. "About ten years older than I. Maybe a little less. He saw me trying to steal some potatoes from a vendor's stand in the marketplace of a town I'd wandered into. When I failed, he followed me back toward the forest. I can still see his long robes billowing as he chased after me. I though he was some sort of officer, come to arrest me.

"But he didn't. He offered me some bread and cheese and told me he knew what I'd suffered. Somehow, I felt he did. He told me he could stop the violence raging through Russia.

That there was a group, a Brotherhood, dedicated to protecting our land and destroying the forces bent on corrupting it. If I joined them, he said, I could do this too. I could protect other families, protect the tsar and his family from the evil that had tried to speak in his name."

"You believed him?"

He nods. "Perhaps I shouldn't have. But I was young and I was frightened. And I was alone. Viktor seemed to be offering a lifeline. I don't remember that I even gave it much thought, although later I knew I should have. I just took it. And I was grateful."

He stands up and paces back toward the counter, leans against it.

The mark on my arm sends out a sudden jolt of pain. I rub it and try to make it go away. Ethan watches but doesn't comment. Then he continues.

"I had nothing," Ethan says. "He offered me—everything. And so I accepted.

"I was fed, clothed. I learned Russian history and philosophy and literature. I studied theology. And I was taught the ancient magic."

"Exactly how much magic?" Even as I ask the question, I'm not really sure I want to know.

"Enough," he says simply. "Mostly basic protection spells. Some a little more complicated. A few more dangerous than that." His blue eyes darken a bit at that last part.

He knows I can see that there's much more to this than he is letting on. But I keep quiet—for now.

"It's not something I enjoy. But it is something I have learned to use—when I need to."

"Like back there, in the park, with those men?"

"Yes," he says. "Like that." He looks at me closely—and then closer still. "You know I didn't kill them, don't you? Just slowed them down a bit so we could get away."

"All right," I tell him. "So you're this monk—well, former monk, I guess, who knows some magic. And your job was to protect the tsar."

I pause because, let's face it, I know what happened to the Romanovs, and I'm sensing that protecting the tsar and his family is probably not high on the super-secret Brotherhood success stories list.

"But the dreams, Ethan. And these marks on our arms. And my hand glowing. Where does all that—where do I fit in to this story?"

"It's coming," Ethan says. He walks back to the table and sits down again. He leans his elbows on the wood and clasps his hands together so that, for a second, it looks like he's praying. "I just need you to see all the pieces. Hell, at this point, I think I need to see them again too. Because even after I'm done telling you this part, I still have to figure out who—or what—is after us. And why."

"Figure out? Like, you really don't know?"

"Like, I need to finish telling you so you'll understand." There's an edge to his tone, but he smiles at me.

"Sorry," I say, even though I'm pretty sure he knows I'm not. "It's just taking a long time."

"You're young," he says, as though that explains it.

"Getting older," I tell him. "So go on."

"A few years before the Revolution, Brother Viktor began to talk of a prophecy. He spoke of forces corrupting Russia from within—dangerous forces that would do anything to destroy the tsar and his family. They were everywhere, he said, even within the Brotherhood itself.

"I found nothing shocking in the idea of a corrupted Russia. How could I when my family was murdered in cold blood? But that this corruption had somehow seeped its way into the sacred Brotherhood? I wasn't sure what to think. These were the men who had taken me in, fed me, protected me. Could one of them—maybe more than one—really be my enemy?"

"Was it that Rasputin guy? I mean, from what I read, he seemed to have a bunch of control over the tsar's wife. And the way he died—all that poison and being shot, and then finally they had to drown him in the river. He certainly sounds like a candidate for corruption. Not to mention a makeover. That whole robe and hair thing—not exactly working for him."

Ethan reaches up and smooths his own hair, then grins at me, which I guess is a good sign, or at least a sign that he knows how he looked back then.

"You've done some research," he says. "But no, it wasn't Father Grigory. You are right—the tsarina trusted that crazy fellow, mostly, I think, because he offered her hope for her son, Alexei."

"I know," I tell him. What I don't say is that I've also seen what it's like for a mother when she realizes that she can't save her son.

"So who then?" I sit up straighter and roll my shoulders a bit, trying to relax my muscles.

"We never did know for certain," he says. "I suspected a younger monk, Ivan. He'd become strange, avoiding Viktor, refusing to take his meals with the others. He would stay away from the monastery for weeks on end and come back wild-eyed, as if he hadn't slept in days. Right before the assassination, he simply disappeared. And then—then things changed, and there was no point in looking for him."

Somewhere outside, a car honks, and we both look toward the window across the room. I'm not sure what *he's* thinking, but I know what's going through my head. *How in the world can he really be as old as I think he is?* Of course, I haven't looked in a mirror since this all started. It's possible that he's looking at me and thinking that I look about a thousand right now.

I push my bangs off my forehead. I just can't get my head around this. Even if he is old but looks young, why? How?

"Then what?" I ask him. Suddenly I'm even more impatient to hear the rest of it.

"Eventually it didn't matter. The Revolution was coming, and nothing—not even magic—was going to stop it. But Viktor told us there was one slim hope. He said there was a chance that we could save one person. That there was magic, old magic, that could help us. If we used them, we might be able to keep at least one member of the royal family safe."

"It was Anastasia, right? The one. I mean that's horrible. But she was the one, wasn't she? That's what people have said all along, anyway. There are all those rumors that she's not dead. People think there's this whole conspiracy or something. Only now—what I asked you back in the park—you're telling me it's true, just not how people think?"

Ethan nods. "Yes," he says, "she was the one. I didn't question that part of it. I mean, why her, and not one of her sisters or the boy? It simply was going to be her, and we all knew it. But even with that, Viktor told us this act would not be possible without a price. I suppose that's the way of the world, really, isn't it? I mean, in my experience…well, there's always a price. And mine—well, mine was my life."

"Your life? But you're not…"

"Dead? No." Ethan smiles at me. "Very much alive. And, as you can see, very much the same."

"The same, as in how old? And why? What does one have to do with the other?"

The questions tumble out of me, but as they do, I get the feeling that once I hear the answers, there's no going back. Once he tells me the rest of it, I can't just pretend that none of this is happening.

"I had just turned eighteen that year," Ethan says.

Eighteen. I start to do the math in my head. "So that would make you—"

He cuts me off. "A great deal older than you." He stands up and paces to the window, then stands there, staring out into the street.

My pulse is racing again. He looks eighteen—a really good eighteen, by the way, with those eyes and that longish hair— that probably got a little sweaty while we were running so it's curling up a bit at his neck—and everything else that's packed into those normal-looking, dark-wash jeans he's wearing with a long-sleeved light blue shirt. But he's over one hundred years old! And then something else occurs to me, so I say it aloud.

"So what you're saying is that you'll stay like this—young— forever, until you find her? You've been like this—all this time?"

"Yes." He turns from the window to meet my gaze. "That was our pledge. Viktor would use the ancient spells to compel Baba Yaga to help us. I know it all sounds impossible to believe.

That's how I felt then too. Magic was one thing. I'd learned it. I knew how it worked. But a fairy tale come to life? I couldn't get my mind around it. Yet it was true. In that room—the hands, Baba Yaga's hands. They—"

"I know," I tell him. "I saw it. In my dream. It was like I was there in that room with you. With all of them. With her."

A shiver works its way through my body. Dreaming all this was bad enough. Knowing that this poor girl actually experienced what I had seen down to the last detail was much, much worse.

"So that was it." Ethan continues to stand by the window. "We could protect the grand duchess—that's her title, by the way—even if all the others died. And if it worked, our lives would not be our own until one of us freed her. She, at least, could keep the Romanov line alive."

I stand and walk over to Ethan. "And you were okay with that? You were willing to give up your freedom for hers?"

"Yes." He runs both of his hands through that thick, shaggy hair of his, blows out a breath. "Yes, I was. I've thought about that since then. I suppose I've had—well, I've had a number of years to think. I was just a child when my family was murdered. I couldn't stop it. If I could stop this, I—well, it seemed like something I had to do."

"All right," I say. The mark on my arm gives another sharp burn, and my heart gives another smack in my chest. "Let's say I believe it all. That it's all true. It still leaves out the main question. Why me? Why do you need me? Why am I suddenly in the middle of all this?"

"The prophecy spoke of a girl—one connected in some way to the bloodline of the Brotherhood. She would be the one who could free Anastasia. We wouldn't know where she lived, or even when. But there would be hints, bits of other writings that would help us. If we stayed true to our cause, eventually, we would find her."

Ethan's still talking when the spike of temper edges its way into me. I don't know if it's his calm tone or what he's saying or maybe a little of both.

"But how can that be me?" I realize I'm shouting at him, and I have no plans to lower my voice anytime soon. "You seriously expect me to believe that I'm related to some anonymous someone in a secret Russian religious order? And that you and God knows who else have been searching for me for—well, a number of decades? You have got to be kidding."

Ethan has the grace to look slightly flustered, but he continues to speak in that same even tone, that tone that's making me want to smack him. "Yes," he says. "That is exactly what you need to believe—because it is the truth."

And then he stops being quite so calm.

He moves closer to me and grabs my arm. "Look at it!" He's holding my arm harder than I'd like. He points to the mark that continues to burn and glow a deep red. "It is the one true sign that Brother Viktor spoke of. He said that if—when—we found the girl, her mark would appear and match our own. He said we would feel it, know it."

I try to wrench my arm away, but Ethan's grip holds firm. The tiny part of me that has still been treating all this like a game of some sort knows now that it is no game.

Ethan's voice has become low and kind of ragged. "Many times over the years, I thought I'd found her. But always, always, I was wrong. This time, I'm not wrong. I know you are the one. I just need you to know it too."

111

He lets go of my arm, then takes both my hands tightly in his. "Believe, Anne. Believe. It is your destiny."

"Destiny? I'm sixteen years old. I don't want a destiny. I go to high school. Until you started following me around, my biggest problem was whether or not I'd studied for my chemistry test. Now I'm running from crazy witches. People are shooting at us. With bullets. And it's all your fault."

"It's not my fault," Ethan says. "It's what has to be. It's what you're supposed to do."

"And who put you in charge of me?"

"Well, I…you—"

"I, you, what? That's the best you can do? You're telling me that you've been around since horse-and-buggy days, checking out every likely girl who comes your way to see if she's the one, and that's the best you can do? I? You? Give me a break, Ethan. I mean, seriously."

"It is serious. It's all very serious. Anastasia's life hangs in the balance. What you decide to do right now is of ultimate importance."

"Like I said, so? What if I don't? Can you, like, make me?"

I'm going to run, I think. Or slap him. Or something.

Only then I look down at our hands.

Slowly, steadily, their color is changing. Ethan's hands and my hands are both radiating the same blue-white glow that my hand had at home last night. The color shifts to the sapphire hue of the sparks that flew from Ethan's fingers back at the park.

Destiny.

And this time, it's not just a glow. I can feel the intense warmth of power residing just below the surface of my skin. Once again, everything in my world shifts.

"It's okay," Ethan tells me as the tears spill out of my eyes and trickle down my cheeks. "It will be okay," he says again.

I've heard that sentence a lot lately. But I'm not sure I believe it. In fact, I'm not sure of much of anything at this point. I'm certainly not sure that I'm special enough to have all this suddenly thrust upon my shoulders.

But it seems to be here whether I want it or not.

"How did you know?" I ask him. "I accept that you felt something when you saw me, but how did you know where I was? It's a big world, Ethan."

"There were documents." He walks back over to the table and starts to clear our tea mugs. "A professor friend that I met in Europe showed me…"

He pauses, places the mugs in the sink, and begins to rinse them. "He's expecting us to come see him. He—"

I'm no longer listening. I walk over to the window. A flash has caught my eye.

Whatever is now pulsing inside me pulses a little faster.

"Ethan," I say, interrupting him, "if Baba Yaga is protecting Anastasia, why did she come after us back at school? Is that all part of this whole thing? I mean, is she coming for me so I can free Anastasia? Or is she trying to hurt us?"

"I honestly don't know," he says. "That part took me by surprise as much as it did you."

The fact that he doesn't know is not thrilling me. Neither is the black limousine—a familiar limousine—that has now glided past the building for a second time.

I turn away from the window.

I feel the pulsing get even faster. "I think now would be a

113

very good time for you to tell me who you think those men are who were chasing us."

His answer is exactly what I hoped it wouldn't be. "I'm not entirely certain," he says, his expression grim. "I think they may have been sent by Brother Viktor."

"But aren't you and he on the same side?" My voice rises so fast it actually squeaks.

"There is a possibility," says the man who is quickly—very quickly—screwing up my entire existence, "that I was wrong about that."

I glance out the window again. Sure enough, two familiar figures dart across the street toward Ethan's building. Well, that's just great.

"It took you over eighty years to realize he might be the bad guy?" I take my gaze away from the window to glare at him.

Ethan opens his mouth to respond. Then he cocks his head, listening. His eyes—those two cute little pools of blue—are now flashing like two angry blue crystals.

"Get down!" he shouts. He grabs my arm and we both slam into the floor together as bullets begin to pound the window.

Wednesday, 1:45 PM

Ethan

I t's those same men!" Anne shouts above the din of bullets raining against the glass. I offer up a silent thanks as they bounce harmlessly off and back down toward the street. My magic may be a bit rusty, but the wards are holding.

For now.

"Follow me," I tell her. We're still flattened to the wooden floor of the loft. My arm is slung across her back. I can feel the rapid pace of her breathing, the wild thundering of her heart. She turns her head and looks at me, those deep, brown eyes filled with fear. A look that has me realizing that I may be in over my head. On many levels.

"Stay down." I reach over and grab her hand. "I don't know how long the protection's going to hold." Her eyes widen more at that last part.

We belly across the floor through the kitchen area. As we reach the table, the pounding of bullets stops. But I know it's far from over.

"Did they give up?" Anne's voice is barely a whisper.

A vicious pounding at the door is our answer. The floor vibrates beneath our bodies with the impact of whatever is now attacking from the hallway.

My mind is racing. We don't have much time. No ward is invincible, and the forces slamming into ours will soon power their way through. I shift my gaze to the door and watch in dismay as a thin crack edges its way steadily from the door's bottom up toward the ceiling. The entire room begins to sway.

"What's happening?" Anne tightens her grip on my hand and reaches for her backpack with the other. The floor rocks so violently that the motion rolls us from under the table and tumbles us in a tangle of limbs out toward the center of the loft. Her pack flies in the opposite direction.

"It's not going to hold," I yell over the noise that seems to be filling everything around us. Rusty or not, my magic is strong. But whatever this is, it's stronger yet.

I pull myself up, dragging Anne with me. "We've got to get out. Now!"

"Out? Out where? How?" Her voice—barely audible above the buzz of sound and vibration—is shrill, terrified.

There's no time to explain, and she wouldn't be able to hear me even if there was.

"Come on!" I tighten my grip on her arm and pull her toward the other end of the loft. "This way!"

I can barely think over the roar of noise. We slip and slide over the swaying wooden floor. Above us, a light fixture shatters, and shards of glass spray everywhere. I curse—in a couple of languages—and move faster, dragging Anne behind me as I go.

"Ethan!" she cries. "The door!"

I whip my head around. The thin crack in the door has widened. It's splitting open. The door itself is bulging inward, propelled by some huge force. Whatever this is, it's enormous. And that's not good.

The floor undulates, and again we start to slide toward the middle of the room. I can feel Anne's fear, feel the pulse leaping in her wrist as I clutch it and—with an audible grunt—drag us to the far wall.

Then the noise that has continued to surge and pound around us changes. I can hear it gather itself into one chugging center, an impossibly loud rushing sound. It's as though the very air inside the room is being sucked forward into some invisible whirlpool—a whirlpool that's going to swallow us whole if I don't do something soon.

Very soon.

But even as I consider my rather limited options, it's too late. The door bursts open, and a swirling vortex of mist and cloud muscles its way inside.

WEDNESDAY, 2:00 PM

ANNE

IT'S BABA YAGA," I SCREAM AT ETHAN. THE WIND SWALLOWS my words. "The hands! They're going to come again."

But they don't. Whatever this is, it's not that.

Ethan tightens his hold on my arm. His fingers dig into my wrist. The wind keeps rushing at us, stinging, biting. My eyes close to thin slits. Through them, I make out Ethan searching the wall for something. He reaches with his free hand, and I see he's grabbed onto a small metal circle protruding from the wall.

"*Ya dolzhen!*" he calls into the howling wind. "*Ya dolzhen!*" He calls it out again, this time in English. "I must!"

He yanks again at the metal ring. I see it give a little, and he yanks some more, a grim slant of a smile playing on his lips. A piece of the wall, like a panel or something, gives way. It slides slowly but steadily, revealing an old freight elevator.

"I have to let go of you," Ethan tells me. "Something's blocking the spell." His voice cracks in the wind. "Brace yourself."

I nod, letting him know I've heard him, then space my feet to find my balance. I nod again. His gaze on mine, he lets go. I stand there, the wind sweeping around me.

Ethan shoves at the elevator door. It gives a little, but not enough. Whatever he's trying, it's no match for the whirling winds.

I look down at my hands. They're sparking, blue melding into a pure, clear white—an elemental force that's working its way up from inside me. Some of the sparks careen from my fingertips and bounce off the metal bars of the elevator.

"Let me help," I say. "I can do this, Ethan." Everything inside me is pulsing. I don't understand any of it, really. But I know it wants out.

"You're not ready." He yanks at the elevator door again. Nothing. "You can't control your power. Not now. Not yet."

I don't stop to answer. Whatever's boiling up inside me needs me to use it. I position my hands next to his on the metal bars of the freight elevator. "On three," I shout over the roaring of the wind. I have no earthly idea why I feel I can do this. I just know I can.

I count. The wind snatches each number as it exits my mouth. On three, we push together.

The door doesn't budge.

This time the wind whips so fiercely around us that I lose my grip and feel myself being sucked backward. Ethan grabs for my wrist, pulls me to him.

"Again!" he shouts to me. "Let's try it again!"

We center ourselves and push. The crazy blue-white sparks fly off my fingers like a thousand Fourth of July sparklers. For a few seconds, nothing else changes. Then I feel something move. With a giant creak, the elevator door slides open. We tumble inside, the door clanging shut behind us. Ethan slams his fist on the control panel, and with a lurch, the elevator begins its descent.

Behind us, the seething mass of energy explodes into the rest of the loft.

119

WEDNESDAY, 2:30 PM

ETHAN

"WE NEED TO KEEP MOVING," I TELL ANNE AS THE ELEVATOR bounces to a stop in the basement. Her hands are still glowing with power—a great deal of it.

"Just go," she says. "Go. I can keep up with you."

I hesitate, then run. She keeps pace, following behind me across the wide expanse of the concrete-floored basement until we skid to a stop at the outside door.

"Hang on." I hold up my arm. "They may still be out there."

I move from the door to a pile of wooden crates stacked unevenly on the side wall. I mount the lowest crate, scaling the pile of boxes so I can peer out the small window above us. They bobble back and forth beneath my feet, threatening to give way with each step I take.

Perched on top, I scan the street, then feel a muscle in my jaw tic as I see what I hoped I wouldn't.

"Are they out there?" Anne asks from below me. "What do you see?"

I don't answer, just turn and climb down. A wave of exhaustion flows over me. This is getting worse and worse, and I still have no idea why.

"They're Viktor's men," I tell Anne. "I thought I recognized one of them at the park. Now I'm certain."

"You're sure?" Her voice rises. I pace the floor as she continues. "It doesn't make any sense. Why would they suddenly turn against you?"

"I'm sure," I say. My jaw clenches again. "The one I know—his name is Dimitri. He—he was once a monk, as I was. But I haven't seen him since—well, for a very long time. Over the years, the search kept us all apart. It's only our contact with Viktor that connects us anymore."

"But are you really positive? I mean, if it's been that long, you might be wrong. He might be—"

"I'm not wrong." I rub my hand over my face, trying to get a grip on what's happened here. "I—I think they want to stop you. Stop us from getting to Anastasia."

Anne's voice rises again. I can feel the panic echoing off her in waves.

"Getting to Anastasia? But we don't even know where she is, Ethan. You think she's in Baba Yaga's hut, but where's that? It's not like I'm going to just walk down the street or take the train downtown and ask for directions. Even if this place really does exist, even if Anastasia is really somehow still alive, how the hell do I find her? So tell them it's no big deal. They don't have to kill us. I'll never be able to do it anyway."

"Of course you can," I tell her. I struggle to keep my voice calm, my tone even. "It's your—"

"Don't. Don't you dare tell me that it's my damn destiny!" she shouts at me. Her panic seems to have shifted to anger. "Tell me something I don't know. Tell me we weren't really about to die up there! Tell me why the hell Viktor wants to stop us! You can't possibly be telling me everything, Ethan. There's no way."

"I'm telling you all I can," I say. I ease toward the door. If she's about to run, I need to stop her. "I'm telling you all I know."

"Well, all you know just isn't enough, damn it!" She stalks over to me, stands toe to toe. I can feel the warmth of her—and the confusion. "It's not enough to drag me here to die for something that, for all I know, is some demented delusion on your part!"

"Delusion?" I grab her wrists. Her hands are still glowing. "Look at your hands, Anne. You opened that elevator door, remember? Oh, I helped you, but you know the truth. Most of that power came from you. Look at that mark on your arm again. Look at that windstorm that just destroyed my loft."

She pulls her hands from mine. "I don't want to look at it! I told you before. I don't want any of it. How do I know that they're not the good guys? Maybe you're the bad one. Maybe Dimitri and his friend want *you* dead and not me."

"You know that's not true." I place my hands on her shoulders, realizing I have absolutely no idea how to reassure her. "Come. We'll get out of here, and I'll take you to see my friend Olensky. Maybe together, we can all make some sense—"

"No!" she shouts at me. "No. This is *so* not where I want to be. How in the world could I have been so stupid? I'm not going anywhere else with you."

"Please, Anne," I tell her. "You have to calm down. Let me take you to Olensky."

"I said no," she tells me between gritted teeth. "And I mean *no!*"

In case I wasn't totally sure, she places her hands on my chest and shoves. The force lifts me from my feet and hurtles me the length of the basement. My head slams into the far wall. I feel my teeth rattle together.

Anne stares at me for a few seconds, then opens the door and runs.

WEDNESDAY, 3:00 PM

ANNE

I'm an idiot, I TELL MYSELF AS I LISTEN TO THE ECHO OF MY own footsteps pounding the empty pavement. I let this man take me here to a loft in this mostly deserted neighborhood. I have no transportation, no backpack, no cell phone, and no one to ask for help.

And what would I tell anyone who happened by anyway? That I knew this guy for all of two seconds and bought into his whole X-Men scenario? Yeah, right. We all want to wake up one day and suddenly have some kind of superpower. But I just want to get—

Like in the movies—the ones where the stupid girl goes into the scary haunted house even though the entire audience is screaming at her not to—I'm suddenly aware that there are other footsteps smacking the sidewalk besides mine.

A rough hand slaps itself across my mouth, and someone's arm wraps itself around me, jerking me backward. The unexpected blow to my momentum sends me tripping and tumbling to the sidewalk. I land hard, pulling my attacker down with me. Too scared even to scream, I look over into the hard, slate gray eyes of the man Ethan had identified as Dimitri.

WEDNESDAY, 3:00 PM

ETHAN

MY LEGS BUCKLE AS I STAND UP AND TRY TO FOLLOW ANNE. I lean against the cold cement wall and shake my head, trying to clear my vision. I'm still seeing double, and there's an ache in my jaw that I don't think is going to fade anytime soon.

I close my eyes. The image of Anne's face looms in front of me—the fear, the confusion, and, of course, the anger as she threw me across the room into a wall. I should never have asked her to help me with the elevator. It's too much, too soon. All that power—

Truth is, a small voice in my aching head reminds me, *without her power, we'd have never gotten out of there.*

I hoist myself off the floor. I've got to find her. She's in danger that neither of us fully understand—danger I should have anticipated but didn't. *Zalupa.*

And then I drop back down to the floor as a bullet grazes my arm. Dimitri's partner strides toward me, gun drawn.

"Your girl is ours now, Etanovich," he says. He's speaking in English, but I can hear a trace of the old country in his accent. "Face it. You have outlived your cause."

He fires again, but the bullet flies over my head as I roll out of range. I have no time for this Russian melodrama. Since he's shooting at me, it's clear that he has no clue who or what he's signed on to help—no clue about me. If he's telling the truth—and God, don't they always tell the truth when they think you're not going to live long enough to do anything about it—they have Anne, and she is not like me. If I let him go, he could kill her.

"She may be yours for now," I say as I push myself up in one fluid motion and turn to face him. "But," I add as he fires again and a bullet lodges itself in my left shoulder, "I think you've forgotten that I've outlived almost everyone. Including you."

His eyes widen as I stride over to him. He shoots again. I jolt as the bullet burns its way into the right side of my chest, but I keep moving. Then I rip the gun from his grasp and pocket it.

I hurry to the door, my fingers weaving a spell behind me. In seconds, the man is kneeling helplessly on the basement floor, clutching his throat as an invisible force tightens around it.

"Stop," he squeezes out.

But I don't. Something raw and fearsome has shifted inside me. Whatever we've been playing at here, the rules have changed.

"Guess you weren't one of us," I say as I open the door. Behind me, I can hear the man gasping for air, but I keep moving. "Guess Dimitri didn't explain that pesky immortality clause as carefully as he could have."

I head out the door without looking back.

WEDNESDAY, 3:05 PM

ANNE

Y OU'VE GOT THE WRONG PERSON, MISTER," I TELL DIMITRI. I'm certain neither of us believe that for a second, but he's dragging me up off the sidewalk toward the black limousine that's pulled up out of nowhere, so I figure I'm entitled to protest. "Let me go!"

"I do not think so," Dimitri mutters. He's got me clutched up tightly against him. His grip is like iron. I can feel his breath against my neck, smell the tangy odor of his leather jacket.

"Now be a good girl," he says, "and I won't hurt you."

"You're already hurting me," I say. "Let me go. Now!" I manage to twist enough to execute a sharp kick to one of his shins.

"Why, you little—!" He grabs a fistful of my hair and pulls hard. The tiny bit of me that's not consumed by fear and confusion wonders if this is going to turn into a chick fight.

"Viktor said you'd be a fiery one," he says, and shoves me a few steps closer to the limo. Its back door opens. "I don't know how you escaped that loft, but this time, you're not getting away." He pushes me again. I can see the black interior of the limo looming in front of me.

I swallow down the bitter bile that's risen in my throat. It's occurred to me in the last few minutes that I've just run from the wrong person—not to mention that I've slammed him into a wall. Which makes me realize that I might not have to put up with this burly Russian who's trying to kidnap me.

"Listen, Boris," I tell him, even though I know his name is Dimitri. He's already pissed at me, so what do I care what he thinks now? "I said you were hurting me!" Blue-white sparks fly from my fingers as I wrench free of him and maneuver quickly out of reach. Inside me, the power surges, replacing my fear with something darker, stronger.

Dimitri tries to grab me again, but I'm too quick for him. I turn and sprint back toward Ethan's building. Footsteps pound the pavement behind me.

Still running, I turn to peek over my shoulder. Sure enough, Dimitri is closing in on me again, his hand reaching for something in his pocket. I may have developed superstrength, but somehow, I'm pretty sure I'm not impervious to bullets. My heart lurches in my chest as I push myself to run even faster.

Then I see it: Ethan's car—with Ethan in it, I hope—screeches to a halt across the street. I sprint over to it, not even looking to see if anything else—a big limo, perhaps—is in my path.

Ethan—the man I tried to squash not minutes ago—leans across and shoves open the passenger door. He's already got his foot on the gas pedal as I leap in and crash into the seat. I bounce around some more as he executes a sharp U-turn, and we speed off, leaving Dimitri cursing on the sidewalk behind us.

My most precious Mama—

Like my sisters, you are a believer in love, and like me, you have secrets. But mostly, you are my mother. The woman who gave birth to four daughters before she finally brought a son into this world. A son for whom you would have given your life if you could. I saw your face crumble each time—and there were many— that Papa reminded you that his little tsarevitch had inherited his illness through your side of the family.

Hemophilia—passed down through mothers who carry it but do not suffer it themselves. Passed down through your grandmother, Queen Victoria, to your mother, Alice, to you, and finally, to Alexei. This is the truth that is part of what this journal has always been about: blood. The truth that changed everything for us.

Your blood failed you, Mama. I might not have always said this to you so bluntly, so directly, but now—well, now I cannot help but do so. It failed you, and you failed Alexei, and even if it is not the best of truths, it is what happened.

"Father Grigory will help us," you said. You always called Rasputin by his religious name, gave him that respect, even though at some point you must have seen, must have known how most of us saw him. That long, greasy hair, those close-set eyes that held secrets and desires much more terrible than ours. Those eyes that would not let go when he looked at me.

But he told you he could cure Alexei, and you believed him. And I think, now, it is because you thought you had no other choice.

So you let that monster into our lives, thinking he was the only one who could save your son. That creature, Rasputin, who called himself Father Grigory and stood in our room for so long one night while we girls were already in our nightgowns that my cheeks grew hot from anger and embarrassment and the servants began to gossip about his intentions. During the war, when the Russian people began to turn against Papa and against us because we were his, there was even worse. The stories printed in the papers that you hid from me but I found anyway. The ones that said Rasputin had taken my sisters and me and even you as his lovers, stories so horrible that I thought I would die from the mortification of it all.

But still you had faith, until finally, Cousin Felix and the others took matters into their own hands and— well, you know how it ended for Rasputin. I need not remind you of what occurred before they pulled his dead body from the river.

So if you were here in front of me, precious Mama, here is what I would ask you. When did you know? When did you know that your husband—the man who wanted you desperately—when did you know that he had another son? Did you marry him knowing about Viktor? Did you see this young boy visiting year after year and finally ask him? Did Papa tell you himself?

Because it all comes down to that, doesn't it? That your blood would be a death sentence to a son. And that Papa's blood already flowed in another child that wasn't yours. And the rest—well, the rest is now what it is.

How did you see yourself, Mama? As a mother doing what she could to save her child? Or like Vasilisa in that story you loved to read to me? Given no choice but to go to the monsters and hope you could bring back light?

Wherever you are, Mama, do not think I do not understand. Because I do.

And here is the rest of the truth. I followed your example. I believed my half brother Viktor when he told me that his Brotherhood would save us, but only if I did what he asked. How could I refuse? Especially I, who thought she was so smart, so clever. I could save my family and show them the value of the man they had rejected.

Only we were both wrong, of course, and now you're dead and I am worse than dead. Because, Mama, I was only seventeen. I had seen suffering and war and soldiers return with missing limbs and eyes and inner wounds that would not heal. I had seen my own brother on the brink of death. But still I did not understand what I had agreed to do. I did not know how long a life could be.

I saw only a handsome face I thought I loved—only the injustice I felt had been done to him.

I did not see who he really was. I did not see the truth.

I saw only myself. Brave Anastasia who would do what she needed to save her family. The girl whose mother gave her a matroyshka doll and told her it would keep her safe.

Did you know what I had promised when you gave that doll to me? The doll I use now to store this journal—written on the thinnest wisps of paper—with its many secrets? Hidden deep inside, like the truths of our family, its smiling face revealing nothing? Or was it just a doll? Did the magic come later?

Or perhaps it never has, and I truly have gone mad.

What did you know, precious Mama? What did you know?

And why did you never tell me your truth?

I remain, as always,

Your Anastasia

WEDNESDAY, 4:48 PM

ANNE

I'M FINE," I SAY INTO ETHAN'S CELL PHONE. "TESS, YOU'VE just got to chill. There's some real weird stuff going on, but I'm—we're okay."

"*We're* okay?" She bellows so loudly that I actually move the phone away from my ear. "Did you actually say *we're?* Do you think for one second that I give a rat's ass about that guy? He's dragged you into some kind of freakish, soap-opera plot, and you're worried about his health? Give me a break, Michaelson."

I can see her point. In her shoes, I'd be shouting the same thing. The truth is, I still don't know if I can really trust Ethan, but at the moment, I think I can, and that's all I have to go on.

"I just need you to cover for me," I say when I can get a word in. "I left a message on the house phone saying that I'm eating dinner at your house, and that we're going to study together. That way, they won't expect me until at least nine thirty or so. Maybe even ten. They probably won't call, but they might, so you need to know the deal."

Even as I'm telling this to Tess, the dutiful-daughter portion of my brain is warning me that my mother is going to be majorly pissed that I didn't leave the message on her cell. And I don't even want to think about how she'll react if she calls *my* cell and it keeps flipping over to voice mail, since it's still trapped in my backpack in Ethan's loft. That is, of course, unless it's been commandeered by Viktor and all his evil pals, who are even at this very moment racking up enough extra minutes to get me grounded until I'm thirty.

Not a pretty picture.

"I'll cover for you," Tess is saying now. "But I'm not happy about it."

"You're the best."

"Yeah, yeah," she sighs. "Where did you say you were again?"

"We're at Northwestern. We're out by the lake right now. But when this Professor Olensky that Ethan knows is done with class in a few minutes, we're going to see him. Ethan thinks he can help us sort this whole thing out, figure out what's going on."

I hear Tess sigh again noisily. "What's going on with witches and giant hands and people shooting at you and whirlwinds trying to suck you away and a guy who may have been around during the Russian Revolution?" she says. "Is that what he's going to figure out?"

Clearly my decision to give her the CliffsNotes version of my little adventure has not eased her mind about anything—including my mental status.

"I'll talk to you later, Tess," I say. "Seriously, I owe you. Big time." I can see Ethan heading back to where I'm sitting on one of the huge rocks that flank Lake Michigan near the NU campus. Since we arrived, he's been sort of anxiously stalking around like the tigers at Lincoln Park Zoo right before feeding time. That is, if tigers chain-smoked Marlboros, which is something else he's been doing. But it's given me some privacy to make my phone calls—or as much privacy as I can get, since it seems clear he has no intention of letting me out of his line of vision anytime soon.

"Love you, Annie," Tess says. "Be careful."

"I will," I tell her, and then I flip the phone closed before she can say anything else.

Ethan stubs out his cigarette, then picks his way across the uneven rocks and sits down next to me. I hand his phone back to him, and he tucks it into his jeans pocket.

"You want any more of these?" I ask him, holding up the remains of the sandwiches we'd purchased at the student union. I'd eaten most of one because Ethan insisted, but right now, I can't even remember what was in it.

He shakes his head, then glances—for what I think is the nine-thousandth time—at his watch.

We both just sit there for a bit, staring out at the lake. Lake Michigan is so huge that it's always seemed more like an ocean to me, and today is no exception. Even though it's still early in October, the water's already turned that wintry, blue-gray color, and the waves spit out a rough froth each time they rush against the beach.

We'd come out here, my mom and I, one freezing afternoon in February, just a couple weeks after David died. It was cold—that frigid, breath-stopping, Chicago winter cold—and I remember watching the little foggy huffs of our breath as we walked. It was so cold that some of the waves had actually frozen solid in mid-roll toward the shore. I had walked next to my mother, my mittened hand holding hers, thinking that those waves were just how I felt: frozen and trapped and waiting for something to thaw me out, make me move and feel again.

Like Ethan, I realize with a jolt that has me looking over at him, studying that face with its strong jaw and sharp cheek-bones—the face that should look old but can't, that is stopped and unable to go on until some force he can't really control allows him to.

"We should head over there now," he says, interrupting my thoughts. "His afternoon class is set to let out at five thirty." He crumples the remains of our sandwich wrappers in one hand along with the now empty Marlboro pack, unfolds his long legs, and stands up.

"You know those are going to kill you, right?" I point at the crushed Marlboro pack.

There's a silence until he realizes that I'm joking. I can see him working over in his head whether or not he needs to lecture me about how this is all not really funny—which, obviously, it's not. I mean, we're both aware that we'd probably love to be somewhere else right now—and probably not together.

But what he chooses to do is smile and hold out his other hand.

I clasp it. His palm feels warm against mine, and this time, we don't send any punch of aftershocks through each other. We're just two people holding hands, which is definitely a lot easier on both of us than when I was flinging him across the basement.

I look at his face again. Whatever he's thinking, he's keeping it to himself, but I know something else happened with him and the other guy in the basement after I bolted and almost got captured by Dimitri.

"He won't be coming after us," is all he's told me once I caught my breath and even thought to ask.

What I haven't asked about is why he has what clearly seem to be bullet holes in his blue cotton shirt—at least two blood-stained ragged holes with no visible wounds underneath. That's the one part of this whole story that I didn't—couldn't—share with Tess. But now, as we walk together up the path that leads to the building called Harris Hall where the professor is conducting class, I think I know.

"You had to kill him, didn't you?" I ask him, but it's really more a statement than a question. I'm shocked I can say it so calmly.

Ethan stays silent. We keep walking together under the trees that line the path. When we pass a trash can, he dumps in the sandwich wrappers. He's still holding my hand, and his palm is still warm against mine. A few students pass us, laughing and chatting. A man rides by on an old bicycle, his briefcase tucked into a metal basket behind him. On the tower of a nearby building, a clock begins to strike the half hour.

We stop in front of a large, stone-façade building. "Yes," Ethan says. He lets go of my hand and turns his head to look at me. His gaze gives away nothing. "Yes, I did."

The starkness of his confession settles silently between us.

Students begin to trickle out of the various buildings. I'm suddenly overcome by feelings it will take a while to sort out. But one of them seems to be gratitude.

"You saved my life," I tell Ethan softly. "If you killed him," I touch one of my hands to the ragged hole in the middle of his shirt near his heart, "it's because you had no other choice."

Ethan searches my face for a second with those blue eyes, places his hand over mine. "There's always a choice," he says. "You need to remember that, Anne. There's always—"

He doesn't finish his sentence but instead lets go and walks behind me. "Alex!" he calls out.

I turn to see him waving at a stout, older man with wildly wavy gray hair who is just emerging from Harris Hall.

"Ah, Ethan," he says. He walks over to us, a smile spreading across his lined face. "I—" And then he stops. I can feel my face flush as the professor stares openly at me.

"So this is really…" He reaches over and actually places his hands on my face, gazing at me like a kid who thinks he's met the real Santa Claus or something. Then, just as I'm about to shove him out of my personal space bubble, he steps back and rakes one hand through that wild hair.

Ethan, thankfully, intervenes. "Professor Aleksander Olensky," he says, "I would like you to meet Anne Michaelson."

Olensky pumps my hand for a bit until I finally yank it away. Not that I want to ruin his good time rejoicing over my presence or anything, but enough is enough.

"Come," he says then. "I understand we've got some research to do." He points to our right. "My office is just over there." He sets off at a brisk pace in the direction he's pointed.

"So," I ask Ethan as we hustle to follow the professor, "you're sure this guy can really help us?"

"Positive." Ethan grins more broadly than I've seen him do. "Trust me. You'll see."

"Yeah, yeah," I say. "Trust you. 'Cause that's going so well."

Ethan narrows his blue eyes. "You'll see," he says again. "Really."

Budapest, Hungary,
Three Months Ago

ETHAN

"TRUST ME," KATYA SAYS. "YOU'RE GOING TO THINK HE'S fantastic." A smile lights up her pale face. She pushes a tumble of blond curls, a bit damp from the summer's heat, off her forehead.

Katya, who's a student here at the local university, grabs my hand, and we cross the street to a small café. Katya, according to my sources, was most definitely the girl I had been looking for all these decades.

Sadly, she wasn't really the right one. The information I had received had proved to be false.

But it's a beautiful summer afternoon, and I'm not leaving until tomorrow. So Katya and I will eat, drink some coffee, and listen to this professor she admires so much. At least she'll have a good memory of the afternoon when she tries to find me a few days from now and realizes that I have disappeared without a word.

We pay for our coffee and cake at the counter, weave our way through the packed café, and settle into two empty seats at a small, round table.

"There he is," Katya says after she swallows a bite of the rich chocolate torte in front of her. She points across the room to an elderly man with a wild shock of gray hair who's sitting not too far from us.

"Aleksander Olensky. Everyone loves him so much that he's started conducting these informal little talks here about once a week. You can sit and have something to eat and just get to know him. So much better than sitting in that stuffy lecture hall." She forks up another mouthful of torte and sighs happily.

I nod my head and take a sip of my coffee. The crowd is mostly university students, with a few older faces and a handful of international backpacker types scattered among them. As if by some invisible signal, they grow quiet and turn themselves in Professor Olensky's direction. He smiles and clears his throat.

A few minutes later, I'm sorry that I've let Katya convince me to join her, because the last thing I really want to do is sit here and listen to Olensky discuss the Romanovs and their downfall, which, it turns out, is the subject he's chosen for today's talk. But clearly, everyone else in the room is hanging on his every word, listening with rapt attention to his current story about young Alexei and his spaniel, Joy.

I'm certain that I am the only one sitting here wondering if he knows how annoying that ridiculous little dog really was.

"Those were magnificent days," Olensky says, taking a sip of whatever he's drinking. "Magnificent. And then came the Revolution. Of course, Lenin and Marx are fascinating subjects too. Did you know that Karl Marx was a student of—?"

He stops and turns to look at me—most likely, I realize, because I have sworn under my breath at the mention of Marx's name. Next to me, Katya wears an expression that seems to be part amusement and part embarrassment.

"Did you have a comment, friend?" Olensky stares at me quizzically.

What the hell? I think. *I'll be gone tomorrow.*

"Marx?" I say. "That charlatan?" And unexpectedly, I find myself sparring history with Olensky, rambling on far longer than I should, until many, many minutes later, I finally sputter to a stop—much to Katya's relief, I'm sure.

"So," Olensky says to me, looking at me far more closely than he had at first. "How is it that a gentleman of your youth is so knowledgeable about people who lived so long ago? You must be an avid student of history, my friend."

"Something like that," I tell him. I am very much aware at this moment of how young I look and how incongruous this is with the level of knowledge I have displayed. *Perhaps,* I think dismally, *he'll just think I'm a prodigy.*

But later, as I part ways with Katya—more easily now that she's mostly furious at my behavior—and head out into the gathering dusk, Olensky catches up with me. Our subsequent conversation lasts many hours and includes many drinks of a decidedly stronger nature than coffee.

Hours later, I sit staring at him in amazement. My brain is on fire, and not just from the one too many shots of vodka.

"You are one of them," Olensky says. He has had a few too many vodkas of his own. His face is glowing red with alcohol and excitement. "I can feel it. I know it."

I sit there for a moment, then down another vodka and run my hand unsteadily through my hair. Trusting someone not of the Brotherhood does not come easily. In fact, it is unthinkable. Yet this man, this excited old man, seems to hold the key that can free me from the mission that has held me for too long.

Aleksander Olensky, it turns out, is a man with a quest of his own—a man who believes in the tales his grandfather told him of a Russian Brotherhood, and of a royal Romanov daughter who never really died. He had become a scholar with access to the archives of the world's greatest universities and libraries, and even as he believed, he had thought it all could be a lie. Until today.

He reaches into his battered leather briefcase and pulls out a sheaf of papers. "I found them in a library in the former East Berlin," he tells me. "The librarian simply allowed me to copy the entire file. You see, no one places much significance on matters of the Revolution anymore—not since the fall of the Berlin Wall in the eighties."

He swallows some more vodka. "I could hardly believe my good fortune. They had no idea…" He pauses and looks me in the eyes. "Papers can say anything, I suppose. That doesn't make it the truth. So tell me, Mr. Kozninsky, what is the truth? Am I just a silly, superstitious old man in love with tales from his youth?"

I cannot tell whether what I say next comes from my need to tell it or from the shocking number of vodkas I have consumed.

Probably, it is a bit of both.

"Believe," I tell Alex Olensky. "Believe. I am the truth."

And with that, he gathers the papers—the culmination of his life's work—and hands them across the table to me.

Chicago,
The Present

WEDNESDAY, 6:00 PM

ETHAN

WHAT'S WITH YOU GUYS AND THE WHOLE TEA THING?" Anne whispers. "Is it the caffeine or something? 'Cause you know, at this point, a shot of Jack Daniels might be better."

I shrug. Personally, I'd prefer some vodka, but now is not the time.

We're sitting next to each other in two battered leather chairs across from Alex's oversized oak desk. Bookshelves line the room, overflowing with texts of various shapes, sizes, and conditions. The room bears the distinct aromas of paper, tea, and tobacco. At least a dozen cigarette butts threaten to overflow a small, green, ceramic ashtray resting perilously close to the edge of the desk.

Alex is still rotating around Anne like a personal satellite, oblivious to her discomfort. He's recounted the story of our meeting in Prague—with enough detail that for a moment, I was certain he was going to pull out paper and illustrate it with sketches—and offered her tea, two varieties of cookies, and a piece of hard candy he pulled out of his pocket.

"I'm afraid that's all I have, my dear," he says. "Unless you can think of anything else that you—"

"I'm good." Anne holds up her teacup. "Really. It's delicious, Professor." She takes another sip as if to prove her point, then looks relieved when Alex finally returns to his desk, sweeps a swath of workspace out of the clutter, and settles himself in his ancient armchair.

"So." He unearths a half-filled pack of Winstons from underneath a pile of student essays, then glances at Anne again, drops the pack back on the desk, leans back in his chair, and crosses his arms. "Tell me what has happened." He looks at both of us intently. "Do not leave anything out."

We tell him everything: Anne's dreams; her vision of Baba Yaga on the street the other night; Baba Yaga's hands; Viktor's men; the whirlwind in my loft; Anne's increasing power—all of it.

I hesitate only once, and that is with the telling of what happened in the basement—the moment I found that I was capable of taking a life.

Alex listens carefully, jotting down notes on a yellow legal pad as we speak. At that last part, a slight shadow crosses his face.

He's still adding to his notes when, about thirty-five minutes later, I rise to stretch and peer out the window into the growing darkness. I yawn. It's been a couple of nights since I've slept more than a few hours, and until we get this thing done, I don't see much more sleep in my future.

I turn from the window at the sound of a match striking. At his desk, Olensky lights one of his Winstons.

"What do you think?" Anne says to him. She slips off the band holding her hair, shakes it out, then gathers it back up. It's a small action, but her hands move gracefully, and without warning, tenderness tugs at me. I've searched for so long, I'd given up thinking about what I would feel once I actually found her.

I push the thought away.

Alex takes another drag, blows out the smoke. "I keep meaning to quit," he says, and smiles, "but I like it too much."

He sighs, then stubs out the rest of the cigarette in the green ashtray. "It's clear that these worlds are colliding. The magical is rubbing up against the everyday. I would think that it's a sign that the time is here. That if Anastasia can be rescued, it will be now. Soon." He picks up the legal pad and thumbs through his pages of notes. "All these years, as far you know, Ethan—nothing has happened like this?"

I shake my head. "Never."

"And you're certain that those men were sent by Viktor?"

"Yes," Anne and I speak in unison.

"When Dimitri grabbed me," Anne says, "right before I kicked him, he said Viktor's name—something about how Viktor had told him I'd be a fiery one. I guess he might have said more, only that's when I kicked him."

"Smart girl." Olensky smiles, then casts a longing look at the cigarette he's abandoned in the ashtray.

"But if Viktor knows I'm the one, why does he want to stop me?" She turns her full attention to me. "You said that you and he and those others pledged your lives to find the person who could get to Baba Yaga's hut and rescue Anastasia. So if I'm the one who can do it, why try to kill me? Why give me all this power and then try to keep me from using it?"

I ease back down into my chair. "She's right," I say. "It makes no sense. Why try to prevent something we've worked to accomplish for almost a century? Why stop Anne from getting to Anastasia?"

"Obviously there's some connection," Alex replies. "If my years of research have taught me one thing, it's that the answer is always there somewhere. We just need to know where to look and what to see when we get there."

"It's certainly not reflected in the documents you gave me," I tell him. "At least not as far as I can tell. Those papers seem focused only on predictions of where and when the right girl might appear."

Anne shifts her gaze to Olensky. "Predictions? About me? You mean like someone predicted that I'd be here to do this? Me, specifically?"

He grins. This is the kind of thing Alex absolutely adores. "It's quite fascinating, Miss Michaelson, truly. What they did, you see, is use a series of predictive charts, not unlike what astrologers use, to conclude that if the Brotherhood's prophecy was true—if Anastasia was truly alive and a girl who could rescue her and who was connected to this same Brotherhood did exist—there were definitive mathematical odds that she would live somewhere in this area during this period of time. Actually, they posited more than one set of circumstances, but since the time frame for almost all of those has already passed, it seemed clear that you might be here." He flashes another broad smile at her. "You see?" he asks.

"I, uh—well, sure," she says, but her voice indicates otherwise.

"And what is even better, my friend," Alex says, and his voice is filled with excitement, "what is truly amazing is that if our Anne here really is the key, then you get a fresh start.

Imagine, Ethan! Knowing what you know and starting over at eighteen. It's, it's—"

"It's just weird," Anne says.

"Weird?" Olensky raises his eyebrows.

"Yeah. I don't know if I'd want that," she tells him. She looks at me as well, since it's my life they're discussing. "To have lived it all and then live it again. I mean, it sounds great, but is it? You know too much to be really young, but you'll actually be young, so you can't be old, and…" She pauses and seems to consider something.

"That's how it is for Anastasia too isn't it?" Anne says then. "You're both the same. If this is all like you say it is, then she's exactly the same as she was, even though everyone else—well, not you and those other Brotherhood guys—but everyone else is way older or dead. If we—when we—bring her back, she'll be just like she was, only not quite like she was."

"Yes." I nod. It seems I have underestimated this girl in any number of ways. "Yes, she will."

"And—well, do you think that's okay?"

"You're young." I scrub a hand over my face and get up from my chair, because suddenly, I can no longer sit still. Olensky stays quiet.

"Well, excuse me for not being a hundred or whatever it is you are. It's not like you've figured everything out, Ethan. I mean, I know you're old, even if you don't look it. Even if, like the professor just said, you get to start over. But you are seriously stupid."

"Oh?" Suddenly, I'm feeling a lot less empathetic. I work to keep my voice even, pluck my lips up in a smile that I'm sure doesn't reach to my eyes.

"I mean, what if she doesn't want that?" Anne asks me. She's up from her chair now and standing in front of me.

"Why wouldn't she?" I ask her back.

"Uh, I don't know. Family—dead. Friends—dead. The year 1918? Almost a hundred years ago."

"Dear girl," Olensky begins, "why don't we—"

If he finishes, I don't hear him. The truth I've held on to for so long rises out of me before I can pull it back. "You think I don't know that?" I ask her. "Is that what you think? Well, think again. You're right. I was stupid. I trusted someone I shouldn't have because I didn't have anyone else to trust. So now imagine something else, Anne. Imagine that as soon as you made a choice like that, you knew—without hesitation, without doubt—that you had agreed to something that you never, ever should have agreed to. Only now it's done. It's over. And it's too damn late to do anything but go along with it."

"Ethan," Olensky starts. "This is not—"

"Not what? Not the time? She's into this with us over her head. But she has to be. So I want her to know. And it's not your place to decide. Because, let's face it, Alex, even you—some part of you—wonders what it would be like to look in the mirror every morning and see the exact same face you've been seeing. You may think you even want it. Well, trust me, friend. You don't. I thought I was saving that girl. I wasn't. I was dooming her to something worse than death. Only I was eighteen, and I had no idea what I was playing with."

Anne watches me with those pretty, brown eyes. "I didn't mean—"

"No," I tell her. "You did mean it. And I mean what I'm saying too. And you know what else? I still can't fix it. I can never fix it. That's the bitch of it. I can only try to get her out of there, and I need you to do it for me. That's the way it's got to work. That's the only way it can work, the only way that we—"

I look at her again and realize now that she's right in what she said before. This morning, her life was hers to control. Now I'm calling the shots. Just like Viktor—

"Anne. I'll just take you home or wherever you want to go. This isn't your battle. It's mine. Win or lose, I did it to her. I'm not going to do it to you too. I have no idea what this will cost you. Or even how to get you to Baba Yaga's hut. And I'm not willing to find out."

Anne stays silent for a long while. I stand with Olensky and watch the various emotions cross her face. *She is so very young*, I think again. This time I don't say it aloud.

"You didn't do it," she says finally. "Viktor did. Or Baba Yaga. Or both of them. You just promised to try to get her back. That's not the same thing at all. So stop telling me to leave. I'm not going anywhere."

"I was in that basement," I say. "I said the words Viktor taught me. I helped compel Baba Yaga to come."

"Maybe you did." She holds up her hands. They're pulsing again—blue and white sparks of color as the power shifts and readies itself inside her. "But so what? Do you just expect me to go home and pretend none of this happened? I think it's a little late for that, don't you?"

"She's right," Olensky adds. "So enough of all this. You can stand there and yell at the girl and regret the past all you want, but it won't change why you came here. It won't stop what we know has been set into motion." He walks to his desk and starts rifling through the piles of paper strewn there. "Although honestly, I'd feel better if we really did understand Viktor's involvement."

"So would I. And I wasn't yelling," I say and both of them stare at me like I've lost my mind. "I was just—all right. Maybe I was yelling." I rub my hand over my face. "I'm sorry. It's just that you—"

"That I what?" Anne angles her chin in a way that says my answer better not start this all up again.

"It's this." I roll up my sleeve. The mark that connects us flushes red on my arm. "And that." I point to her hands, still flexing with what's resting just under the skin. "This link that's now between us. It's not like me to tell people what I just told you. Those things are mine. I had no intention of burdening you with them. But obviously, I just did. So the professor is right. Everything is in motion. I don't think we could stop it if we wanted to, though we still don't know all the answers. And I suppose, even after all this time, that scares me. Because it's no longer just me. It's you too. And as long as Viktor seems determined to stop us, you're in danger."

The three of us stand there, silently digesting all that.

"So," Anne says, breaking the quiet. "Where are those documents, anyway?" She walks over to Olensky's desk.

"My copies are in the loft," I say. It is entirely possible, I then realize with a jolt, that Viktor has gained access to our information.

"Luckily," Olensky says with a small smile, "a good researcher never gives up his sources without a backup." He shuffles through the tallest pile on his desk and extracts a manila folder.

"May I look at them?" Anne asks. "I know you've both read them, and I know they led you to me, but I'm the one who has the power. Anastasia's been in my dreams. So has Baba Yaga. She's even appeared to me on the street, remember? So if it's all about me, then maybe I'm the only one who can see all the signs." She reaches across the desk and places her hand on Olensky's folder. "You said before that we just need to know where to look and what to see when we get there. Well, maybe if I really am related to someone in the Brotherhood bloodline, then I'm the only one who knows exactly what to see."

I stare at her, startled. Of all the many things that have occurred to me, this has not been one of them. Perhaps that's the real reason I've lived so long—to figure out how absurdly shortsighted I've been.

"Go ahead," Alex says to Anne. "Let's see what you can find."

The small clock on Alex's desk clicks on seven as Anne opens the folder, extracts the sheaf of papers, and settles back in her chair to read. And although it has been a very long time since I have prayed, I utter prayers now for this beautiful young woman who just might find some of the answers we need.

The Forest, Evening

Anastasia

AUNTIE'S CAT CURLS UP AGAINST ME, HIS YELLOW EYES GLOWING with something I cannot even begin to name. My fingers search the pocket of my dress, feeling for the small bit of bread I have placed there. The tiny offering my *matroyshka* has said I might need.

"Here, *koshka*." I hold out my hand as the doll has taught me, palm up, the coarse brown crumbs lying in the center.

The animal sniffs, considers. Then his small mouth opens, and he bends his head over my hand. My skin prickles as his wet, rough tongue runs across my palm.

In the fire, the images flicker. Baba Yaga and I watch and listen.

"Where is he, Dimitri?" Viktor rages at a man I do not know. His anger pours out of him. And I think of the day I found him pacing the stone chapel, the knuckles of his right hand dotted with his own blood, the skin shredded from pounding against one of those stone walls. That was the day he told me he had warned Papa of what was coming. The day Papa had dismissed him with a brief wave of the hand.

"He is dead," the man called Dimitri says to Viktor. "Vladimir is gone. Ethan must have...he never came out of the building."

"And Ethan and the girl?"

"They escaped. But it should not be too hard to find them. You've thrown Ethan off his game. I'm sure he thinks the whirlwind was Baba Yaga's doing, not ours."

"Of course he does," Viktor says. "He thinks whatever I make him think. He always has. But the girl—we will need to be much more careful in how we go about this."

"She is strong," Dimitri says. "And her strength—it is growing. If we are to stop her, we must do it soon."

"We will," Viktor tells him. "Oh, we will."

Next to me, Auntie laughs, a wild sound that fills the room like a howl. "He thinks he knows," she says, "because he was able to use us. Use the one they call Ethan too. But he has no idea about the girl's power. He thinks he understands. But he does not."

"Understands what?" I ask Auntie Yaga.

"Many things," the witch tells me. "But the one he understands the least is destiny."

WEDNESDAY, 8:10 PM

ANNE

I UNFOLD MYSELF FROM THE CHAIR, ARCH MY BACK, AND STRETCH, trying to ease the knots out of my muscles.

Professor Olensky and Ethan are still hunched side by side, elbows on the desk, studying something on the computer monitor. They've been pulling up website after website, document after document. None of them seems to be doing us any good. We still don't know how to get to Baba Yaga's or why Viktor seems determined to stop us. I may have all this power, but I still have no idea how I'm going to use it, which let me say, is not thrilling me.

"Any luck, my dear?" The professor looks up from whatever they're reading.

"None," I tell him. "Less than none. I thought—well, I thought it would help if I looked. But I guess I'm just as clueless as the two of you."

A muscle in Ethan's jaw clenches at the word *clueless*, but he doesn't say anything.

"I know all this is supposed to be about me," I say, "but you guys know it's ridiculously boring, right? All the 'When there shalt cometh' kind of stuff over and over? How much of that can you read before you just feel like falling into a coma or something?"

I ignore Ethan's glare. And Professor Olensky's.

It's getting late, my eyes hurt, and I'm going to need to forge a note to explain why I wasn't in my classes this afternoon. Pretty soon, either I'll need to call and talk to my mother or father or show up at home, or I can kiss ever being a licensed driver good-bye.

"I'm going to have to get home soon," I say. "Even with my parents thinking I'm at Tess's, they'll expect me back by nine or so. Ever since—" I pause, realizing that I haven't told Ethan about my brother. A part of me wonders if he somehow already knows. "My parents worry easily," I say instead. It's the truth, even if it's not all of it. "There's only so much Tess can say to cover for me if they call her house."

Ethan's face tightens. "I'm not happy about letting you out of my sight," he says. "It's too dangerous right now."

What does he honestly expect? That I'll just say okay, let me go pack a bag, and I'll move into your destroyed loft? Or perhaps bunk here with the professor for a few months? Or however long it takes to—?

My heart rams its way into my throat at the firm knock at the professor's office door. Ethan grabs me and yanks me behind him. "Stay back," he hisses at me. "It might be—"

"Anne?" a familiar voice bellows through the professor's door. "Anne, are you in there? Say something. Open up, or just shout if you're there."

"Stand down, Wolverine." I shove Ethan aside, walk over, and unlock the door. "It's okay."

And with that, Tess—carrying a delicious-smelling bag with the Wrap Hut logo in one hand and her little Burberry purse in the other—enters.

"Well," she says, setting the bag down on the professor's desk, where it immediately starts to ooze grease all over some student's essay, "you weren't that hard to find. I just asked a couple of frat guys headed for a party if they'd heard of some professor named Olensky, and they walked me right over here."

I guess I'd told her Olensky's name when I called her. On Ethan's cell phone.

"I figured if you were saving the world or whatever," she rattles on, "you probably needed snacks by now. Plus, to be honest, I couldn't handle another phone call from your mother." She places her hand on my arm. "Remember when you get home that the sandwich she packed for your lunch gave you food poisoning or something. So we kept studying, but you were in the bathroom puking every time she called."

I've been standing, my mouth hanging open, just kind of gaping at this vision that is Tess. I sneak a sideways glance at Ethan and the professor and see that they're pretty much doing the same thing.

"How did you get here?" I move the bag off the papers and try to mop up the grease with the palm of my hand. "You can't drive alone yet."

"I called Sarah," she says to me, even though she's not really looking at me. Instead, she's eyeballing Ethan with that same evil, squinty look she'd directed toward Neal Patterson and Kate Harris earlier. "She dropped me off in front of the campus. I told her I'd get a ride home from the guy you were with."

She stomps over to Ethan, stretches up on tiptoe—something she does quite gracefully, by the way—and directs her glare straight into his blue eyes. "You *are* going to take us home in a minute, you know. She may believe all this crap you've been telling her. And who knows? It may all be true. But she hasn't known you very long, and I don't trust you. So you guys will finish up whatever you're working on, eat the sandwiches I brought, and then we're out of here. Get it?"

I think she's done speaking, and so does Ethan, who opens up his mouth to respond. But Tess—well, she's Tess, and she doesn't stop until she's gone a few steps too far.

"Last summer," she says, still eyeball to eyeball with Ethan— who's looking amazingly uneasy for a man who just recently used magic to *kill* someone—"I was stupid enough to have sex with a guy who wasn't who I thought he was, which was someone who wouldn't cheat on me. So I don't care what you've been telling my best friend here, or *how* hot you look—I'm not going to stand by and let something like that happen to her."

Oh. My. God. Tess.

Ethan flushes from the part of his chest I can see at the top of his blue shirt to the roots of his chestnut hair. Then he flushes some more. It's the reddest I've ever seen anyone's face—and that includes my third-grade teacher, Mrs. Klinger, who once bent over to pick up something from the floor and farted—loudly—in front of our entire class during story hour.

Professor Olensky gives a snorting sound, then claps his hand over his mouth.

And I stand there thinking that being scooped up by a giant pair of hands or devoured by some magical whirlwind might not be so bad right now.

"She...you...she simply can't be here right now!" Ethan sputters. His gaze seems to be fixed on some invisible point in the air. "Is this who you called when I gave you my cell phone?

You told me you were leaving a message for your mother, not calling all your little friends."

"This is Tess, Ethan. Not *all* my friends. Just one. And she cares about what happens to me. She—"

"This isn't a damn game, Anne!" He whirls to face me, his blue eyes darkening. "Do you actually still think we're just playing here? That this is still something you can go home and gossip to your girlfriends about? You think that's what this is? After what's already happened? After what you've seen? After what I—This is real, Anne. And now you've put your friend in danger by having her come here."

"She didn't tell me to come," Tess says. Her voice quavers, but she continues. "I came on my own, because I was worried about her. And I still am. You're right. None of this is a game—not to me. She may think she trusts you, but *I* don't trust you. I don't know you. I've seen you at the ballet, and once at school. I don't know anything about you."

"Tess," I say. "Let me—"

"No." Tess flashes me her pissiest look. "You let me finish." Her gaze snaps back to Ethan. "Anne's told me what you think she can do. That she's supposed to save Anastasia, who's trapped somewhere and didn't really die back in nineteen-whenever-it-was. Well, I'm not buying a word of it—but let's say it's true. Let's say that Anastasia did live through that massacre, like you say. So? This is the twenty-first century. What possible difference could it make? There's no more Russian aristocracy. Hell, there's no more Soviet Union. It's all a bunch of little whats-it-stans and places like the Ukraine."

"Not all that little," Olensky observes dryly. "My dear, Russia spans eleven time zones."

"Well, yeah." Tess begrudges him that. "But still—what do they need Anastasia for? Why the hell would you want to save her?"

I don't know what stuns me most—the fact that Ethan backs off and stands there silently, as does Olensky, or the fact that Tess actually seems to know something—most of it seemingly accurate—about Russian current events.

But whatever it is that's pulsing in my hands does its thing again as I answer. "Because she's a person," I say. "Because Anastasia was a seventeen-year-old girl who never got a chance. She lost everything she ever had, everybody she ever loved. If she really still is alive, she's been trapped this entire time, unable to do anything she was supposed to. No one deserves to lose it all like that. No one."

I'm thinking about David, about what it's like to watch someone fade away and become just a shadow of what he used to be. By the look on her face right now, I'm pretty sure Tess knows that too. And since she's my best friend, she probably also knows I'm scared—and I'm tired and hungry and seriously overwhelmed by this whole destiny thing.

I look past Tess, over to Ethan. "I'm sorry," I tell him, even though with Tess here now, I'm wondering again if I can really trust him. "I know I should have told you that I called Tess too. But it's done now, and we need to just deal with it. You're not making it any better by yelling again. We're not getting any closer to the answers."

"I wasn't—I mean…" Ethan blows out a breath. "At the beginning, it was about restoring a Romanov to power. That was our mission. That's what I believed when I pledged to do this thing—the Romanovs were the rightful rulers of Mother Russia, even if

Nicholas was a poor excuse for a tsar. They were believers. They deserved our help. It made sense to me then. So when Viktor told me what needed to happen, I accepted it. I was eighteen. Lots of crazy things made sense then." His lips pucker in a little half-smile. "But now—well, we're all asking ourselves those same questions. Why Anastasia? And why Anne for that matter?"

He clenches his hands, then unclenches them. "I just want us to get through this safely," he says finally. "There are so many unknowns that I think we should—"

"What I think we should do, Ethan," Professor Olensky cuts in, "is rest for a moment and eat the food that this young woman has so kindly brought for us. Surely we can take some time to refuel. Then we will put our heads back together and figure out what to do next."

I'm waiting for Ethan to argue with him, but he doesn't. He just sighs hugely and nods his head.

So we eat. I hadn't been hungry before, but now I'm ravenous. Tess, thankfully, has brought enough for a small army. We break into the bag, dividing up the pita wraps, gyros, and little bags of chips. Professor Olensky goes into his whole tea routine again, and everyone digs in. Tess and I flop down on the carpet and spread our food on some napkins. Ethan and the professor stay at the desk, where the professor continues to scroll through a website while he eats.

"I can't believe you," I whisper to Tess as I watch her pick the onions out of her half of the gyro sandwich. "How could you look him in the eye and say all that stuff? Did you see his face? God, Tess."

She plucks out another sliver of onion and lays it next to the others she's got lined up neatly on a Wrap Hut napkin.

She's made a cute little onion border around the picture of the pita shaped like a little cottage.

She shrugs. "It's the truth, isn't it? Neal's an ass, but this Ethan guy is seriously yummy looking—don't deny it." She grins at me. "I can't remember ever seeing anyone turn that color red. That was amazing. So don't even try to tell me that he hasn't been thinking about you as anything other than the super special savior of old-timey Russia. I don't buy it."

"Lower your voice," I hiss at her. "He can't possibly. No. I mean he's—well, no way."

I take a bite of my half of the gyro and busy myself with chewing. Nothing like the thought of dating your great-great-grandfather to make you a little queasy.

"So," Tess says. I'm grateful when she swivels her attention to a topic other than hooking me up with the world's oldest teenager. "Tell me about this witch again. Baba Yaga—the one from the Russian fairy tale who has supposedly carried off Anastasia."

"What about her?" I crumple up my dirty napkins and sandwich crumbs and toss them into the wastebasket next to Olensky's desk—well, I try to, anyway. What I actually do is toss my garbage on Ethan's foot.

He sighs—his favorite form of communication since Tess's arrival—then picks up the garbage and places it in the can. Then he scoots his chair over to sit with us. Olensky remains where he is, hunched over the computer, sort of muttering under his breath.

"Well," Tess says, "she's a witch. So—with all due respect to the *Wizard of Oz*—is she a good witch or a bad witch? I mean, if she's saved someone, that would make her a good witch. But if she's trying to hurt you, then she's not so good. It's confusing."

"It's part of what we're trying to figure out," Ethan says. I guess he's resigned himself to including Tess in our conversations as long as she's here. "She's not really good, at least not in all the legends. When she—well, when the Brotherhood's magic compelled her to help us, she did a good thing, but it was forced on her. She is still compelled by that magic, as far as I know. Where she stands now on the spectrum of good and evil—that's a lot harder to say."

There is way more of a gray area here than I'd like. At least in *Swan Lake*, when Prince Siegfried screwed up, it was just because he was a stupid twit, not because Rothbart was evil only on odd days of the month or something.

"So when she chased us back at school," I say, "you're saying it's possible that she *wasn't* trying to hurt us?"

Ethan nods his head. "It's possible. Until I know for sure how much Viktor is involved in everything that's just happened, I can't really say."

"Anyway," Tess says, "this Baba Yaga—she's supposed to live in that little cottage with the chicken legs, right? And you said the legs were so she could move her house from place to place. So how's Anne going to find her? I mean, even if Anne *is* descended from some magical dynasty, if Baba Yaga moves around all the time, how will she know where to look?"

Ethan rubs his jaw. "We're working on it," he says, and gets up to rejoin the professor.

"Terrific," Tess says as she gathers the remains of her sandwich and wrapper. She lowers her voice. "Are you okay?" she asks me. "I mean, really? God, Anne, this is all so crazy.

And what's even crazier is that I'm starting to believe it along with you. I mean, things like this just don't happen—only they *are* happening."

"I'm okay," I say. "I'm just so tired." All at once, I really was. "I'm going to close my eyes for a minute, okay? I think it will help me clear my head."

"I can call Sarah," Tess says. "We'll just say you have to go, and we'll meet her and…"

Tess continues talking, but the exhaustion washes over me, as thick as fog. I stretch out on the carpet and cradle my head in my arms. When the dream begins, I know it, but I can't open my eyes to stop it.

I'm dreaming that I'm Anastasia again, and it's like I've dreamed before. I'm her, inside her body, her mind, there in that basement with her family when the killing begins. I can feel her panic. My heart is beating as hers is—unbearably fast. Her thoughts are racing. In those moments of my dream, we become one. Her flashes of memory become my own, and I know what I'm seeing as though I am her. Playing with my dog. Edging away from Rasputin when he comes into the room. Holding my brother Alexei's hand. Worrying that he will get sick again. Looking at myself in a dressing-table mirror. Laughing with my three sisters.

And talking in the park to a man named Viktor. He's tall and thin, with an angular face and dark, dark eyes—so dark they're almost black. "It will work," he says to me. He's speaking Russian, I think, but because I am not me, I understand him. "I promise you. You just need to be brave, like the girl in that story you love: Vasilisa. Be brave, and do this for your family— and they will live."

"Are you sure, my brother?" I ask him.

"I promise you, Anastasia," he says. "I promise. I give you my word."

These are the thoughts that fly through my head as I dream of Anastasia. In that horrible basement, the killing continues. *You lied to me, brother,* I think, and I see Viktor in my head as I say it. Then, in the corner of the room, I see someone in a long, brown robe crouched out of the line of fire. I feel my heart surge a little. Viktor. He is here. He will do as he promised. It will all work as he said. But even as I think it, I know it can't be true. My father is already lying on the ground, blood pouring from his wounds. My sisters are dead as well. Surely he must know this. Why isn't he stopping it?

Now I look closer. It's not Viktor. It is someone else—not my brother who made me that promise, but some stranger with blue eyes who is muttering words and looking at me with tears in his eyes. And I know what's about to come next. I know she's coming for me. Baba Yaga. But nothing else is like Viktor said it would be. My family is dead. When the hands come down to pull me away, all I'm thinking is that I want to die too.

"Anne!" Tess is shaking me. "God, Anne, wake up! Please. Wake up!"

I open my eyes. Tess is bent over me, just inches from my face, her eyes really, really wide. Although I don't mention it, she's breathing gyro breath in my face, and let me say, it's pretty rank.

"You were crying," Ethan says. I realize he's kneeling on the other side of me.

I reach up and touch my cheeks. They're wet with tears.

Then I shove Tess away and sit bolt upright as it all comes rushing back to me. "She knew him," I say. "Anastasia. She knew Viktor. I was dreaming I was her again. She knew who he was."

Ethan shrugs, even though I can see he looks relieved that I'm sitting up. "He probably wasn't a stranger to her. I know he went to the royal palace now and then. Nicholas—the tsar—was not unfamiliar with the workings of the Brotherhood. We existed to protect the royal family."

"No, Ethan. I don't mean like that—not like she saw him around the palace or even got introduced to him and knew his name. She *knew* him—really knew him. At least, that's how I saw it. She kept calling him her brother, but it didn't feel like a title—not like when you use it and call him Brother Viktor. I could feel that she thought of him as an actual brother, like her brother Alexei, only not exactly the same. He'd promised her something. She was remembering how she talked to him. They were standing in a huge park, I think. 'You just have to be brave,' he told her. 'Like Vasilisa.' He said if she was brave, then she could save her family, and that's what she was thinking while she watched them die—that he'd promised her, and she'd agreed, and she knew Baba Yaga was coming for her. Only he'd lied. He'd lied, and you were there instead of Viktor, and everyone was dead."

In that moment, it's like a whole bunch of things suddenly make sense to him in a way they just haven't before. Professor Olensky is at my other side now, glancing back and forth between me and Ethan and looking like he's about to jump out of his skin with excitement.

As for Tess, she just looks relieved that I'm conscious.

"You're very clear about this?" Ethan says then. "That Anastasia wasn't surprised? That she knew—at least in some way—what was about to happen to her?"

I nod. "Yeah. There was nothing uncertain about it. She knew. And she knew him. And when she realized it was you in the corner, she—well, that's when she started thinking that he'd lied to her. I mean, I know it's a dream, so I'm not sure if we can—"

"We must believe it," the professor says. "We're dealing with magic and folklore here, so we must accept those parameters— let them mesh with our world and see what happens. Your dreams are part of it, so we have to take them as they are. In literature, you'd call it a suspension of disbelief. For example, we have to accept that in a fairy tale, animals can talk. For our purposes, it's really the same thing. We figure out the rules and accept them."

"He sent me," Ethan says, and I can see him going back there in his head. "Viktor knew the tsar, but he sent *me* that day. He told me he wasn't even positive the assassination would occur right then, but he'd heard rumors that the time was close, and he wanted me to be there. He didn't go himself. If he knew how crucial this was, why would he teach me the words? Why would he set up something this monumental and then not go himself?"

"So what then?" Tess stands up, then reaches out her hand and hauls me off the floor too. Ethan and the professor follow our example. "Did this Viktor guy have something to hide? I mean, why would he not want to be there? Maybe he just couldn't watch it happen. If he knew her like you said, maybe he just couldn't stand to be there. You guys were supposed to be protecting them, right? So if he knew most of them were going to die, maybe he just couldn't handle watching it."

"But she kept thinking that he'd promised her she could save them—and that he'd broken his promise," I say. "She was really clear on that. It wasn't just that it didn't work out, but that he'd lied to her."

"Well, that's original." Tess snorts. "A guy going back on his promise. Big deal. Men are bastards. Nothing new about that." Her eyes go squinty again, and I'm pretty sure she's thinking about Neal.

"Oh," the professor says. "Oh! I can't believe I didn't—oh!" He claps Tess on the back a couple of times. "Young lady, you're a genius, an absolute genius!" He's grinning hugely at her, and his eyes are lit up like two little candles.

"Because I said men are bastards? Present company excepted and all that, but is that like a surprise to you? Being that you're a guy, I figured you already knew." Tess shrugs Olensky's hand away.

"Alex," Ethan says. "What are you—? Oh!" Whatever it is that the professor has figured out, Ethan seems to be on the same wavelength. "Oh my God! It's the first thing that finally makes sense."

"Not to me," I say. "Want to clue us in?"

"Viktor was her brother," Ethan says.

"Well, I told you she thought about him like that, kept calling him her—oh. I get it. I mean, I think I do. You mean like—"

"Like Tsar Nicholas had an illegitimate son," Professor Olensky says. "Viktor. And Anastasia knew."

"Whoa," Tess says. "You mean *that* kind of bastard. This is finally getting really interesting."

"Yeah," I say. "But would it have been a secret all this time? Wouldn't other people have known?"

"Yes and no," the professor says. "First of all, you have to remember that this was the late 1800s and early 1900s. No Internet. No instant communication. No cell phones snapping pictures and sending them around the world in the time it takes for you to press a button. And no media like we know today. This was tsarist Russia. No freedom of the press either, like here in America."

"And the yes part?" I ask.

"The yes part," Professor Olensky says, "is that the history books are filled with stories about Tsar Nicholas and his possible affairs—particularly because his father, the previous tsar, didn't want him to marry Alexandra. We know, for example, that Nicholas had a well-documented affair with a dancer from the royal ballet. But there have been rumors for years that there were other affairs, other women. It seems very possible that one of these other women was Viktor's mother."

"Do you think Viktor knew? Who he was, I mean?"

Ethan blows out a breath. "Of course he knew. And he told Anastasia. It all makes sense. It explains what you saw in your dream and why she would have trusted him. Who knows? Maybe that's why they all trusted him. Maybe they went down there like lambs to the slaughter because of it."

"I don't think so," I say to him. "I know you were there and I wasn't, but every time I relive it—it's not like that, Ethan. It's only her. She's the only one who's looking for it to happen."

Ethan shrugs. "Nicholas had to have known who Viktor was. He had four daughters before the tsarina finally gave birth to Alexei, to a son. If he had another boy out there, he'd have known it. But I don't see any way for us to find that out for sure—at least for now. Even if we go on the assumption that this is the truth—that Viktor was Anastasia's illegitimate half brother—it still doesn't tell us why he wants to stop us—why he wants to keep her trapped. Or why I was so blind to it all back then."

"It's the Neal factor," Tess says. "People tell you one thing, but they're really doing another. Not everyone is a good guy."

Ethan rolls his eyes at that.

"Enough with Neal," I tell Tess. "Seriously. Give it a rest."

"It's relevant," she says. "You can't deny it. Besides," she eyeballs Ethan, "Anne says that you were a monk back then, right? So you wouldn't have been thinking about all that kind of stuff anyway, would you? Tsars fooling around and all that?"

"No," Ethan says evenly. "I suppose not."

We all ponder that for a minute. In the silence, Professor Olensky strolls back to his computer.

"So how does this all lead back to Anne?" Tess grabs up her purse from the chair where she'd tossed it, pulls out her lip gloss, and re-glosses her lips.

"I guess I could be related to any of you," I say. "How many brothers were there, anyway?" I direct my question to Ethan. "Come to think of it, I could even be related to you somehow, couldn't I?"

"Yeah," Tess adds, then dumps the lip gloss back in her purse. "You've been around a long time. Maybe you've got some love child out there you don't know about."

Ethan scowls. I press my hand over Tess's mouth and then take it away all covered with peach-colored gloss. "Gross," I tell her, and I'm not sure whether I mean the gloss or the love-child comment.

"You're not the only people to ask questions like that," the professor says as he settles himself back in his chair and starts clicking the mouse again. "So when we research, we work systematically—cross off stories that aren't really plausible and work with what is. Like those stories that existed for years about the woman named Anna Anderson who claimed she was actually Anastasia. Some people believed. Others examined the evidence—eventually even DNA evidence—and declared she was a fake. The tale of Anastasia is so powerful, it seems to attract people and stories like a magnet."

"Imagine if anyone knew all the stuff you guys are talking about," Tess says. "You wonder if they'd believe you or think it was just too crazy."

"You'd be surprised at what people are capable of accepting, whether it's true or not," Olensky says. "For instance, there was a woman who contacted me a few years ago through one of my colleagues in Prague. Nadia Tauman was her name. She sent me—here let me show you." He gestures for us to join him at the computer and brings up a document for us to see.

"It's a family tree she sent me. I've received dozens like this over the years, but this was one of the most intriguing, even if ultimately it was a dead end. Now, I suppose, we could insert Viktor's name into it, see if that took us anywhere different—although it's a time-consuming task and—well, look."

Ethan, Tess, and I read the letter over the professor's shoulder. Nadia Tauman, it seemed, had helped her friend Lily give up Lily's newborn baby girl for adoption. By itself, that wouldn't be out of the ordinary—just sad, maybe, because Lily didn't want to give the baby away. But her husband had been gunned down in a jewelry-store robbery in Chicago, and she had no means of support to keep her baby. Nadia was claiming that there was more to the story. Her cousin in Prague had heard Olensky lecture about the Romanovs and given her his email, because according to Nadia, Lily was not just any ordinary young widowed mother. She claimed she was the great-granddaughter of the last tsar of Russia.

"Huh," I say. Something about the story has tickled the back of my brain, but I have no idea what it is, and I'm on such information overload right now that it's probably nothing. "You get letters like this all the time? People claiming these connections to the Romanovs?"

The professor nods. "Yes," he says, "although this one was particularly heartbreaking to read."

Ethan points to the monitor. "Like you say, Alex, we could certainly contemplate the possibility that if the great-grandfather was Nicholas, then there is also a relation to Viktor—although I'm not sure where that gets us."

"Plus," says Tess, "how would you know? She's listed only mothers' names here."

I read through the names with Tess. Lily, daughter of Natasha, granddaughter of a ballerina named Irina, great-granddaughter of an unnamed woman who had an affair with Tsar Nicholas.

"So if Nicholas was really Viktor's father, then this Irina could have been Viktor's lover," Tess says. "Cool."

I glance over at Ethan on that one. His expression is pretty guarded—which makes sense, since what do you say when someone you've known and trusted turns out to be someone else entirely?

"We could only make that connection if we were certain these claims were valid," Professor Olensky says, and there's an edge of frustration in his voice. "But I lost contact with Nadia, and through her, Lily. There's really no way to document any of this at this point."

"What about the baby?" I ask as I get to the bottom of the page. "Does it say what happened to the poor baby?"

Olensky scrolls to the next page. "According to this, she was adopted by a family here in Chicago," he says. "See?" He points to a sentence in the middle of the next page. "Baby girl, Laura, born in 1965. Closed adoption."

I read the sentence. And then I read it again. My hands turn to ice. I know what was tickling at the back of my brain.

"Oh," I say. "I think I'm going to be sick." I swallow hard, fighting back the bile that's rising in my throat. I'd told them that maybe I was the only one who could see the clues. I didn't know what it would feel like to be right.

"What's wrong?" Ethan places his hand on my shoulder. Tess and Olensky are both looking at me as well.

"What is it?" Tess asks. "Anne, what's going on?"

"Lily," I say. "She had a daughter named Laura, born in 1965 and given up for adoption."

"I got that," Ethan says slowly, as though if he speaks too fast, I might just freak out and bolt away. "Anne, what is it?"

I close my eyes and breathe in deeply. But when I open them, the words on the screen still say the same thing.

"It's my mother," I tell them. "Laura—she's my mother. I—I'm Lily's granddaughter."

WEDNESDAY, 9:15 PM

ETHAN

Lily's granddaughter?" I say to Anne. "Explain yourself. Certainly you know your grandparents."

"Well, no, I don't. Not really." Anne's face has drained of color. She looks scared and young—too young.

"Oh," says Tess, and once more, I have to resist the overwhelming urge to just throttle the girl. "This is the Grandma Ellen story, isn't it? You guys are gonna love this one. Her grandmother is the biggest bi—"

"For God's sake, please, please just let her tell it." I grab the pack of Winstons from the desk. "May I?" I ask Alex, although I'm already pulling matches from my pocket.

"Go on," I tell Anne as Alex nods, and I slide a cigarette from the pack, light up, and take a deep drag. "Let's hear it."

"Two years ago," she begins, "my older brother David died of cancer." She bites her lip, and I know the telling of this tale is costing her. It is a price I understand all too well.

"It was horrible," she says, "and it was quick. Too quick. One day at football practice, he went out for a pass, and he dropped it. Coach yelled at him, 'Michaelson, what the hell are you doing?' David told us he wondered the same thing. But he had this horrible pain under his arm when he reached up to catch the ball, and when the trainer felt around to see if it was a muscle tear, he found this lump."

Anne pauses, and once again, her eyes well with tears. "Turns out he had lymphoma. So the doctors began treatment, and he was supposed to be okay. He was young and an athlete. Only it didn't matter because the cancer had spread to his lungs and his brain. That was September. We buried him that following January. It was the worst thing our family had ever gone through. It still is."

A tear traces its way down Anne's cheek, and as it does, the images of my own family flicker through my memory. I take another drag of the cigarette and flick ashes into a mug that still holds a few swallows of old tea. After so many years, I'm still surprised that the longing can be so great.

"Here," Alex says to Anne. He fumbles around, unearths an empty tissue box, then finally hands her a couple of unused napkins. She smiles, takes one, and dabs at her eyes.

"Thanks," she says. "I hate getting all…I hate being that person—the one everybody feels sorry for. You know, that was my first thought when David died. We walked out of his hospital room, and we had to start calling people. To tell them. And I—I kept thinking how I didn't want to do that, because once we told them, I wouldn't be just Anne anymore. I'd be Anne whose brother David died. And I hated it."

"But what does this have to do with the woman named Lily?" Olensky asks.

"I'm getting to that," Anne says, "but you need to see the whole story to understand. After the funeral, we were all back at our house. The neighbors had brought food, and Grandma Ellen was trying to get my mother to eat something. 'Just *something,*' she said to her. I remember she tried to hand my mother a deviled egg. Now, my mother hates deviled eggs, but Grandma Ellen said to her, 'Laura, dear, Mrs. Lewis made these. She's such a lovely young woman.' And suddenly, my mother was screaming. See, you have to understand, my Grandma Ellen is the type of person who's super-polite on the surface. It's all about appearances with her. You don't raise your voice, you call everyone a lovely young man or woman. It drives us all crazy. So my mother was screaming. She knocked the egg out of Grandma's hand, and it splattered all over the floor. 'I don't want to eat!' she yelled at Grandma Ellen. 'My son is dead! I don't want a goddamned deviled egg!'"

"See what I mean?" Tess interrupts. "Her grandma—"

"Let her finish, dear," Olensky tells her. He reaches over and pats Tess on the arm. Then he fixes his gaze back on Anne.

"So my grandma," Anne says, "she just looked at my mom like she'd slapped her. And that's when my mother said it. She yelled, 'Maybe you don't understand what it's like to lose a child, but *she* would! Lily would. You've never understood me, and you've proven that today!' Then she ran, crying, into her bedroom."

Slowly, I drop the remains of the Winston in the teacup. If this is the same Lily, then Anne, and Viktor, and, yes, Anastasia, all come from the same line. The girl I've been trying to save, the man who's betrayed me, and the young woman who's sitting here telling her story—all of them Romanovs.

Olensky's gaze catches mine. His eyes are shining.

"After that," Anne says, "it was like we all pretended it hadn't happened. I guess we were too busy pulling the pieces of our lives back together—trying to be a family again after

David's death. But later the next month, my mom and I spent a day together. She seemed to want to tell me something, so even though it was freezing out, I went walking with her on the beach—not too far from where we just were, in fact. And that's when she told me she was adopted, that Grandma Ellen and Grandpa Sam weren't her birth parents. I guess when she was little, you didn't talk about stuff like that—not like we do today."

"But what did she know?" A note of urgency creeps into Olensky's voice. "About Lily, I mean?"

"Not much." Anne shrugs her shoulders. "But she said her birth mom's name was Lily, and that her birth father had died, and Lily couldn't raise her on her own. That all seems to agree with what that Nadia wrote to you. My mom didn't really dwell on the details much. She just wanted me to understand why she'd said what she did the day of the funeral, let me know that even though Grandma drives her insane, she still loves her. After that, we never really talked about it. But when I read the name Lily, I knew I'd heard it."

Anne sucks in a quick breath. "Oh my God," she says. "My mother—do you know she used to dream she was Anastasia? That's what she told me. This morning, before school, when I was—well, freaking out, I asked her if she'd ever dreamed something over and over. I don't know why I said it, except she looked worried about me, so I had to say something. And she didn't even hesitate. She just blurted out that, oh, yeah, she used to have this recurring dream that she was Anastasia."

"It sort of makes sense," Tess says. "I mean, she's your mother and—hey, wait a second." Tess stares at Anne. Her eyes grow huge. "If you're really related to Lily, then that means…

that would mean that you're—" Tess just stares, her mouth popping open and closed, like a fish out of water.

"A princess," Olensky says. He's beaming. "A princess."

"Well," Anne tells him, "let's get it right. An illegitimate princess. Not quite the same thing."

"Way better," Tess says. "Much more interesting. Think about it. Maybe Coach Wicker will let you guest lecture in world history or something."

"Just shut up," Anne tells her and then laughs. "Seriously."

I just stand there. Surely there is more than one woman in the world named Lily who gave her baby up for adoption. But more than one who gave birth in the same year, in the same place, to a girl named Laura? Who just happened to have had a dream that mirrored her own daughter's?

Viktor's secret affair, and the tryst of his father before him, have resulted in the very person the Brotherhood had pledged to find.

It is a pledge that Viktor now seems determined to break.

But why? And how much of this does Viktor actually know? Does he have knowledge of Anne's lineage? Or does he just see her as the girl foretold by prophecy?

"We still don't understand why Viktor has turned," I say. Dozens of questions hurtle their way through my brain— dozens of questions, but no answers.

"I'm having trouble wrapping my brain around the idea that some witch from a fairy tale really managed to somehow change history," Anne says. "Even if I've seen her. It just seems so damn impossible—but I guess so did seeing her hut move on that Russian lacquer box." She smiles. "You know, my mother figured I was so fascinated with that box that she bought it for me. She gave it to me this morning. It really is beautiful. And I love that little key shape inside."

"Key?" My heart gives a little thump. "The box has a key?"

"It does now," Anne says, and my heart smacks again because this is something new. "Raised up in the center. Like if you could just find a way to get it out, you could—"

This time, all four of us suck in a breath almost simultaneously.

"So what now?" Tess asks. "You figure out a way to get that key out, and you can let yourself into the witch's house and spring Anastasia—if, that is, you can find the place?"

Alex strides over to his bookshelves, scans through the volumes, then reaches up for a thick volume on the top shelf. "Why didn't I think of this before?" he says.

He turns to me, his eyes glittering. "It's a story, Ethan. We've never thought of it that way, but it is." He taps two thick fingers on the book he's pulled from the shelf, *Slavic Folklore*. "We've been treating Baba Yaga as though she's real. It's never occurred to us to think about her as though she's not. It's the story, Ethan. That's where the clues lie. I'm sure of it. A pattern of some sort in the fairy tales like Vasilisa's. How Baba Yaga's hut is accessed in those stories. Maybe it's as simple as that."

My pulse skips a beat. "Then we need to read," I tell him. "Figure this out. Here." I take the book from his hand. "Let me—"

Alex glances at the clock. I do the same. It's after ten. He pulls the book back from me. "What an evening this has been, my friend. Take these two lovely young women home. Let Anne get some rest. I'm certain her parents are worried about her by now. Give me some time alone with all this." He raises a graying eyebrow. "Without distraction."

I hesitate. We need to go to Anne's house at some point, if only for the lacquer box. But if Viktor's men came after us once, they can find us again. It's safer for us to stay together.

Nevertheless, Alex is right. Anne's parents are probably more than worried at this point, and with good reason, if only because they've already lost one child.

"Okay," I say, even though I don't think it's okay at all. "Come on." I motion to Anne and Tess. "Get all your things. I'll drive you home."

I reach in my jacket pocket and pull out the gun I'd taken from Dimitri's partner. "Here." I toss the gun to Olensky. "If you need it. I'll be back in a few hours. I'll drop them off and then go check the loft. That should give you enough time to search this out." I start to say more, but he's already settled at his desk with the book. His thick fingers rustle through the pages.

So I leave him, and, with Anne and her friend in tow, head out into the night.

Wednesday, 10:48 PM

Anne

Y OU SIMPLY CAN'T INVOLVE HER IN THIS ANYMORE," ETHAN mutters as we watch Tess make her way up the driveway to her house. "This whole situation is dangerous enough without adding another person to the mix. You have some power now to protect yourself, Anne. Tess doesn't. She's a smart girl, but that's not going to matter if something comes after her."

Ethan's mood has darkened ever since we left the professor's office, stopping first so Ethan could ward it with his magic. Not that those wards had stopped Viktor at Ethan's loft, which is something neither of us has mentioned.

"It's not like I forced her to come find us," I say. My own temper spikes a bit at his annoyance, but I stamp the irritation back down. It's late, I'm exhausted, and he's right—at least, mostly. Regardless of what he thinks about Tess, he's right to be concerned about her safety and her impulsive behavior.

He shifts the Mercedes back in gear and starts to pull away from the curb in front of Tess's house. "Hey, wait," I remind him. "Aren't you going to do the same hocus-pocus protection thing you did when we left the professor's? You know—the warding spell?"

"Don't treat the magic like it's something frivolous," Ethan says as he parks again and turns off the engine. "It's not some party game or circus trick. It is never, ever something to take lightly." A scold-the-stupid-schoolgirl tone edges into his voice. He pushes the driver's door open, unfolds from the car, and stalks off in the direction of Tess's house.

I open my door, slide out, and jog after him until he stops in the deep shadows of the large spruce tree on the far edge of Tess's front yard. "Ethan," I say quietly. "Wait."

I place my hand on his arm. He shakes it off. "Let's get this done," he says tersely. "We need to get you home, remember? And then I need to swing by the loft and then back to Olensky's." He looks like he's about to say more, but he doesn't. He just stands there, jaw clenched, and starts to stretch out his arms to do the spell. The air around us begins to crackle.

"Wait," I say again. "Stop, Ethan."

I can see him pull back into himself. The air settles. Next to me, the spruce actually gives a little shiver and sprinkles some of its needles on the ground. "What?" That dangerous tone in his voice moves from simmer to boil. Even in the darkness, I can see the straight line of his mouth.

I decide to ignore the pissy gaze he's giving me. "Show me," I say. I place my hand back on his arm. "I need to know what you're doing, Ethan. If—well, if I've got all this power juicing up inside me, don't I need to know how to use it? I mean, isn't that the point? That I need to understand how to control what's there so I can use it—somehow—to save Anastasia?"

Like the spruce tree next to us, Ethan gives a little shake. I can see some of the tension slough off him. A sliver of a smile plucks at his lips, and for what I suppose is the millionth time tonight, he sighs.

"Yes," he says, running a hand over his chin. "Yes, you do."

"Well, yay," I say, although I'm certain there's a more sophisticated response floating around in my brain somewhere. Unfortunately, I can't think of it.

"Here." He moves so I'm in front of him. "We'll do this together."

We stand in the blue-black shadows of the spruce tree. Ethan edges forward, not quite pressing against me, but close enough that I can feel the warmth of his breath against my neck as he speaks.

"Place your arms in front of you," Ethan tells me. "I need you to concentrate. You need to feel the power inside you. And then you—well, you need to imagine what you want it to do."

Ignoring the fact that I can still feel his breath tickling the hairs on the back of my neck and the fact that he's so close I can smell the cotton of his blue shirt and the sort of woodsy, musky smell that's him inside it, I do as he asks. At first, I don't feel much. I can hear the wind rustling through the spruce, a few cars whooshing by on the main street a few blocks over, and the even sound of Ethan's breathing behind me. I close my eyes and try to block out everything but what's inside me.

Think, I tell myself. I picture what my hands looked like when I first saw that blue-white glow; when the sparks flickered as we fought to open that elevator door back in the loft; when I'd shoved Ethan and watched him fly across the room; when I'd realized that maybe whatever was now mine gave me the power to escape Dimitri.

When it begins, it feels like something fluttering lightly in my chest. Not my heart beating, but sort of similar. It's electrical and pulsing. And powerful.

"That's it," Ethan says. He stretches his arms out and rests his hands gently on top of mine. His palms are warm, like they'd been when he held my hand out at the lake.

"Now you just have to use it," he says quietly. "Look over at the house, and imagine a wall around it—something sturdy that will keep out things that don't belong there."

In my mind, I build that wall. Big, gray bricks, thick and wide. Heavy mortar slathered between them. All around Tess's house it stretches, towering to the rooftop and then a short way beyond. My eyes still closed, I add more bricks, feel their heft and weight as they strengthen the barrier. Around me, I can feel the wind pick up just a little. The spruce tree wavers, its fresh, green scent perfuming the air.

I open my eyes. In front of me, Tess's house looks just like it always does—a two-story Cape Cod model with brown wood and white trim. But as I look down at my hands, still buzzing with that good old glow, and at Ethan's hands, doing the same, I know the house isn't exactly the same as it was. I can't see it, but I can feel it—the wall I've constructed is there, under the surface of things, keeping Tess safe.

"Wow," I say, and let out a breath I didn't even realizing I was holding. "Wow." Ethan drops his arms, steps back.

Without thinking about it, I turn around and hug him. "I did it!" I say as I squeeze my arms around him. "I could feel it. It's amazing! I—I had no idea. I just didn't—is it real? I mean, did I really do that? Is that wall really there, even though we can't see it?"

"Hope so," he says. His face is very close to mine when he smiles at me. "Yes, it's there. Not forever, remember. But for now—if anything tries to harm people in that house, it will stop them, keep them from getting inside. By force or by magic."

Even in the darkness, I see a flicker of worry cross his face. We both know that the whirlwind in his loft got through despite Ethan's magic.

"Let's get you home now." He steps back from me—and for one tiny second, I think I might wish he hadn't. But only for a second.

We head back to the car, then drive the couple of blocks to my house, stopping a few doors down so that, if I'm lucky, I won't have to explain my getting out of a stranger's car over an hour past my weeknight curfew of ten o'clock. I may be able to put a magic wall around Tess's entire house, but if there's a spell for dealing with two irate parents, Ethan hasn't mentioned it.

"I'll put the wards around your house too," is what he does say. "And you need to get that lacquer box. Don't let it out of your sight."

"Look for my backpack," I tell him as I ease quietly out of the car. "My parents are going to freak if I lose that cell phone."

He just shakes his head and gives what sounds like a little laugh. "I'll see what I can do," he tells me. "Try to get some sleep, if you can. The magic drains you. You need to—well, recharge."

I don't hear him turn over the engine until I'm at the door, trying to insert my house key as noiselessly as possible. Then the door yanks open from the other side, my mother frowns at me, and my normal world hits me like a pile of those bricks I just conjured up a few minutes before.

Thursday, 12:05 am

Anne

I LEAN BACK AGAINST MY PILLOW AND STUDY THE LACQUER box. No matter how many times I've flipped it open and run my finger over the key shape on the inside, it remains just that—a shape. Just a little raised outline painted on the inside bottom of the box.

I've even gone so far as to close my eyes and rev up my new, special glow hands to see if that would do anything, but all I managed to do was singe my sheets a little. Now, among my many other worries, I can add one that has my parents thinking that I'm smoking in bed.

Down the hall, I can hear the muffled sounds of my parents talking as they get ready for bed. "I'm sure Tess will have them in the car when she picks me up tomorrow," I'd told my mother when she'd started ranting not only about my late arrival but also the conspicuous absence of both my backpack and my cell phone. Her response had included a wide variety of reasons why I no longer needed a cell phone—or a life outside the house, for that matter.

"Your mother's right," my father had added. It's never a good sign when he takes Mom's side. "I know you think that phone is something you absolutely must have, but trust me, I'm more than willing to let you learn that you can get along just fine without it. Especially if you're just going to use it to make excuses as to why you can't come home at a decent hour."

"And don't think we don't realize that you and Tess weren't at her house the entire time." My mother lowered her voice ominously. "If you're going to tell lies, Anne, at least have the grace to come up with something more believable than Tess saying that you're having a bout of food poisoning but not to worry because you're still studying. Give me a break, Anne. I'm not an idiot."

What could I say to defend myself other than the truth, which would just loop us back to her telling me to come up with something more believable? So I held my tongue. In fact, I just about bit it off until they both ran out of steam and I could take a shower and crawl into bed.

That's where I am now, poking at the stupid box and wondering where Ethan is—if he's still at the loft or back at the professor's. I'm ignoring the thought that his hands felt kind of good when he placed them on top of mine, because that is far too weird for me to handle.

So is the sudden shuffle of footsteps in the hall outside my room. My pulse skips a couple of beats, and a montage of doom—Viktor and Dimitri coming to get me riding on Baba Yaga's hands—races through my head. But it's not supernatural doom lurking outside my room. It's just my mother.

"Anne?" Her tone has settled down considerably since we last spoke. "Are you still up?" Light filters in from the hallway as my mother, wrapped in her long, blue robe, opens the door.

"Yeah," I say, shoving the lacquer box under the covers on the far side of the bed and scooting over so she can sit next to me. "Wide awake."

"So." When my mom reaches up to brush her bangs off her forehead, her hand is thin enough that I can see the outlines of the bones, the blue veins pulsing under her skin. "Tell me what's going on."

"Going on?" I stall, because I don't know what to say. *Hey, Mom, did you know your birth mother's probably descended from the Russian Romanovs through a magic-monk-turned-bad-guy named Viktor? And remember how you used to dream about Anastasia? Well, guess what? I'm the one who can actually spring her—yes, that's right, the princess you thought was dead—from the hut of Baba Yaga, where she's been in a sort of holding zone since 1918. And oh, yeah, Baba Yaga—the one whose hut is on that funky lacquer box you gave me? She's real. And by the way, I've run for my life a couple times since yesterday, I've also developed glowing hands and super powers, and a minute ago, I think I just got warm and fuzzy feelings for a man who's—let's see—close to ninety years my senior.*

Any place I begin is going to have Mom running for the Prozac prescription.

"Something's clearly not right," she says to me. Even with just the dim light from the hallway, I can see the worry in her eyes. "This morning—well, I guess it was yesterday morning, at this point—you were worried about some dream, and then coming in so late tonight. And lying to me about where you were—"

"Mom," I start.

"No." She rests a hand—gently, but firmly—on my shoulder. "I know you weren't telling the truth. End of story. And it's not like you, Anne. You and I—we tell each other the truth. I thought that's how it was."

"It's nothing, Mom," I say, knowing even as I speak that it's just as she's said—a lie. "I was late, and I'm sorry. I know you worry more about me since—well, I was just late. That's all it was."

"I'm not going to push you on this, Anne," my mother says stiffly, "but if something really is wrong, I'd hope you'd tell me. And I promise to listen."

The emotions churning inside me bubble their way to the surface. I lean in and hug her. "I love you, Mom. I—I just can't tell you right now. When I know what to say, I will. You're just going to have to trust me. Really."

"Is it Tess, honey?" she asks, clearly not willing to let me slide as quickly as I'd hoped. "Or someone else you know? Anne, is someone in trouble?"

"Yes," I say, trying for some semblance of honesty. "I think someone is. But I—I'm not sure if there's anything I can really do about it."

My mother plucks at the material on the lap of her robe, pinching it and letting go in a pulsing sort of rhythm. "Sometimes, you can help people, Anne," she says, "and some-times, you can't." She takes a deep breath. I'm clear where this is going, and when she looks at me, I almost want to turn away.

But I don't.

"I never told you what I'm going to tell you now," she says. She reaches over and takes my hands in hers, holds tight. The edge of her wedding ring cuts a little against one of my fingers. "But maybe," she tells me quietly, "it will help you with whatever's going on."

I nod silently and wait for her to continue.

"On the day that David died, you and your dad had gone to get some coffee. David was sleeping, and I finally dozed off in the chair next to his bed. I was dreaming that I was at one of his football games, and there he was, running for the ball. He caught it and raced across the goal line. I watched him jump up and down, this big smile across his face. He looked up into the stands and shouted, 'Mom! I did it, Mom! I did it!' And I was so excited that I leaped up and ran out of the stands and down onto the field to hug him. But when I got to the field, I couldn't cross the sideline. I kept running and running, but David kept getting farther and farther away."

"Oh, Mom," I manage. My own voice breaks as I say it.

"I woke up then. My heart was racing a mile a minute. When I looked over at the bed, David's eyes were open. He smiled, and—and he said to me, 'Mom, it's okay. You're going to have to let me go. I can't stay here much longer.' Then he went back to sleep. And a few hours later—well, you were there."

My mother lets go of my hands. For a moment, her eyes are distant.

"Anne." She stops and swallows. "Letting David go was the hardest thing I've ever had to do—but it was what he needed from me."

"Like Lily," I blurt out, surprising both of us. My mother angles her head to look at me. "She had to let you go so you'd have a better life. She didn't have any choice either, did she?"

"Now what in the world made you think of that?" A curious expression crosses her face. "We haven't talked about that since—well, for a long time." She pauses. "But yes, I guess it is like Lily. I hadn't really thought about it. But I guess it is. You're right about that. But, Anne, you're not right about one thing. There's always a choice—but sometimes, it's not an easy one."

She leans over and brushes her lips against my forehead. Then she eases off the bed and stands up.

195

"Get some sleep, honey. We can talk more tomorrow. Just remember, whatever it is, your father and I are here for you. We love you."

"Me too, Mom," I say. I watch as she walks to the door and shuts it behind her as she steps out into the hallway. A floorboard creaks as she heads back to the master bedroom. Then everything is quiet.

I slip the box out from under the covers. "Tell me what to do," I whisper to Vasilisa, the girl on the cover, the one who was able to find and defeat Baba Yaga. "Tell me how to find Anastasia." I look at the other figures on the box—the tiny doll, the three horsemen, one white, one red, one black. Silently, I ask them each the same question.

The only answer is the quiet hum of my ceiling fan. I'm still holding the box in my hand as I finally drift off to sleep.

THURSDAY, 2:00 AM

ETHAN

I ANGLE THE SHOWER HEAD, CLOSE MY EYES, AND LET THE warm water stream over me. I figure I could stand here for a week, toss back more than a few shots of vodka, and smoke my way through another pack of Marlboros before the tension screaming in my muscles begins to ease.

I'd found the loft eerily silent—no sign of the whirlwind that almost sucked us into its jaws a few hours ago, but also no mistaking its aftermath. Furniture scattered wildly. Cups, plates, light fixtures shattered on the floor. But the building—and the loft itself—remain fully intact.

Anne's backpack turned up in a far corner, ragged and tattered but in one piece, her cell phone still tucked inside. And I'd found my copy of Olensky's documents just where I'd left them—hidden in a box under a false panel at the bottom of the heavy, wooden armoire in the back of the room. The entire piece had tipped and fallen, but the panel hadn't given way.

Viktor—and whatever forces he'd harnessed to attack us—had wanted us, not our possessions. And he'd almost been successful.

I massage the back of my neck, then rub one aching shoulder. Even under the pounding water, I can still hear the faint crackle in the air from the powerful magic I'd conjured to reward these rooms, still sense the electrical pulsing that lingers.

I press harder at my shoulder, my fingers tingling ever so slightly as they brush the mark of the Brotherhood, a small tattoo of a lion's head etched into my back. Yet another reminder of the past that has held me so tightly—the bonds that I know now were just lies, illusions. All gone now, just like—I open my eyes and scan my chest and arms—the bullet holes that have also disappeared.

I'm just an ordinary eighteen-year-old again.

Only I'm not—not anything close. And right now, I feel every one of my hundred-plus years. The man I once trusted with my very life has betrayed me. No one in the Brotherhood, it seems, can be trusted. I'm not certain of any of the things that I'd been sure of for so long—including my belief that taking a life was something I could never do.

And then there's Anne.

I glance down at the mark still visible on my forearm, now faded to a dim red circle—the mark that links me to this girl, who has for so long been just a ghost, just a vague hope year after year. But now, I've found her. She's real, solid, and more powerful than she understands.

In the past two days, I've taken her entire life and managed to turn it inside out.

I turn my face back to the stream of water. Anne Michaelson is absolutely nothing like what I had expected—but she is the girl I need to keep safe. We need to complete this mission that, despite everything, still needs completing.

Only problem is, I realize with a shock that's not entirely unwelcome, what I seem to want more than anything right now is to kiss her.

I slam the water shut and step from the shower, then towel off and rummage through the heap of clothes that has spilled from the armoire for jeans and a gray pullover sweater. Then I swipe the towel over my hair a few more times, drop it to the floor, and head to the front of the loft.

I glance at my watch. I need to get back to Olensky. On the other hand, I think wearily, he'd have contacted me if he'd made a breakthrough. Perhaps another hour or so. Let him have the time he needs.

I lug the mattress back onto the frame and sit down on the edge of my bed. Unlike the flimsy wooden chairs, the iron-post construction had kept it from being destroyed. *Just for a second*, I think—I'll rest for just a little bit, then I'll head out to check on Alex. I lie back on the mattress and stretch out.

I sleep.

Thursday, 4:30 am

Anne

IN MY DREAM, I'M WALKING IN A FOREST. IT'S THICK WITH TREES so dense that they're blocking the light, and it smells of rot, of things left too long in one place. Behind me, I hear the crunch of dead leaves as something—or someone—stamps them into the ground. Ahead of me, I just barely see the outline of a small cottage. It's Baba Yaga's hut, I think. I try walking faster. I can see lights flickering in front of it and a small, white fence.

Then the dream shifts. I'm not in Baba Yaga's forest anymore. I'm standing in the middle of Second Street, staring at the Wrap Hut, right next door to my mother's jewelry store. Tess is in front. She's flinging onions over a small, white fence. "Try it," she tells me. "It's so much fun."

I take an onion from her, heft it in my hand, getting ready to throw.

"Here," Tess tells me. "Take these." She tosses two more onions at me. "Three's the charm, you know."

I look at the three onions I'm clutching in my hands. And suddenly, they're not onions at all. They're skulls—three small skulls, each one with hideously glowing eyes.

I scream. The skull-onions drop from my hands. When they hit the ground, I'm back in the forest. Baba Yaga's hut—at least, I think it's her hut—is in front of me. It's balanced on two hen's legs. Their pointy, nailed feet keep digging into the earth beneath them. I look on the ground for the three skulls, but they've disappeared. In their place is the small, black lacquer box with the forest—this forest—on the cover and Baba Yaga's hut tucked behind the trees.

I pick up the box, turn it over and over in my hand. *The secret,* I think, *must be inside.* I open it up and run my finger over the raised key painted on the bottom. *Three's the charm.* But three what? If I just think hard enough, I can figure this out, but it's so hard to think here. The forest so heavy and dim and thick that I can barely breathe.

I look up from the box. Anastasia, in a white dress dotted with blood, stands in front of me. Her long, light brown hair is tied back with a ribbon, and her face is very, very pale. In her hand is a small, wooden doll with a brightly painted face.

She smiles sadly at me—reaches out, but doesn't take my hand.

In a blink of my eyes, I'm no longer in the forest. I'm with Anastasia inside Baba Yaga's hut. The bed, the fireplace, the rocking chair—everything I saw in my dream is there. *But it's not a dream,* I think. Not real either. Something in between.

"Sit," Baba Yaga tells me. "Both of my girls, sit now." Her iron teeth gleam in the firelight as she smiles. My heart is beating impossibly fast. She reaches out one huge, wrinkled hand. I place my hand in hers. Her skin is rough and leathery and very warm. She leads me to a small table flanked by two wooden chairs. Anastasia walks next to me.

We sit. In the fireplace behind Baba Yaga, a skull floats in the flames. Its empty eye sockets stare at us from the bleached white bones.

Something soft rubs against my ankles. I look down. A black cat looks up at me with gleaming yellow eyes. He yawns, and I see his pink tongue and the sharp little teeth lining his mouth. He licks my ankle. His tongue feels rough, like it's coated with tiny pins.

"Leave her, *koshka*." The witch swats at the cat with one enormous hand. He slinks off to some corner I can't quite see.

Outside the hut, there's a pounding sound. Hooves, I think. Yes, hooves. I look around for the lacquer box. There were three horsemen on the cover, weren't there? But I can't find it.

"You hear them, eh?" Baba Yaga says. She stares down at me over her long nose. Her eyes burn darkly. "Do you know the story of my horsemen?"

Silently, I shake my head no.

"Then, child, I will tell you. It is a good story, as all my stories are. Although the ending—well, that will be up to you, eh?" Baba Yaga laughs and slaps one of those enormous hands on the table. The room shudders around us from the vibration.

"There are three of them, each one tall and handsome. Like your Ethan. The one who has helped you find your power. Yes, child, handsome men like that. Each with his own horse—one red, one white, one black. In the early morning comes the one on the bloodred horse. Three times he circles my hut as the sun rises. Three times on his bloodred horse. He brings the morning with him."

Three. The number keeps echoing in my head as she speaks. Three's the charm. Three times round. It has to mean something. If I could wake up, maybe I'd know what.

"The next one arrives at noon," Baba Yaga tells me then.

Her voice keeps filling me up, as if I were in a car with the bass on the radio pumping too loudly. "His horse is white," she says. "Pure and snowy. He brings the day. Three times round he circles this hut. Three times round on his snow white horse."

I want to look away from her, but I can't. Those dark eyes keep burning into me like they did when I saw her on the street in front of Miss Amy's, each pupil a tiny skull that wavers like a flame. As I watch her, a word pops into my head. *Auntie*. It's what Anastasia calls her—Anastasia who is sitting across from me at this tiny wooden table. *Auntie Yaga*. I don't understand how I know this. I just do.

"In the darkness," the witch continues, "the third horseman visits. His cloak is the deep blue of shadows, his horse black as night. As soon as three stars flicker in the sky, I hear his horse galloping swiftly toward me. Round and round the hut he goes—once, twice, three times. He calls in the night, and his voice is as deep as the hollows on the moon that is rising."

She bends to look at me. Her face blocks out everything else in the room. "Do you like the story so far?" she asks. But she does not wait for me to answer.

"We do not have much time, child, so I will finish my tale. But I will not tell you everything. You do not want to know too much. Not yet. The horsemen are my servants. They ride where I tell them. Remember this. You will need it soon. Three horseman, young Anne. Do not forget. I will have to try to stop you. That's the way my story goes—at least for now. That is the way it must be here. But they are not bound as I am. That is one of my secrets, and I'm sharing it with you."

She reaches out and cups my chin with one impossibly enormous hand. "'Once there was a brave young girl,'" she says. "That's how the story starts. But now there are two of you. Anne and Anastasia. We will see what ending you both decide. You are part of each other, you know. That is a piece of your story too. Her blood, your blood."

Baba Yaga grabs my hand and scrapes one long fingernail across my palm. Blood oozes out—one drop, then two, then three, falling like tears on the wooden table. I'm too surprised to feel any pain.

"It all comes down to that," she says as I pull back my hand. "So many choices. Round and round and round, like my three horsemen. To save or to sacrifice? Matters of blood are never simple. You can take, but you must also give up."

"I don't understand," I say. The words croak out of me. I hold my bleeding hand against my chest. I watch as the blood soaks my nightshirt. I turn to ask Anastasia, "Am I supposed to understand?"

The room grows hazy then, like the screen fading out at the end of a movie. I look around. I'm back in the forest, and Baba Yaga's hut is in front of me. It twirls wildly. When it stops, the door is no longer facing me. I'm looking at the back of the hut.

Behind me, there's a ripping sound, like someone tearing a giant piece of paper. Everything shimmers.

I need to get back inside, I think. *Rescue Anastasia.* The lacquer box—I'd been thinking about the lacquer box. And the story. Baba Yaga told me a story, but now I can't remember it. Three times—three times something. What was I thinking? What do I need to do?

"You can do it," a voice says from behind me. "Just open the box again, Anne. I know you can figure it out. You can get us back inside."

I turn around. Ethan's standing behind me. His eyes are so blue they almost make me dizzy. When I look at him, it's like I'm sinking, falling into some endless blue pool. He holds out his hand, palm up. "C'mon," he tells me, and his voice sounds different somehow—farther away. "C'mon. I'll show you."

I don't feel afraid as I take his hand, but it doesn't feel like what I want either. Those long fingers entwine with mine, and heat seeps through my palm and up my arm.

"It's so warm," I tell him. I'm speaking so softly that I can barely hear the sound of my own voice. "I feel like I'm burning."

"Me too," Ethan says. He unlinks his fingers from mine and reaches up to strip off the gray sweater he's wearing. "There." He lets it drop to the damp forest floor, where it sinks into the leaves. "That's better." Then he walks ahead of me toward Baba Yaga's hut.

He just took his shirt off, I think vaguely. I know this should alert me or excite me or do *something* to me, but I can't find the on switch for my emotions. On his naked back, near his shoulder, I can make out the tattoo of a lion. I watch, fascinated, as it sort of wavers back and forth with each step he takes.

Ethan turns his head to look at me. His blue eyes—God, they are so very, very blue—are shimmering. "Don't lag behind," he tells me. "You've got to come now. We've got to save her."

Save her? Save who? Wasn't I just in that hut? My mind is a muddle. Who the hell is it I'm supposed to save? All I can see are those blue eyes. All I can feel is the heat that's rippling off him and out across the forest.

"But I'm afraid," I tell him. And suddenly, I am. My heart races like a jackrabbit in my chest. Still, I can't take my gaze off him, can't move. I try to walk forward, but my feet feel like they're encased in lead. "Something's not right," I say. "I don't know what it is, but something feels wrong."

Ethan will fix it, I think. *Whatever this is. Whatever's making me feel this way. He'll make it better.*

"Don't worry." Ethan walks back to me, wraps his hand around mine again. "It's nothing. Don't worry. I'll help you." His touch is so hot that it blisters my palm. I try to yank my hand away, but I can't.

This isn't right, I think muzzily. *It hurts. This just isn't right.*

"Oh, but it is," Ethan says, as if he's read my mind. "It's what's meant to be." He gathers me in his arms, presses me to him. Is this what I want? Isn't this what I thought I wanted to happen?

I look into his face, and again, it's as though I'm falling— falling and falling as Ethan's eyes grow bluer, as the heat around us shimmers even faster.

He brings my face to his. "I need you," he says, his lips brushing my forehead, the heat of him flooding into me. "I need you." And then he lowers his mouth to mine and kisses me.

I close my eyes. I can feel Ethan's lips press against mine, feel myself kissing him back. His breath is warm, so very warm, and I think my knees are actually about to buckle.

"It's okay, Anne," Ethan tells me, his mouth still rubbing against mine. "It will be over soon."

"Over? But I don't under—" His mouth crushes against mine. I try to wrench myself out of his arms, but he's too strong. His arms tighten around me. Steadily, he's drawing the breath from my body.

No, I think dimly. *No. He wouldn't. Not Ethan. It's not Ethan.* But the vise around my lungs is growing tighter, and tighter still with each breath he takes.

I force my eyes to open and look into Ethan's eyes—two pools of black.

No, I think again. *He wouldn't do this to me.*

"You're right," a voice says. "He wouldn't. But *I* would."

Thursday, 4:30 am

Ethan

Ican't open my eyes. I know I need to wake up, but somehow, I just keep sleeping.

"Don't go," a familiar voice tells me. It's Anne, I think. I need to help her, to go to her, but I simply cannot move.

"It's so nice here," Anne's voice says. "You need to rest."

My eyes are heavy, weighted down—so heavy that they ache as I force them to open. But I have to, I think, even if she's telling me not to. She needs me. My lids flutter slowly, as bit by bit, I struggle to raise them.

Finally, I can see. I'm in a forest of some sort, thick with trees. My nostrils fill with the heavy odor of rotting wood and leaves—and something else, something thick and sweet. Too sweet. My memory flashes to the day I came home to find my family murdered, to the jars of plum preserves my mother had just made, the fruit still warm from the stove. They lay broken and spattered on the floor, their pungent aroma mingling thickly with my family's blood as it seeped back into the earth through the cracks in our wooden floor. It was the smell of death.

I hear a soft rustle behind me. When I turn, Anne is standing in front of me. Even with the scent of rot around us, I can smell the freshness of her skin, the soap she's used, something that smells of peaches and vanilla. She's wearing a thin, blue nightshirt that falls to about mid-thigh. Her legs are bare, and that auburn hair I've always seen pulled back falls softly about her face. She doesn't belong here, I know, but all I can think is that she looks so good, so young, so pretty.

"I've been waiting for you," she says. "I thought you'd never wake up."

She walks over me, cups her slender hands around my face. "Oh, Ethan," she murmurs, her face bending in to mine. "Hold me."

Some small part of my brain is telling me this isn't real, that I'm in danger, that we're both in danger. But still, I reach out and wrap my arms around her, embrace her. My body thrums with the feel of her against me. I've needed her for so long, I think, and even as I think it, it seems true. How could I have existed without her? So many years without her.

I close my eyes again and just breathe in her scent.

"Kiss me," Anne says. Her lips brush against mine.

So I kiss her. Her mouth is warm and wonderfully soft. *I could stay like this forever,* I think. Dimly, I know something is wrong, but the thought doesn't stay with me long.

Anne pulls back. I raise my heavy eyelids again. She looks at me with those deep brown eyes, reaches up, and runs a finger across my lips.

"Don't leave me," she says. "Promise me you won't leave."

I dip my head and kiss her again. "I won't," I tell her. My head is spinning. I'm finding it hard to put words to thoughts. I wanted to kiss her, but this feels forced. Off. As if someone else is controlling what I think, what I do, what I desire.

209

"I'm supposed to do something," I say. Her lips are still on mine, warmer now, burning against my mouth. "I know there's something. I just can't remember. Do you know what I'm supposed to do?"

"Of course," Anne says. My hands slide up to stroke her neck. "Of course I know. Do you want me to tell you?"

"Yes," I say. "Please tell me. I need to know."

But when she opens her mouth to speak, no words come out. I stare into her eyes and realize they've gone dark and blank.

Then, against my own will, my hands tighten around her neck.

Thursday, 4:45 am

ANNE

Searing panic fills me as I pound my hands against Ethan's chest. His mouth burns against mine, pulling the life from me. His hands are squeezing my neck, cutting off my air.

Stay calm, I tell myself. *It's just another dream.* This can't be real. It simply can't be. I've seen those movies. I love them— the ones where the hero gets rid of the bad guy by realizing that he's just a vision or a hologram or something.

But I can't breathe. I can't think.

"It will be over soon," a voice says. It's not Ethan's voice, but someone else's—someone else's voice vying for space in my rapidly emptying brain.

"Let go." The voice slithers softly into my ears. "It won't hurt so much if you just give in."

I have no breath left to say no. All I can do is shake my head. *No,* I think. *No. I can't die this way.*

My hands keep pounding against Ethan's chest. He clutches me to him, his mouth wresting the breath from my body, his hands squeezing tighter and tighter around my neck.

It's an illusion. I know it's just an illusion, just a dream. But I still feel like I'm dying.

Ethan's hands squeeze even tighter.

"You trusted him," the voice says. "You trusted him, and now see how he's repaying you." At that moment, I know who's speaking: the man who wants me dead, who doesn't want me to reach Anastasia. Viktor, my own distant ancestor, who seems determined to get rid of me. He's found some way to get into my head, into my dreams. Ethan—the real Ethan—would never do this. But that won't matter if I can't stop it. I'll still be dead.

Dead.

I let my hands slide limply to my sides, will my body to go heavy.

Viktor takes the bait.

The dream Ethan lifts his mouth from mine just a fraction of an inch. His grip loosens.

Wonderful air rushes back into my lungs.

"I'm not quite as dead as you think, Grandpa," I tell Viktor, wherever he is, and this time, it's my own voice that echoes in my ears. I yank the dream Ethan's arms away from me and shove my fists into and through his chest.

The illusion explodes.

Gasping, I sit up in bed, awake and alive.

THURSDAY, 4:47 AM

ETHAN

CHRIST. I WRENCH MYSELF AWAKE. MY HANDS STILL FEEL like they're around Anne's neck. I'm up and off the bed, shoving on my shoes and jacket even before my legs are steady underneath me.

I stumble into what's left of the kitchen, turn on the faucet at the sink, bend over, and gulp some mouthfuls of water. My throat is dry as dust.

He'd used me against her—stretched out his will with magic, burrowed into my head, and made me…

I flip on the light over the sink, the one fixture that still has a working bulb after yesterday's whirlwind, and look at my watch. It's almost morning. Shit. I've got to get to her.

I pull my cell phone from my jacket pocket. My hands shake as I fumble to open it. I take a breath and punch in the numbers for Olensky's office. I need to get to him, but I need to get to Anne first.

"Ethan?" Alex's voice sounds thick with exhaustion.

"Are you all right?" I ask him, skipping any other preliminaries. "Is anything wrong there?"

"Wrong? No, friend, nothing is wrong. What—what time is it?" In the background, I hear him shuffling some papers.

"It's almost morning, Alex. Viktor came after Anne. He made me—I can't explain now—there's no time. I need to go to her. Stay where you are. We'll be there soon."

I don't wait for a response. I simply flip the phone closed and jam it in my pocket. Then I grab Anne's battered backpack from the floor and head out. This time, I don't bother with a warding spell. I have nothing left worth protecting.

Except the girl I hope remains safe until I can reach her.

THURSDAY, 5:30 AM

ETHAN

I BARELY TAKE THE TIME TO PULL THE KEYS FROM THE IGNITION when I park the Mercedes in front of Anne's house. I should be more cautious, park out of view, but I don't care about any of that—only that Anne is safe.

I scan the house. Through the blinds of a window facing the street—a bedroom?—I can see a vague glow of light. Other than that, the front of the house is dark.

Somewhere down the block, a dog barks as I walk around to the back of Anne's house, open the gate, and slip into the yard. Then I stop dead in my tracks as the unmistakable odor of cigarette smoke filters through the damp morning air.

Anne's mother is standing on the patio smoking. Through the dim morning light, I can make out the red tip of her cigarette; I watch it flicker as she inhales. I edge closer. She sighs as she exhales and pulls her long robe tighter around her slender figure.

It's not just the lingering odor of the tobacco that stops me. Right now, not even a cigarette would undo the tension that's knotted itself into every fiber of my body. It's her. She just looks so—sad. I can see it in her stance, hear it in her sigh. It cloaks itself about her like a mist.

A few seconds later, she senses me, looks up, and screams. A loud, piercing scream, in fact.

So much for sympathy. Or stealth.

"Who are you?" She drops the cigarette to the patio floor and stomps into the yard until she's directly in front of me. I'm more than a little aware that Anne has not developed her personality out of thin air.

"I—uh, I'm Ethan," I say. "Ethan." God, could I sound any more foolish? "A friend of Anne's from school."

"I've never heard her mention you," she says. There's an edge to her voice that I'd rather not be hearing.

"I—well, I'm new. We don't live too far from here." I gesture vaguely to my right.

"Uh-huh." She places her hands on her hips, which I'm assuming is not a good sign. Even in the dim light, I can see the frown in her eyes. "So, Ethan who doesn't live very far from here, what are you doing in my yard at five thirty in the morning?" Her tone is sharp enough that I find myself backing up a few steps.

Unfortunately, she follows me.

"Yard? Well, I—uh…" I pause, hoping wildly for inspiration. Anne's mother continues to glare at me, her eyes flashing. An idea flits though my head, and I grab it like a life preserver.

"I—I told Anne I'd give her ride to school today. I've been tutoring her in history and she has a test today. She wanted to review before school."

"Really?" she says. "You know, most mornings I have to drag my daughter out of bed. You truly want me to believe that she arranged to meet you before dawn so she could study for history?"

216

Well, yes. But clearly, she's not buying it. And if I'm not mistaken, she's also sizing up the idea that I was part of whatever made her daughter so late last night. I suppose at this point I might as well drag the backpack and cell phone out my car, dangle them in front of her, and just call it a day.

I'm still contemplating a response when the patio door creaks and then opens. Anne emerges, a thick terry-cloth robe wrapped around her, auburn hair wet and slicked back. Relief floods through me.

"Mom?" she says. Her voice is tired but steady. "Is something wrong?" She sniffs the air. "Are you smoking again? You promised me—" She stops and peers beyond her mother to me.

"Ethan?" Anne angles her head slightly. She glances from me to her mother and back again.

Now I'm grinning like an idiot. "Anne," I say, and start to walk to her. "Anne, you're—"

Mrs. Michaelson's slender arm is remarkably sturdy as it snakes out and grabs me by the shoulder. "Not so fast, Ethan," she says.

And then she tightens her grip on me.

The Forest, Early Morning

Anastasia

THROUGH THE EYES OF THE SKULL AS IT HOVERS IN THE FLAMES, Ethan smiles at Anne. I am happy to know their names now. To know the name of the man who was there that day. The one I was sure was part of Viktor's betrayal, but who, it seems, is not what I thought at all.

My face is still wet with tears. I felt Viktor rip Anne from this hut, or rather, from the vision of it that Auntie had given her. Felt the violation of her body, of her mind. Just as she has felt what I feel in her dreams, so did I feel this now. He tried to make her believe that Ethan would hurt her. But she was too strong for him. Too clever.

She is what I hoped to be but learned I am not.

Still, I remember what it is to be the tsar's daughter. *Ya khachu videt,* I commanded this skull. "I want to see." And so, while Auntie stands outside, speaking to her horsemen, I get what I want. I watch this girl who is trying so desperately to figure out how to free me. Even if I no longer know what freedom means.

My father's blood is in me still. As is my mother's. Royal lines that go back many generations. Ruler after ruler now reduced to bleached white bones like this skull. It too was once covered with flesh. Blood pulsed through its veins. As somehow blood still courses through me.

Baba Yaga is right. It all comes down to blood. The blood of royal lines. The blood of an ordinary man who wants more than he deserves. Anne's blood, spilling on this table as Baba Yaga sliced into her flesh. The blood of family, slaughtered without regard.

Outside the hut, Auntie's body casts a shadow over the skulls that line the yard on their wooden spikes. Her hands feed oats to the three horses—one red, one white, one black. They scuttle back and forth on their calloused fingertips to the bucket that rests near the gate, scooping out handfuls of brown grain.

My secret brother, Viktor, is not done. My own blood—the thing that connects us, even if I wish it did not—tells me this. He will go after them again. I do not know how, but I know he will. He has always wanted what he could not have. Only too late have I understood that the price for what he wanted was my life.

Like Auntie Yaga, I stretch out my arms. I take one last glance at Ethan and Anne and at the woman I think must be her mother. As my precious *matroyshka*—the doll my own mother gave me so long ago—shifts inside my pocket, I wait for the skull to float back to me.

Thursday, 6:30 am

Anne

I CAN'T BELIEVE THEY LET ME GO WITH YOU." I BUCKLE MY seat belt as Ethan pulls away from my house. "I figured once they started tag teaming, it'd be all over, but they really seemed to like you."

No kidding. Within a few minutes of listening to Ethan's story about his father the petroleum engineer who'd moved the family to Russia for a few years and had now brought them back to the States, my parents were feeding him orange juice and doughnuts and talking to him like he was an old pal or something—which really had me freaked, until I reminded myself that he *was* them, and then some. Not too hard to relate to the adults in the room when you've been one for longer than they've been alive.

Of course, my concentration during the entire event wasn't helped by the fact that Ethan was wearing a pair of jeans that hung low at his hips and the same gray sweater he'd stripped off in my dream. I was wondering—okay, *obsessing* would be a better description—if that sexy little lion's-head tattoo was really there on his well-muscled shoulder.

"Are you okay?" he'd whispered to me as we'd settled around the kitchen table and my mother had continued to fix him with one of those make-a-move-toward-my-daughter-and-I'll-drop-you-in-your-tracks looks. He'd rested his hand on my thigh under the table and studied me with those blue eyes.

I'd nodded my head, then sipped my juice and tried to ignore the hand on my leg. And the memory of his naked back and funky tattoo.

What I couldn't ignore was that unless I was really mistaken, I had almost died. And great-great-grandpa Viktor—if that's what he really is—had wanted me to think it was Ethan. That was the thing that had my throat so dry and my hands so clammy I could barely bring the juice to my lips, barely swallow it down.

Now, here in Ethan's car, I'm still finding it hard to swallow. My head's still swimming. I'm wearing a clean sweater under my denim jacket, but my jeans have now graduated to three-day jeans from two, because they were all I could manage to find after I put on the sweater.

Near-death experiences don't exactly encourage high fashion standards.

Ethan, having kept a cheery smile on his face at my house, looks as grim as I feel. He sort of glanced at me out of the corner of his eye after my comment about my parents liking him but said nothing. Still silent, he's clutching the steering wheel tightly enough to make his knuckles white. His face is drawn and pale, and those blue eyes are clouded with a frown that doesn't seem like it's going to disappear anytime soon.

In the life I used to live, I'd have been in Tess's car right now, her dad at the wheel. I'd be worried about the homework I just remembered I didn't do and the test I didn't study for. But in this new life, where witches bring visions of their huts and mad monks try to kill me in my sleep, I called Tess from upstairs while I was getting dressed. I left her a voice mail when she didn't answer and told her I was going to go with Ethan. I also told her that I would probably be skipping school for another day—something the old me would never have done either—and felt my throat constrict when I told her I'd be careful. Because after what just happened, I'm not sure if that's even possible.

"We've got to get back to Olensky's," Ethan says, breaking his silence. I watch his jaw muscles move as he speaks. "I talked to him before I came for you, and he was fine. We'll get back there, see what he's found. I—" He keeps one hand on the wheel and rakes the other one through his hair. "I'm sorry, Anne," he says. His eyes stay focused on the road. "I'm sorry you had to go through that, have someone—God, that you had to have someone in your head like that. He used me against you. So I'm sorry."

I run one hand along the sleeve of my jacket, pull at a stray thread on the hem. The look on his face is so painful that it hurts to watch him. "Don't be sorry, Ethan," I say, rolling the thread into a ball in the palm of my hand. "He did it to you too. I—I knew it was him and not you. You would never do that to me. I may not be certain of much right now, but I'm pretty clear on that." I roll the ball of thread some more until it's a hard little knot.

Ethan puts both hands back on the wheel, then yanks it hard to the right and maneuvers the car into a parking space. With a suddenness that whooshes the breath from my body—thankfully, not in a bad way this time—he reaches over and wraps me in his arms. My stomach does a nifty little free-fall thing.

"You're right," he tells me, although it's hard to listen because he's hugging me, and unlike last night in front of Tess's house, this hug feels like he means it. "I would never hurt you. You have to believe that, Anne. I know you barely know me, but you really have to believe that."

I do believe it, and I tell him so. And in that moment, I remember something.

"There was more to the dream," I say to Ethan. He's still got his arms wrapped around me, so I kind of give him a shove so he'll give it a rest. He pulls away from me and I continue. "Before Viktor got in our heads and tried to get you to suck the life out of me, I was at Baba Yaga's. I can't believe that I almost forgot that part. Ethan, it felt like I was really in there with her. Anastasia too. Baba Yaga was telling me all this stuff about blood. Then she took her nail and sliced into my hand, and it started to drip blood on the table. And she told me a story about her three horsemen—you know, like the ones on the Vasilisa the Brave lacquer box that my—shit. I forgot the box. Ethan, we need to go back."

"Not now," he says abruptly. He starts the car and pulls out into traffic. "There's no time. We'll have to get it later. We need to get back to Alex and see what he's figured out. I'm hoping it will line up with what you've just been telling me. So keep trying to remember all the details."

"Okay," I say as Ethan rockets the Mercedes down Lake Street.

But it's hard to just sit here and say nothing. So I choose a distraction.

"Ethan," I say as he veers left, passing a Suburban and two Range Rovers before cutting back to the right lane, "do you really have a tattoo of a lion on your shoulder?"

The silence in the car is—well, deafening.

"Yes," he says finally, both hands firmly on the wheel. "We all do. The Brotherhood. It stands for our strength and unity. Or at least, it did."

"Oh," I say, keeping what I hope is a casual tone.

"Saw it in the dream, did you?" he asks after another moment or two.

"Uh-huh," I tell him.

"Well," he says, and keeps on driving.

To Papa—

I have saved the last of my truths for you. Truths so filled with anger and longing and bitterness that I fear they will rise up from the page and wrap around me, squeezing tighter and tighter until my last breath is gone.

Cruel irony, Papa, since where I am, that could not happen—even if I hoped for it. Prayed for it—if I still prayed, which I used to, like my mother, but now I do not.

Even with all that, Papa, I love you. You are my papa still. The father who knew how much I loved the smell of lilacs. With whom I spoke Russian, even though Mama preferred English. I know you wanted a son when I was born. Your Anastasia, your fourth daughter. The story goes that you had to take a walk outside to compose yourself after your disappointment that day. Maybe that explains how restless I always was. How much I wanted to be moving, running, laughing. As though the boy you hoped for lived a little inside me and made girlish pursuits dull.

If you were here with me now, Papa, I would tell

you this: I forgive you for wanting me to be what I could not be. And I forgive you your weaknesses, as I hope you have forgiven me mine. As I love you, my papa, I believe in my heart that you loved me, loved Mama and our family. That you wanted the best for us and for Russia and its people. These things are true.

But here is another truth, Papa. One that is harder to forgive. A truth from your fourth daughter, who knew more than you thought she did and less than she needed to.

You did not love your first son. The one who came before all of us girls, before Alexei, and before you married Mama. You did not love Viktor. Or if you did, you tucked that love inside yourself so deep and far away that you could no longer find it. Like I am hidden here at the witch Baba Yaga's, deep in her forest and ever on the move so that even if someone wanted to reach me, the search would be nearly impossible.

So I say again—you did not love him. But I did. Even more, I think, because he was forbidden. I do believe now that his being outcast was part of it. Because as much as daughters love their fathers, a part of them longs to rebel. To become women in their own right and not just someone's daughter or someone's grand duchess.

If the history books ever write of me, I wonder what

they will say. How will they know of this small rebellion that became something I never wanted? And if they do, how will they see me? Like the American women I used to look at in the newspapers. The ones who bobbed their hair or the ones who chained themselves to the White House fence the year I turned sixteen so the American president, Woodrow Wilson, would know how serious they were about wanting the right to vote? If somehow my story is told, will people think I was strong like them?

Or will they only see me as another sad, young Russian woman, like that silly Anna Karenina created by Mr. Tolstoy—just another Russian woman who loved badly and paid the price, even if mine was not a romantic love, but a love for a brother, a love for someone she thought deserved more than what he had been given?

Do you like stories, Papa? Well, let me tell you one you have not heard. It is my story, the tale of the tsar's youngest daughter, a wild, headstrong girl. A girl you named Anastasia. Your daughter with the light brown hair you said was so pretty and the blue eyes exactly like your own. Your youngest girl, who liked games and races and listening to her mother's tales. It is the story of my life as it used to be. A wonderful life.

Until it was not.

Until things changed for us, and I went in search of the brother I knew I had. The one whose eyes were dark—not the clear blue of a summer's day like yours, Papa—but whose veins held your blood nonetheless. My secret brother that no one spoke of. The one whose mother—a mother not the same as my own—had given the name Viktor. Champion.

Because I suppose that is what mothers want for their sons. To win. To prevail.

"Can you help us?" I asked him, because by then, there was no one else, no one who had not turned against you, Papa, even though I know you loved your people dearly.

Viktor thought for a very, very long time before he answered me. So long that I should have known enough to turn and leave. But the blood between us was strong. And so I stayed. And I waited.

"Your father doesn't want my help," he told me when he finally spoke again. "As I have told you before, he does not care for me very much."

What I told him in return, Papa, was that you did not need to know.

"Are you sure you know what you are asking?" he said then. I remember watching as he pushed a lock of hair from where it had fallen over one of his strange, dark eyes.

"They say you know things," I said.

"Who have you been listening to, little sister?" he asked me. "You've seen what happens to those who dabble in the magic. You were there when they pulled Father Grigory from that frozen river."

"He was evil," I said. "You are my brother."

"Are you so sure," my secret brother, Viktor, asked me then, "that I cannot be both?"

I reached out, clasped his hands in mine, and told him I was.

"Remember," he said to me, even as his hands warmed my palms almost to burning, "nothing comes without a cost. Are you willing to pay whatever it takes?"

This is what he asked me, Papa. And I nodded my head and told him yes. Because I was a Romanov. My world was filled with things of value. Even in that horrid house in Ekaterinburg to which we'd been forced. Even there.

Only, Papa, this was not the payment that Viktor had in mind.

"I will do what you ask," he told me. "I will save your family."

"Our family," I reminded him. "Our family."

"Yes," Viktor said. "Yes, Anastasia. Our family. As you say, sister."

So he told me the rest of it. That if I let the witch Baba Yaga keep me for just a short while—witches and magic being real and not imaginary, like my mother had told me—the power of our Romanov blood mingled with the power of the oldest of magic would shift the tide of events. No matter what happened, the magic would protect us. No harm could come to our family if I was brave enough to let myself be taken.

Because I thought I loved him, I believed. And I agreed. "Yes," I told Viktor. "I will do what you say."

Much, much later, of course, Papa, when it was too late to change what I had done, I learned at least part of the truth. By then, this hut in which I sit writing to you had become the only home I had.

"I am here to keep my family safe," I told the witch who had taken me when I was finally no longer too terrified to speak.

"You are a fool," Baba Yaga said. "But so am I. Your family is dead, girl. You saw it with your own eyes, even as I reached down to take you. You are the only one he ever meant to save. You. The girl, Anastasia. The one whose name means 'resurrection.' You are the only one, little girl. Now and always. You are mine. So the magic compelled me. And so you chose. Your brother, it seems, had something else in mind for both of us."

"It cannot be as you say," I screamed, because having found my voice again, screaming was what I wanted to do most. "It cannot be!" I stood in front of her, clutching the matroyshka doll my mother had given me. Baba Yaga's black cat rubbed against my legs and gave an odd cry.

But even as I denied it, I knew it was the truth.

Do you like this story, Papa? Does it please you? Does it make you see what you refused to see?

I hope that it does. But the ending—well, that I do not know. That part of my tale has yet to be written. Blood began this story, and blood may end it still. Like me, my secret brother, Viktor, lives. How that is possible is not something I understand. But it is true nonetheless. He lives, and so do I, and you and Mama and my sisters and my dear, dear Alexei are dead. It is not the story I had hoped for. It is not the story I was promised.

Still, Papa, it is my story. And I am still the tsar's daughter. Your daughter. I may yet finish this tale in a way that honors us all.

Please forgive me, Papa, for trusting the man who betrayed us. For believing what I never should have believed. And as I said as I began this last of my letters, I forgive you as well. It is not a forgiveness that has come easily. You betrayed your first son, and that betrayal came home to you. You insisted that Mama bear a fifth child so you could have your true son, and his illness sent Mama into Rasputin's hands. You were as strong as you could be, but it was not strong enough, and it made me think that I needed to save you.

And, of course, when I did, it all went horribly wrong.

There is nothing left for you and me, my papa, but forgiveness, and so I offer it to you with all that I have left.

Keep me in your thoughts and prayers, dearest Papa. Keep me in your heart. If I see you soon, or if I do not, know always that I remain—

Your daughter in blood and heart,

Anastasia

Thursday, 7:15 am

Ethan

"My cell phone is dead," Anne says as we walk rapidly up the path that leads to Alex's office. She's retrieved it from her backpack and is flipping it around in her hand. The campus is quiet still, just the few early risers, their coffee to-go cups firmly affixed in their hands.

"Stop fiddling with it," I tell her. "Just close it and hold it in your hand."

"But why?" A scowl crosses her face, and those deep brown eyes flicker with frustration. "What difference could that possibly—"

"Shh." I place my hand on her shoulder. "Just do as I say. Close your hand around the cell phone as tightly as you can."

"Okay," she says. Her tone tells me she's simply placating me, but she does as I tell her.

"Now, concentrate," I direct her, once the phone is enclosed in her palm. "Just like last night. Concentrate on what you want it to do." I place my hand over hers. "I'm going to help you."

I feel the power flow from both our hands, feel it mingle, grow stronger. "*Ya dolzhen.*" The words float softly into the air. "I must." The beginning of a simple spell, one that tells the forces around me that I must change something, bend it to my will. One that makes Anne smile.

I take my hand away. "Now, open the phone."

She flips it open, and her smile grows, lighting up her face. "Fully charged," she says gleefully. "Fully charged and five bars. I can't believe it." She makes a sound I can only describe as a squeal. "This is so awesome. Did I really—did we really do that?"

"Seems that way," I say mildly. "But don't fiddle with it again," I tell her as she starts to toy with the device once more.

"Why?" she says with a little laugh. "What could I do? Power it up so much that it explodes?"

"Actually, yes," I say, and I grin as she quickly tucks the phone in her jeans pocket.

The worry comes flooding back then. I've pulled this girl from her family, placed her in the gravest of danger. I have no guarantees I can keep her safe, no guarantees that whatever power and knowledge I have can do more than recharge a cell-phone battery.

We round a bend in the path. I can see the outline of Olensky's office building in the distance.

"What's it like?" Anne glances over at me briefly, then returns her gaze to the path. "Being—the way you are?"

"As in—?"

"As in knowing all this stuff. The magic. As in being able to charge a cell phone with the squeeze of a hand. Or build a mystical protection around someone's house. As in—well, not being able to die."

"Ah," I say. "That."

"You say it like it's nothing."

"I say it like it's something I've grown used to, something that's part of me."

"The magic, maybe. But what about the rest of it? The whole immortal thing? I mean, at least until I do what I'm supposed to and then you get to pick up where you left off."

Even with all that's happened, I'm surprised as the answer rushes out of me before I can censor it. "It's lonely," I tell her. "It's long, and it's lonely. When I was eighteen—who doesn't think he's going to live forever at eighteen? Who doesn't want to? Until you actually do. And then—well, it's the proverbial other story, the story where the guy who looks eighteen suddenly realizes that he can't have friends. He can't even fall in love. Because his friends and his lovers, they'll grow old. And the guy himself can't until he finishes what he started. It, uh—sort of closes certain doors."

"Oh," Anne says. Then she's silent as we continue toward Olensky's building.

I pull my cell phone from my pocket. "I'll let him know we're almost there," I say.

"You could use my phone." Anne grins. "Since it's fully charged and everything."

"Keep that in your pocket where it belongs," I tell her as I press in Alex's number.

I'm smiling at her as his phone begins to ring on the other end. It rings some more.

The smile dies on my lips.

The phone keeps on ringing and then clicks over to voice mail.

"What is it?" Anne asks.

"He's not answering." My throat tightens. I close the phone and blindly shove it back into my pocket.

The door to the front entrance is locked. I grip the handle and concentrate, feel the energy flash through me. The door opens. I take Anne's hand and step inside. Our footsteps echo against the tile floor.

Something is wrong—very, very wrong.

"What is it?" Anne asks again.

"Just stay behind me," I rasp. My mouth has gone dry.

In front of Alex's door, I let go of Anne's hand and motion for her to stay still. I listen. Nothing.

"Alex?" I call. I rap lightly on the door. "Alex. We're back." I turn the knob. The office door is unlocked. This can't be happening. He's asleep at his desk or has gone out for coffee, even though I told him not to. "Alex?" I say again into the silence. Still he doesn't answer. Slowly, I push the door until it swings open.

"What's that smell?" Anne whispers.

I sniff the air and smell something with the tang of copper. Blood.

I reach the desk in two strides. My friend, Alex Olensky, is sprawled next to it. Blood seeps from a hole in his brown cardigan, which is still buttoned neatly around him.

I crumble to my knees next to him. "Alex," I say. His eyes flutter open. There's blood spattered in his silver hair.

"I thought it was you," he gasps. His voice is barely a whisper. "When I opened the door, I—" He coughs. More blood. It oozes thickly down his chin.

Anne kneels down next to us. Her face is ashen. "We need to call an ambulance, Ethan! It's okay, Professor. It'll be okay. We'll call someone and—"

Alex reaches over and places his hand on Anne's arm. "No need, my dear." He coughs up more blood. "No time."

He looks over at me. His eyes are starting to haze over.

"Hang on, Alex." I touch his shoulder gently. "Who did this? Did you see him?"

Alex shakes his head. He reaches down slowly and pats his pants pocket. "I never even got the gun out. He had his own." His lips curl in a bloodied smile. "Ironic, eh? Not how I thought this story would turn out." He coughs again. There's blood everywhere. "I imagined I'd be having tea with Anastasia."

His voice strengthens. For a moment, his gaze is fully lucid. "He took my book, Ethan. So you wouldn't find it. So I couldn't show you. But the book doesn't matter. Not exactly. Not in the way I thought. Anne already has the answer. That's what Viktor couldn't know. To get Anne to Baba Yaga's forest, she just needs her…"

Alex stiffens. His eyes go blank. His hand clutches at the blood seeping from the wound in his chest. His mouth tries to form more words. And then he's gone.

"Alex, no." I hear myself sob.

But it's too late. Alexander Olensky is dead—not by magic, not by some supernatural force I might have undone.

Anne covers her mouth with one hand, then uncovers it, bends over the small trash can next to the desk, and vomits.

I hold her bent body, feeling the grief pulse inside both of us, until she can stand up.

"It was Viktor," she says as she leans against me. "Ethan, I can feel him. Like I could feel him in that dream last night. I can't explain it, but I know he's been here. He did this. Or maybe he sent someone to do it, but it's still the same thing. Oh God, Ethan. Why would he—?"

"Not now," I manage. "Later. You'll tell me later. It doesn't matter now." I pull away from Anne, then bend down over my friend Alex. I gently close his eyelids.

"What's that?" Anne points to a piece of paper under the hand Alex had clapped to his chest.

I slide the paper from under his limp hand. It's a napkin from the meal Tess had brought last night. Around the Wrap Hut logo, drops of Alex's blood stain the paper.

"It's got to mean something," Anne says. "We need to figure out—"

"Not now." I shove the napkin into my pocket. "We need to get out of here. Fast. It's not safe."

"But we can't just leave him here." I hear the horror in Anne's voice.

"We don't have a choice, Anne. Do you think I'd leave him if we did?" I stand up and close my eyes. I cast my hands in a circle and say the words I memorized so long ago. I fight back my own tears as the power flows out of me. My friend is dead because he tried to help me—and none of my magic can bring him back.

"Nothing should be able to violate his body now, or indicate that you and I were here," I tell Anne when I complete the spell. "He has a class in a couple of hours. When he doesn't show, people will come looking for him, and they'll take care of him. It's the best we can do, Anne."

I pull her with me to the door. Then I stop.

"Good-bye, my friend." The words rip painfully from me. "I pray you find peace. I pray you find rest."

It's not much of a eulogy. But no matter what I say, it will never be enough.

The sky is a murky gray as we step outside into the crush of students rushing for nine o'clock classes. Above us, black clouds mass ominously. The air feels charged, pulsing. Thunder booms once, then again. Out over the lake, a jagged bolt of lightning forms, cracking through the tumbling clouds.

Inside me, there's a storm of another sort. Alex is dead—and I allowed it to happen.

"Why was he holding the napkin?" Anne asks. Another peal of thunder echoes above us. "Do you think it means something?"

I try to pull my thoughts together. "It has to. And his book, the folklore book he said was taken. He said the answer isn't exactly in there, but at least if we had the book we could—it's all got to mean something. I just don't know what."

Maybe there's another copy, I think vaguely. Maybe there's one at Alex's apartment or at a library. My thoughts scatter like the leaves blowing around us. I can't see anything but Alex lying there dead.

"My dream," Anne says. "The part with Baba Yaga." We're walking back toward my car, but I have no idea what we'll do when we get there. "We need to figure out what all that means, how it connects to whatever the professor was trying to tell us."

I nod. We need to go somewhere, sit down, collect ourselves, and go through what we know. But where can we go? We're not safe anywhere. I have to keep Anne safe. I have to—

"Ethan!" Anne says. She grabs my arm and pulls me to a stop. "The lacquer box! We have to go back for it, remember? That's where the key is, right? We need to go back to my house. We need that box. We—"

Abruptly, Anne stops. Her gaze focuses just over my left shoulder.

I turn. We don't have time to stop. We need to keep going.

And we certainly don't have time for Tess, who's sprinting toward us, her blond hair flying in the wind.

Or maybe we do. If I'm not mistaken, we've just had one tiny turn of luck, since Tess is clutching the lacquer box tightly in her hand.

Thursday, 8:18 am

Anne

"YOU COULD HAVE AT LEAST CALLED AND TOLD ME YOU weren't going to school today," Tess says when she's caught her breath.

"I did, but I got your voice mail, so I left you a message. Didn't you—?"

"Oh. Well, whatever." Tess grins. "I got to your house, and your mom said you'd already gone with Ethan."

Tess turns to him and narrows her eyes. "How is it that Anne's mom seems just fine with you, by the way? What'd you do, put some mystical Russian whammy on her?"

"Save it, Tess." I put my hand on her shoulder.

She glares at Ethan for a couple more seconds, then gestures at me with the lacquer box. "Anyway, I saw the box on your kitchen table, so I snagged it. Thought you just might need it. I figured I'd find you guys at the professor's." She hands me the box. "Oh, and before you interrogate me about how I got here," she adds, "I got Neal to cut school and take me. Figured he owed me a favor or ten. He's out there circling Sheridan Road for a few minutes—or he better be." She frowns, most likely thinking of ways she'll avenge herself on Neal if he's left her.

"I was researching Baba Yaga some more last night," Tess continues. "Do you know that in Russia, they used to call a girl a *baba* once she lost her virginity? And I am so not a witch—at least, not most of the time." She pauses for breath. "God, it's stormy out here," she says.

Another crack of lightning, followed by a burst of thunder, punctuates her words. I tighten my grip on the lacquer box. Its sharp edges dig into my palm.

"Did the professor figure out anything?" Tess asks. "Do you guys know how to get the key out of the box?"

Her words stab at my heart. "Maybe," I say. "Uh—well, not quite. We…I—"

"He's dead," Ethan says quietly. His voice is flat. "Professor Olensky is dead. We think Viktor killed him. If that young man who brought you is still here, I would suggest you get in the car and let him drive you back to school. It will be safer for you there."

For the first time since her arrival, Tess is silent. But there's no time for silence, no time for grieving. "Go, Tess," I say. "Ethan's right. You've got to get out of here."

I hand the box to Ethan and wrap my arms around Tess. A single tear works its way down her cheek. She makes no move to wipe it away. Around us, people continue to scurry as the clouds billow faster.

"Thank you for coming here, Tess," I tell her. My throat feels so tight that it's hard to get the words out. "There's no one I trust like I trust you."

Ethan blinks—once—at that last part. But it's true.

The rain starts then—huge drops soaking us within seconds. In the distance, I recognize Neal's red Bronco hovering on the street at the edge of campus. "Go on," I yell to Tess above the wind. "Ethan's with me. It'll be okay." I'm lying, of course, but what else can I say?

Then something happens that doesn't normally occur on college campuses in quiet Chicago suburbs. Okay—it doesn't happen anywhere.

With a cracking sound, the clouds open. Baba Yaga appears in front of me, just like she did before—only this time, I'm not the only one who can see her. I'm certain of that, since Tess is grabbing my arm and shrieking.

The witch's face is so close to me, I can feel the heat of her breath, practically see my reflection in those iron teeth. "I told you, girl," she says. "I told you when it began that I'd have to try to stop you. That I would have no choice."

Ethan lunges at her. She swats him away like he's a rag doll. He stumbles backward and lands in the grass.

"Remember, Anne!" Baba Yaga howls over the wind. "Remember all I told you. You will need it now. It is time. It has begun!"

Tess is still screaming. I add some of my own to the mix.

Baba Yaga soars up into the clouds and lands in what looks like a giant tea cup without handles. The mortar streaks off through the clouds.

"What is that?" I shout to Ethan. Between the wind and Tess's screams, I can barely hear myself.

"Her mortar!" he shouts back. "In the stories, that's what she rides in."

And then it gets worse. Because then she flops her humongous hands out of the mortar and sends them hurtling to the sidewalk. They scoot along on their fingertips, heading right for us.

The only thing that's missing is for the witch to zoom across the clouds and skywrite *Surrender, Dorothy.*

"Oh, my God!" Tess shrieks, although I have a hard time hearing her over my own screams. "You really *have* been telling the truth, haven't you? I mean, I believed you, because you're my best friend, but I'm not sure if I *believed you,* believed you!"

The disembodied hands continue to trot down Sheridan Road. A campus bus slams to a halt, and three cars smash into it and each other. I guess the drivers have noticed the freak of anatomy on the sidewalk.

To Neal's credit, he's still got the Bronco waiting at the curb.

"Get the hell out of here!" Ethan snaps.

"You damn well better keep her safe!" Tess tells him. Her eyes narrow again. She wraps me in a quick hug. Then she takes off down the path and throws herself into the Bronco. Neal careens away from the curb, barely avoiding another pile-up with more freaked-out onlookers. Then an all-too-familiar black limousine pulls into the spot he's just vacated.

The hands hesitate, then turn and head toward the limo. It pulls away with a squeal of tires that's audible even from this distance.

"Run!" Ethan says.

I don't need a second invitation.

Thursday, 8:40 am

Ethan

WE SPRINT WEST ACROSS SHERIDAN ROAD. THE LIMO DOES a screeching U-turn and follows us down a side street. Baba Yaga's hands do the same.

Problem is, my car is parked in the opposite direction.

There's no time to rummage up a spell—no time to do anything but keep running.

"The El station!" Anne gasps. She's keeping pace beside me. "Up there."

"Perfect," I manage. "We'll double back somehow when the train stops at Howard."

The El line from Evanston ends at Howard Street. Riders have to transfer to another train if they want to head into Chicago. The El goes just far enough to get us out of reach for a while. Viktor and Baba Yaga could still follow us. Probably will. But right now it's our best option. Until this is over, we're not safe anywhere.

Behind us, tires screech. I glance over my shoulder. Baba Yaga's mortar hovers in front of Viktor's limo. Her hands scuttle back to her. For the moment, she's blocking Viktor's path.

I don't take time to question our good fortune. I just grab Anne's hand and keep running.

We reach the train station. I flash my hand over the pass-card slot. "Cool!" Anne says. We push through the turnstile and dash toward the stairs.

Atop the El platform we look up. Baba Yaga's mortar streaks through the sky. Where Viktor is at this point is anyone's guess. Two black, billowing clouds split apart. The witch flies into the opening. And then as suddenly as she'd appeared, she's gone.

A train pulls to a stop next to us. The car doors slide open. I pull Anne with me into the last car and we flop into two available seats. The doors close. With a jerk, the train pulls from the station and heads toward Chicago.

For the moment, neither of us speaks. We just sit hip to hip in the small seat, rocking with the train.

"She's going to keep coming after me," Anne says when she finally speaks. She ties back her hair that came loose as we ran.

"Seems that way," I say.

"And I get that," she says. "I mean, sort of. She keeps saying that's part of the deal. You guys used magic to compel her to protect Anastasia. She says she's bound to keep doing so. That's what she told me in my dream—that she's going to have to stop me if she can."

"You know, that's not what I thought," I say. "All these years I believed that once we found you—" I don't know what to say next. She already knows that everything I've believed in for so long is a lie.

I close my eyes, but all I can see is Alex lying dead. I open my eyes again.

"You didn't kill him, Ethan," Anne says softly. She reaches over and covers my hand with hers. "Viktor did. You know it, Ethan. Please say you know that."

The grief squeezes at my heart so hard that I wonder if it will just stop beating. The cruel irony is that it can't.

"He wanted to hurt me," I tell Anne, "so badly that I'd stop and just let it all be. So now my dear friend is lying there dead, and I wasn't able to prevent it. Alex trusted me, Anne. Just like you're trusting me. And look where it got him."

"It got him a good friend." Anne shifts in her seat to face me. "Someone he believed would keep trying. Think about it, Ethan. You could have given up searching for me—just enjoyed living forever and gone on. Even if it isn't perfect, it's still immortality, isn't it? If you let Anastasia stay at Baba Yaga's, you get to live forever. But you can't—and not just because it's lonely. You knew someone was counting on you. God, Ethan, you've been strong for all these years. How can you sound like you're going to give up on it all now?"

The answer strikes me with a force that slices through all my self-pity. "That's it!" I say, as much to myself as to Anne. "I can't believe it's never occurred to me!"

"What's it?" Anne raises an eyebrow.

I grab her hands in mine. "It's his immortality, Anne. When we bring Anastasia back, Viktor and I, and the others who took that pledge, will be released. We'll become fully mortal again. We'll start to live our lives. And eventually, like we're supposed to, we'll die. Maybe Viktor wants to keep living, Anne—so much that he's willing to commit murder in order to do so."

Thursday, 9:00 am

Anne

WELL, DUH.

It makes perfect sense. Of course Viktor wants to keep his immortality. It's like it's in the *Bad Guys' Handbook* or something. Keep on ticking as long as possible so you can continue to stay rich and powerful and pretty.

Ethan's right. Knowing that you can't die if you just keep one girl alive—a girl the world thinks is dead anyway—how could that not be tempting? It could even be tempting enough to turn someone into a stone cold murderer.

"We'll find her, Ethan," I say, even though I'm not at all sure that's ever really going to happen. "I mean, you found me, didn't you?"

Underneath my feet, I feel the steady vibration of the train. Ethan leans closer to me—so close that my heart does a little *thump, thump* hop in my chest. I study his face. Those blue eyes. That shaggy chestnut hair that's all tousled from the wind.

"I almost lost you," he says quietly. And all at once, it feels like we're the only two on the train, even though I can see a lady and two little boys a few rows ahead of us. "Here I've finally found you, and Viktor almost—"

It occurs to me that he just might kiss me—and that I just might kiss him back. Which I'm thinking would probably not be the best of ideas right now.

"I don't think so," I tell him. "You—a hundred. Me—sixteen."

"I wasn't—we weren't…" He stumbles into silence. Clearly, he was and we were, and we're both pretty sure that we shouldn't.

Okay, I'm not totally sure—but I'm sure enough. Even though the image of that lion tattoo is dancing in the front of my brain, and I'm certain that he'd have more manners than Adam and all that Corona-inspired groping he was so fond of.

"Hey," I say. It's not the smoothest transition, but it's the best I can come up with.

"Hey, what?" Ethan leans back in his seat. I'm not sure whether he's relieved or disappointed that our lips are no longer in kissing distance.

"Why now?" I ask him. "Baba Yaga told me it's all beginning. Well, why now? What's different now? If you compelled her to keep Anastasia safe, and now she's trying to stop me, does that mean I've got everything I need to get to the hut? Even if Viktor thinks I don't?"

Before he can answer, the train starts to slow. I look out the window. We're at Howard Street.

"C'mon," Ethan says. He stands up, swaying with the motion of the train, and holds out his hand to me. "We need to get someplace safe so we have time to pull this all together. But you're right. Something's changed, and we need to figure out what."

The train stops, and the doors open. Ethan and I step out onto the platform. I'm less than thrilled to be out in the open again. I scan the skies. Lots of thunderclouds, but no Baba Yaga.

Our train moves on so it can turn around and head back to Evanston.

Ethan hesitates, then heads us for the stairs. "Let's get to the street," he says. "We'll be less of a target if we've got more room to run."

His words only make my heart kick an extra beat.

We start down the stairs. I'm not even really looking, just walking on autopilot. My brain is occupied with trying to undo this puzzle before it's too late. I press my free hand to my jacket pocket. The lacquer box is still there. Pieces of my dream start coming back to me. Something about turning the box. Something—

Ethan stiffens. His hand squeezes mine so hard that I yelp.

"Turn around now," he says.

I don't have any choice in the matter. He's already yanking me back up the stairs. I risk a glance behind me and understand why.

Ethan drags me up the last few stairs. Another train is already leaving the platform. Its doors are closed. We lope along the platform next to the moving train. Ethan slams his hand on the doors of the third car. His fingers glow against the metal of the train and he shouts out some words. The doors slide open briefly, and we slip in. They close again as the train picks up speed.

Only then do I risk a glance out the window. Dimitri rushes into view as the train carries us out of his reach.

Thursday, 9:07 am

Ethan

"OH MY GOD, ETHAN." ANNE'S BROWN EYES ARE HUGE. "They know we're on this train. They could get on at the next stop. Or Viktor, he could already—"

She pulls the lacquer box out of her pocket. We're both clear on one thing: We're not safe until this whole thing is done. "Here." She shoves the lacquer box into my hands. "I've already tried everything I could think of. Maybe you'll do better. Tap it, poke it, whatever. See if anything makes that key inside pop out. I'll tell you everything I remember from the last dream. There's got to be a connection to all this. We're just not seeing it."

For a second, our gazes meet. Alex's words hang between us. *The answer is always there somewhere,* he'd told us. Now we need to figure out where.

The train continues to race into the city. I flick my gaze over the other passengers in the car. On the seat to our left, a man in his mid-forties sits, checking his Blackberry. Near the door, a guy in a gray hoodie slumps in his seat, dozing. A stout, elderly woman in a thick, navy wool coat and a head scarf sits near the front of the car.

I can feel Dimitri's presence still, but only in a vague, distant way. I don't sense Viktor either. For the moment, I think we're safe.

I open the box and run my finger along the raised painted key. "Talk," I say to Anne. "Tell me all you remember."

So she does. She tells me Baba Yaga's story of the three horsemen, how each one circles the hut three times. She reminds me of what she told me in the car: the witch had sliced Anne's hand and squeezed out three drops of blood.

"They dropped on the table one by one," Anne says, "and I remember thinking it should hurt, but it didn't. I remember I pressed my hand to my chest and the blood was soaking into my shirt."

As she talks, I experiment with the lacquer box. I close the lid, then open it again. I turn it around in my hand, tap it on the top of the seat in front of me, and even flip it upside down.

Anne watches me. "I've tried all that," she says. "Why won't any of it work? I mean…Hey!"

She grabs the box from my hand. "I just remembered. That dream didn't start in Baba Yaga's hut. It started with me and Tess. We kept shifting back and forth from the Wrap Hut to Baba Yaga's. Tess kept throwing onions, maybe because my brain was thinking of the onions from our sandwiches. Then the onions turned into skulls. And then Tess told me, 'Three's the charm.'"

She looks down at the box and then back up at me. She's grinning. So am I.

"Three," Anne says. "Three. Oh my God, Ethan. It's everywhere in fairy tales, isn't it? Three wishes. Three pigs. Three guesses."

I nod my head. Three horsemen. Three stars. Three drops of blood. Three. It hadn't occurred to us, but Alex figured it out. Three. Our magic number.

"It makes sense," I say. "Maybe if we just do this." I take the box from her and turn it around three times. "Like the three horsemen riding around Baba Yaga's hut. Maybe that's the clue." But when I open the box, there is still no actual key.

Anne's face pales. "The napkin the professor was holding," she says. "The one with the drops of blood. Where is it?"

Grief spears through me as I hand the lacquer box back to Anne, then pull the napkin gently from my pocket. I hold it up so Anne can see. The drops of blood we'd seen around the Wrap Hut logo aren't just random. Not two or four or even ten. Just three.

"He was telling us," I say.

Anne's eyes well with tears, but she's smiling too. "That's what Baba Yaga was telling me too. Ethan, think. She may be compelled to stop me, but I think she's trying to help anyway. She showed me how when she cut my hand. Blood. My blood."

For the first time in a long while, I feel hopeful.

"Do you think that's it then?" Anne asks. "Both those things together? Turn the box three times and bleed on it? Could that really be it? Then we get the key?"

"We won't know until we try," I tell her. I think about something else Baba Yaga said, about how matters of blood are never simple.

"Then let's do it," Anne says. "We'll need something to cut my hand."

I nod and shove the bloodied napkin back in my pocket.

And then I feel the train slow.

I look up. In the front of the car, the guy with the Blackberry stands and moves to the doors. I look out the window. At least twenty people crowd the platform as the train approaches. The train slows some more. The air feels alive, crackling with energy.

"Ethan," Anne says. I can tell she feels it too. "Something—"

"I know." My throat tightens. I can't tell what's happening, but I know it's not good.

The train stops. The doors slide open. Blackberry guy starts to step off.

Then he's slammed across the car, crashing into a window on the other side as the train rushes forward, the doors still hanging open. He slumps to the seat below the window, moaning, and the elderly woman in the blue wool coat begins to scream.

The guy in the gray hoodie lurches from his seat, then tumbles toward the open doors. He scrabbles at the floor, grabbing onto the bottom of one of the seats to keep himself from rolling out.

The train picks up speed.

"Help me!" the guy on the floor screams. His hand is losing its grip on the seat bottom. "Oh God, someone please help me!"

Anne stands. I shove her back in her seat. "Stay here." I inch my way into the aisle and head for the guy in trouble. "Hang on," I call. "Just hang on!"

The train speeds up some more. Everything is whipping by as I weave my way forward. "Grab my hand!" I say when I'm close enough. I grip the bar on top of the last seat and reach down to the man with the gray hoodie. He slides a little closer to the open door.

I stretch out, reach his free hand, then pull. When he's far enough from the door, I drag him back to another seat. "You're okay," I say. "You're okay."

"Do you really think so?" asks a familiar voice behind me.

I whip around to see Viktor holding Anne in front of him, a gun to the back of her head. "Ah, Etanovich," he says. "It's been a while, hasn't it? But it seems you have not changed at all."

THURSDAY, 9:47 AM

ANNE

THE COLOR DRAINS FROM ETHAN'S FACE, AND I'M CERTAIN THAT
I'm not looking too perky either, given that Viktor has his
gun jammed against my neck and is holding me so tightly that
he's cutting off the circulation to my arms. He'd come through
the door from the next car. I'd tried to scream when he grabbed
me from behind, but something—some magic something—
had swallowed up the sound.

"You realize, Brother, that I can't let her go through with
it?" His free hand snakes out so fast that I barely see it move.
Magic slaps the space around us with enough force to jerk us
both backward.

"Ethan!" I watch the spell lift him from the floor and somehow suspend him in midair. Swirling blue ribbons of energy
wrap around him, then squeeze tight. He's still holding his arms
out, as if he's trying to pull me to him. Vaguely, I'm aware that
the old lady in the blue coat is still screaming.

"What the hell is this?" The guy that Ethan has just saved
from sliding onto the tracks stands and starts to edge toward
us. This time, Viktor is so fast I don't even see what he does.
But the guy in the gray hoodie sits down, and the woman
stops screaming.

"You thought you were special, didn't you?" I feel Viktor shake his head as Ethan hovers above us. The train roars past another stop. "That I picked you because you were stronger or smarter? I asked you to pledge your life, and you didn't hesitate for a second. The virtuous Etanovich. So devout and so committed to his cause."

Ethan manages to clench one fist. I can see him straining to break whatever hold Viktor has on him.

"It never occurred to you," Viktor says, "that perhaps I picked you because you were none of those things. Not smart. Not strong. Just young and foolish and weak."

Anger sends the power I still haven't learned to control flooding through me. I can feel my hands burning. I twist and press them against Viktor's sides. He yelps and loosens his grip on me ever so slightly.

In that moment, Ethan breaks through whatever's holding him. In one motion, he drops to the floor and starts to rush toward us.

Viktor grabs me to him again. He flicks a couple of fingers in the air, and pain shoots through me. It's as if the power I'd been trying to direct outward has reversed itself and is trying to burn its way through me. I feel my knees buckle, but Viktor's grasp keeps me standing.

"I will kill her, Ethan. I hope you don't have any doubts about that. So I would stay where you are. You and I may be immortal, but your little girl here isn't."

Like I needed reminding.

"You don't want to do this Viktor," Ethan grinds out, his breath ragged. "Let her go. Deal with me."

"I thought I told you, *Brother*. That's not going to happen." Viktor edges us forward. "You two will fail Anastasia, and she will stay where she is. Just like you failed your friend Olensky. Such a nice man—and so easy to get rid of."

Without warning, I'm in Viktor's head, seeing the professor, watching as he opens the door to a voice in the hall that he thinks is Ethan's.

I hear Baba Yaga's words echo somewhere inside me. *You can take, but you must also give up.* Was the professor's death the price we paid for trying to fix history?

"No!" Viktor whirls me around to face him. His dark eyes glitter as he watches me. "Your girl is meddlesome, Ethan. She thinks she can search my mind. Like that bitch, Baba Yaga. She has no idea what I am capable of!"

A muscle in his jaw tics. His gaze holds mine, and an unseen fist plows its way into me. This time, I do double over. Nausea rises in my throat. Then I'm on the floor, so racked with searing pain that all I can do is clutch the bottom of one of the seats and hang on as the train keeps flying down the track.

"It is such a shame." Viktor turns his attention back to Ethan. His tone is almost pleasant, like we're all just friends having a simple conversation. "You have turned out to be such a disappointment. I gave you the perfect life. You were nothing— just a sniveling, filthy little orphan. I gave you knowledge and power, Ethan. I let you see what it was like to be more than the dirt on some aristocrat's boot. And then I gave you the best gift of all. Immortality."

"You think that was a gift?" I can hear the fury in Ethan's voice. He jerks one hand in the air. Viktor stumbles backward and clutches his head. When he brings his hand away, I see it smeared with his blood. "Is that what you think? That you gave me this great gift? This wonderful thing?"

"And what are you going to tell me, Ethan?" Viktor wipes his hand on his leather jacket. "That it's not? That you'd rather go back to—what were you doing when I first found you? Oh, yes, stealing some rotten potatoes. Sleeping in pigsties. Waiting until starvation or disease or some angry Cossack caught up with you. How silly of me, Ethan, to forget how much I robbed from you." He shakes his head, and with a slow, deliberate motion, he brushes a spot of dirt from the arm of his jacket.

"Enough. This is getting tiresome. Say good-bye to your dear Anne, Ethan. She won't be around for much longer."

"Why not?" I have to work to make my voice come out. I force myself to stand. "Because you want to go on living forever? Because you love immortality so much that you just don't want to give it up? Is that it? And now you have to get rid of me so I don't mess it up for you?"

This time, Viktor doesn't even move a muscle, but the magic flares out at me again and slams another blow to my midsection that leaves me breathless.

"You're a coward, Brother." Ethan's voice rings out over the wind rushing through the train. "And a liar. You used Anastasia. Now you want to hurt Anne. And for what?"

I'm still doubled over, trying to keep my balance as the train hurtles along, but I raise my head. Ethan's gaze is fixed on Viktor. When he speaks again, something inside me just knows it's the truth.

"This whole thing is about Nicholas, isn't it? It's always been about him. Not about saving Anastasia or helping the Romanovs or even living forever. You just wanted to stick it to Tsar Nicholas, didn't you? Dear old Dad wouldn't acknowledge his bastard son, and you couldn't stand that. You son of a bitch. All this because of him. Anastasia's life. Anne's. Mine. Every other brother who let himself be sucked into your lies. All because you just couldn't let it go—because you needed your vengeance."

Viktor's face hardens. He raises one hand and cuts through the air with a slashing motion. A jagged wound opens itself on Ethan's cheek. Blood runs down his face, but the cut begins to close itself. "Do not ever presume to—" Viktor starts.

"Presume to what?" Ethan moves closer yet. "To know that you would take revenge on a man who's been dead and gone for almost a century by trapping his daughter? And," he gestures at me, "by killing an innocent girl whose only crime is fulfilling a mission you made us all believe was real?" Ethan uses his thumb to wipe blood off his chin. His gaze is fixed on Viktor. "By murdering a kind old man in cold blood?"

Viktor doesn't answer. His eyes kind of glaze over, like he's gone back somewhere. "Do you know why I joined the Brotherhood?" he asks. "Because I thought it would please him. But he looked right through me, even when I warned him that the Revolution was at hand. He just laughed and walked away—told me a tsar didn't take orders from a peasant, even if that peasant was his illegitimate son." Viktor laughs—a crazy, bitter, *Demented Relatives—Next on Dr. Phil* sort of laugh. "So his blood flowed," he says, his eyes still in that hazy place, "and he paid for his arrogance."

"And Anastasia?" Ethan crosses the distance between us. "What is *she* supposed to be paying for if you let her rot in Baba Yaga's house so you can go on living?" He slams Viktor—maybe with magic, maybe just with sheer force—against the back wall of the train. The gun clatters to the floor. Ethan motions at it, and it crumbles to pieces. "What gives you the right to play with someone's life like that?"

Ethan grabs my hand and pulls me to him. For about two seconds, I feel relief—until, of course, I realize that the train still hasn't stopped, that we've blown by every stop on the north side of the city. We're headed into the downtown underground tracks, and we're picking up speed.

"Think carefully, my dear Etanovich." Viktor's now looking straight at me, and I don't like what I see in those dark eyes. "Our lovely young woman here—the one you seem to care so much about—did you give her a choice? Can you really tell yourself that she is here completely of her own free will?"

He flicks a finger toward me. The breath rushes from my body. I reach my hands up to my throat, but it's like my dream all over again. Only this time, it's all real. The invisible vise tightens. I can't breathe at all.

"Take a good look at her, Ethan. You'll want to remember that face—remember what it looked like as she died. And then try to convince yourself that you had nothing to do with it."

It's funny what crosses your mind when you think you're dying. And what crosses mine is that I'll never be able to talk to anyone I love before I go. Which makes me think of my cell phone. Which makes me realize I've got one more chance after all.

But Ethan's got a last-ditch idea of his own.

He shoves me in front of him. "You don't know who she is, do you? You think you know everything, Viktor. But I don't think you really do. *You* look at her, Brother. Think. Do you remember a woman named Irina? A ballerina back in Russia?"

I think I see something wash across Viktor's face. Then again, I'm hurtling in this metal box toward certain doom and the life is being sucked out of me, so it's really hard to say for sure.

"Do you know that when you left her, she was pregnant? She had a child, Viktor. Your child. A little girl named Natasha. And Natasha had a daughter, and that daughter had her own child."

The stranglehold on my throat eases enough for me to gulp a little air. I dig my hand into my pocket, wrap it around my cell phone, concentrate with all I've got left, and squeeze.

"That child was named Lily, and she had a daughter too," Ethan says. "And then, Brother, another girl was born. Her name was Anne."

"You can't know this," Viktor says. He clamps down my airway again.

"I told you to look at her, Brother," Ethan shouts. "Look at her eyes, her mouth. Look at her, Viktor! Can you do it? Can you kill your own great-great-granddaughter?"

I feel the heat rise through my fist. Then I yank the cell phone, more than fully charged, from my pocket and aim it at Viktor's head.

It hits him smack in the forehead and explodes in a satisfying burst of flames and smoke.

A small piece of metal from the explosion flies out and slices into the still-outstretched palm of my hand. But my lungs fill with air.

Ethan grabs my hand. "Glad you remembered," he says as we run toward the front of the car.

Yeah—me too. Now if only I can think of something wickedly brilliant to tell my dad when he discovers I've destroyed my cell phone.

I risk a quick glance behind us. Viktor's lying on the floor, his eyes closed, but I know he's not dead. He can't be. Not as long as I'm still on this train and Anastasia is—well, wherever she is.

The guy in the gray hoodie has somehow moved over and is holding the elderly woman in the blue coat. The train door to my right is still gaping open. With a sudden jolt, the train begins to slow.

"Viktor's magic must be breaking," Ethan says, "but I doubt he'll be out for long. Let's put some distance between us."

For one freakish second, I think he's suggesting we jump from the speeding train onto the tracks, but he just pulls open the door that leads to the next car. "Move," he says.

I start to follow him. My heart is pumping wildly. I can feel the slickness of my bleeding hand against Ethan's as he clasps it. I look down. Blood trickles from between our hands and falls to the floor. It leaves a little red trail at my feet.

"Wait." I hold Ethan back. "My hand. Ethan, I'm bleeding. We need to do it now." I grab the lacquer box out of my pocket with my bloody fingers. If Viktor wakes up while we're still on this train, there may not be another opportunity.

Three's the charm, Tess had said in my dream. Three times. Three turns. Three drops of blood.

"Hold the box," I tell Ethan. I shove it into his hand. "You turn it, and I'll do the bleeding." I grin at that last part. If you're about to open a magic box while the bad guy is a few feet away ready to wake up and try to kill you again, you might as well smile.

As if on cue, I hear a groaning. Viktor is trying to sit up. There's no time to argue about it. Three really better be the charm.

He turns the box around and around. I hold my hand over it and bleed. One. Two. Three drops.

The air crackles around us. The box lid snaps open. The key is inside, whole and solid.

Trembling, I pull it out, feel its weight in my hand.

"We did it, Ethan!" I leap up and down on the dusty train floor. "We did it!"

The crackling in the air intensifies. The overhead lights of the train flicker. The guy in the hoodie gives an audible gasp and points at the still-open door on the side of the train.

"Jesus, Mary, and Joseph!" The woman in the blue coat claps a hand over her mouth.

Ethan and I turn. Instead of a dark train tunnel, we're looking into a forest. Ethan pulls me toward it. "Come on," he says. "This is it."

Once again, there's no time to think—only time to hope that the leap we're about to take is the right one. Because otherwise, a trashed cell phone will be the least of my worries.

I shove the box and key back into my pocket and hold tight to Ethan's hand. "Let's do it," I tell him.

I don't think about what's coming next. I just take a deep breath and squeeze Ethan's hand tighter as we fling ourselves from the train into the forest. We land hard on the moss-covered ground. A huge tree root jabs me in the waist as I roll to a stop. I sit up. So does Ethan. We've done it. We're in Baba Yaga's forest.

But so, I realize, as I hear a familiar deep groan behind us, is Viktor.

Thursday, in the Forest

Ethan

How in the hell, I wonder as I raise my knee and jam it full force into Viktor's belly, did I *ever* trust this *zalupa?* I wonder it again as he lands a punch to my cheek.

Son of a bitch.

"Give it up, Ethan," he gasps as I return the favor with a punch of my own, and he staggers backward. "I told you I would stop her. Some things are just not meant to be."

Stop her? We're in Baba Yaga's forest, Anne's got the key, and unless I'm mistaken, our magic isn't quite working here, so we have to resort to good old-fashioned brute violence. Many things may arise to stop Anne—who's just hauled herself up off the ground a few feet away—but I doubt now that Viktor is one of them. "You really don't ever get tired of hearing yourself talk, do you?" My next pop to his jaw sends him sprawling to the ground. And then I'm over him, punching again and again until his face slackens and his eyes roll closed.

"Is he—dead?" Anne's standing over us.

I roll my eyes. "Hardly." I stand up. "Unfortunately, he'll be just fine. Well, at least until we release Anastasia." A man can hope.

"No, really, Ethan." Anne's eyes flick from my face to Viktor's unconscious form and back again. "You can't just kill him. I mean, even if you could."

"I know," I say gently. "I know. He's going to wake up soon, Anne, and we need to find Anastasia before he does."

"So then what? Just leave him here?" Another detail that hadn't quite occurred to me.

"We'll think of something." I grab her hand. "Let's go."

We head off into the forest.

Within seconds, we're hopelessly lost. I can't see where we've started. I can't see ahead of us. It's all just a thick mass of trees and shrubs pressed tightly together. The branches snag our clothing and lash at our arms and legs, and even our faces, as we attempt to walk.

A thick rope of vines whirls down from a low-hanging branch and whips itself around Anne so quickly that it takes my breath away until I can pull her free from its grip. Our feet sink into the wet, spongy ground, and dead leaves and other things stick to our shoes as we walk.

"It's hard to breathe," Anne gasps. Her face is flushed, and her sweat-slicked hair is flattened to her forehead.

Something small and soft brushes by my legs. I look down. It's a cat. I think his fur is black, but it's hard to see because the trees have blocked out all but a few thin rays of light. The cat blinks up at me, his eyes gleaming gold and orange in the darkness.

"*Koshka*," Anne says, startling me. "*Koshka*," she repeats. The Russian word for "cat."

"How do you know that?" I ask her. The cat slips away into the darkness. I can hear his feet against the leaves for only a second or two, and then he's gone.

266

"It's what Baba Yaga called him in the dream." With effort, she pushes a heavily drooping branch out of our way.

The trees around us start to sway violently. The wind picks up.

"We must be close." My eyes narrow to a squint as the wind rakes us.

"Do you think it's Baba Yaga?" Anne stumbles and grabs my arm. The wind gives another vicious howl.

"Yes," I tell her. "We need to keep moving."

What we also need to do is figure out what side Baba Yaga is on. Is she protecting Anastasia? Or has the magic compelled her to side with Viktor and keep us away? Maybe Anne is right and it's somehow both of those at the same time. If we can get to Anastasia, perhaps it will no longer matter.

"Do you see that?" Anne shouts. She's pointing to our right. I peer into the darkness. Small dots of light dance far in the distance.

"Come on." I yank her hand. "This way."

We walk toward the lights. They twinkle and blink as we struggle closer. At one point, I glimpse the cat, the *koshka*. He pokes his black head out from under a bed of rotting leaves and hisses. He flicks his pink tongue at us, then licks it, slowly, over his tiny, sharp teeth.

Above us, there's a swirling sound—the same one I'd heard when Baba Yaga had swooped down on the university campus. "She's coming!" Anne cries out. "I know it, Ethan. It's Baba Yaga!" She pulls at my arm and runs toward the dancing lights that continue to flicker ahead of us. The lights, I realize with a sinking feeling, have not gotten any closer, no matter how far we've walked.

Anne is wrong. It's not Baba Yaga who breaks through the treetops above us.

It's just her hands.

Thursday, in the Forest

Anne

I DON'T EVEN BOTHER TO SCREAM WHEN THE GIANT HANDS come scuttling after us like two mutant hermit crabs or something. I just grab onto Ethan's hand and run. The branches snap at our faces. The hands swish after us. The wind keeps howling like some crazed animal.

We keep moving.

I hear another howling sound, only this time it's not the wind. It's the *koshka*.

He sort of materializes in front of us, then stands there flicking his pink tongue in and out of his mouth, waiting. His black fur ruffles in the gale-force winds. His eyes are two glowing yellow slits. I think back to the dream, to the cat winding around my ankles as I sat at Baba Yaga's table.

In my mind, I see Anastasia. She's sitting in the huge rocker in the hut, gazing at the skull in the fire—watching as two people stand in the middle of a forest. Ethan and me.

"Follow him," Anastasia says. It's a shock to finally hear her voice, even if it's just in a vision. "Follow Auntie's *koshka*. He will lead you to me. You must trust me." And then she's gone.

"Did you see her?" I shout to Ethan over the wind.

"See who?" He stares at me. I simply have got to stop having these visions that only I can see.

"We need to follow him," I say, pointing to the cat.

"You have got to be kidding me," Ethan says. The part of me that's not totally terrified notes that he's sounding more and more like me.

"Oh right," I tell him. "'Cause I have so much time and energy here to make up a joke."

"If you're sure," Ethan says. The cat is already heading off into the trees. "Okay, then, let's go," he says. So we do.

We push deeper into the forest. Sometimes, I hear the hands rushing at us from behind. Sometimes, they seem to be coming from one side or the other. Sometimes, I don't hear them at all. But the *koshka* keeps moving steadily.

And we keep following.

Then I realize that—finally—the row of little lights has gotten closer—close enough for me to realize, in yet another moment that I'm sure will require years of therapy should I actually live through this, that they're more than just pretty little lights. They're a row of glowing skulls, each one on a stick jammed into the ground.

But none of it matters, because it's then that we—the cat, Ethan, and I—stumble to a halt.

Correction: the cat slinks off out of sight, leaving Ethan and me gasping for breath in front of Baba Yaga's hut.

We've made it.

"Get the key," Ethan says to me. His voice is low and tight.

I'm shaking as I reach into my pocket and wrap my hand around it. "Now what?" I ask him. I'm still staring at the hut. It seems to be—well, breathing. Like it's alive or something.

The crooked wooden walls suck in and out as we stand there. Steam puffs in huge bursts from the long, narrow chimney. The chicken legs—yes, it really is standing on chicken legs— kind of quiver every few seconds, like they're getting ready to bolt if the opportunity arises. The one little window on the left wall keeps sort of *winking* at us. Like it sees us. And the skulls—well, they're watching us too. I had thought the skulls were each on a stick of some sort, which would be bad enough—only they're not on sticks. They're each on top of a bone. And these are human-looking bones.

My stomach rolls. For a moment, I think I might throw up. My hands tighten into fists. The edges of the key dig into my already cut palm.

The hands—thankfully—are still nowhere in sight. Nor is Baba Yaga.

"Let's try it," Ethan says.

"Okay." My voice comes out shaky and small. My heart's fluttering around in my chest like a little flag left up in a hurricane.

We move closer. The hut puffs in and out. One second, it's small, and the next, it seems to tower over us. Underneath it, the chicken legs claw at the dirt, scratching up big clumps of it, which they kick at us as we approach.

"I guess we're not in Kansas anymore," I mutter. A crazed-sounding giggle kind of sticks in my throat.

Ethan gives me a quick scowl. "Keep your eye on the door," he says. "In the fairy tales, the hut can—"

"Flip around so we can't get to it?" He's forgotten I've already paid a visit in my dream. We're now looking at the back of the hut, which is still moving in and out like some demented wooden accordion.

Shit.

"What do we do now?" I move past shaky to primal screaming territory. "Tell it to turn around? Like, 'Hey there, hut, turn your front to me'?"

The hut spins wildly—around and around until I'm almost dizzy from watching it—but when it stops, the front door is once again facing us. "Uh, yes," Ethan says. "Something like that."

I guess when you're Destiny Girl, things really do go your way occasionally.

Then I hear a shuffling sound in the woods behind us, and I figure if I'm really going to do this, I better just do it. I place my hand on the small gate in the middle of the skull fence and push. It gives a deafening moan, like all the people who were once attached to these skulls, who probably belong to the bones jammed into the earth, are screaming at once.

"Don't listen to it," Ethan shouts above the moaning and shrieking. "Keep moving!"

I do as he says. We pass through the gate. Still, the voices of the skulls call to us. It's as if their voices are wrapping around me, pulling at me. I stumble backward for an instant. Invisible arms grab at me. "Help us," the voices scream in my head. "Don't leave us here."

But I keep on going, and so does Ethan. We reach the door.

I uncurl my fingers and look at the key nestled in the palm of my hand. There's no going back. If the key doesn't work, it's over. Even if it does, we may not make it out of here.

"Now, Anne," Ethan says softly. "Go on." He squeezes my arm.

My hand is shaking—in fact, all of me is shaking—but I place the key in the lock of the wooden door of Baba Yaga's hut and turn it. I hold my breath.

The door creaks open.

And then she's there. Anastasia.

Not a trick. Not a vision. Not a dream.

She's this pretty girl with a thin face and brown, wavy hair who looks not much older than me. She's wearing a worn, white lace dress that I'm sure was once very beautiful. And she seems to recognize me, just as I recognize her.

I reach out my hands, and she clasps them. "Anastasia," I say to her.

She nods. "And you are Anne," she says, and I'm struck by the sound of her voice. Even after all she's been through, she sounds—well, royal. I'm also struck by something else.

"You speak English," I say, hearing how stupid that sounds as soon as it's out of my mouth. I feel oddly plain and ordinary next to her. Which is totally weird after all I've been through.

"My mother taught me," she says softly. "She taught all of us. So we could converse with our European relatives. But I haven't used it in—well, I suppose you will be able to tell me how long it's truly been."

My stomach rolls when I hear that last part.

Behind me, I hear Ethan clear his throat. The small-talk part of the visit is over.

"I guess I'm supposed to get you out of here now," I say. "I think that's how it works. You can't leave until I come for you. Well, I did. I'm here. So you don't have to stay any longer."

"I would like that," Anastasia says. "I would like that very much." She gives my hands a squeeze. "But wait. I must not forget. I need to get something. I think it will be fine if you come with me. I—I do not want you to let go. Do not worry. It will not take long."

This is not something I'd expected. I'd made my visit to this cabin more than enough times. But as Anastasia pulls me over the threshold with her, I realize I've got one more visit to make.

It's all as I had seen it: the rocker, the fireplace, even the skull floating in the flames. I swallow my panic and hang on to Anastasia. Her hand feels small and thin in mine.

"Here," she says, and plucks a small, wooden doll with painted red lips from the bed in the corner. It's exactly like the one on my lacquer box. "It is my *matroyshka*," Anastasia tells me. "My mother gave her to me. I cannot leave her here." She tucks the little doll in the pocket of her dress.

My panic returns. We need to get out of here. Viktor's going to wake up, and Baba Yaga could come back at any time. This is *so* not where I want to be when any of that happens.

I tug gently on her hand. "Come," I say. "It really is time for us to go." Skin to skin, our palms feel almost electric. My hand does its glow thing. I pull her toward me, and slowly, ever so slowly, she lets me guide her out of Baba Yaga's hut.

Everything rushes through me then—joy and amazement and an incredibly deep sadness that this girl has been hidden away for so long that I wonder if she had given up hope.

"You didn't let him stop you," she says. "I have been able to watch through Auntie's magic."

"Him? Oh, you mean Viktor, don't you? Well, he tried. Oh boy, did he try. But we—"

"Anastasia," Ethan says. I'd almost forgotten he was still here. His face looks like I feel. Every emotion flitting across it in rapid succession.

We all stand there, looking at each other, and then Anastasia lets go of my hand and walks to Ethan. I smile as he wraps his arms around her, says something to her that I can't hear. Then he reaches up and smooths her hair. "We came for you," he says, "just as we promised."

Anastasia tilts her head and looks up at Ethan. "I am not particularly fond of promises anymore," she says. "But you are here, and the rest will sort itself out now that you are."

I want to ask what she means by that, but suddenly there's no more time for our little reunion. We hear the all-too-familiar whooshing sound that can mean only one thing: Baba Yaga is coming.

Anastasia gestures toward the back of the hut. She shouts something to Ethan in Russian.

"What?" I scream at them. "What's she saying? Ethan, what's she telling you?" And why the heck did she have to switch to Russian? Other than it being her native tongue and all…

"She says the three horsemen are back there," he replies. "They'll take us out of here. She says her Auntie Yaga promised her they'd help."

Auntie. Just like I'd heard her say in my dream.

Above us, black clouds rush in over the treetops. The whooshing sound grows louder, closer.

"We must ride now," Anastasia says to me. "We need to go before she returns." She's switched back to English again.

She looks at me. There I am, face to face with the girl whose bloodline runs through me too—who lost everything so her half brother could have it all. It's more than unfair. And not, I think as I watch her, like that Russian fairy tale at all. Vasilisa the Brave got a happy ending.

Anastasia deserves one too.

In the sky above the hut, thunder rumbles, and a bolt of

pure white lightning streaks through the clouds. We race to the other side of the hut. Three horses stand in a circle: one white, one red, one black. Three horsemen sit on their backs.

Anastasia digs into her pocket and brings out a fistful of what looks like oats. She approaches each horse in turn, croons something to them that I don't understand, and feeds each one from the palm of her hand.

The horsemen dismount. They bow and gesture toward their horses.

"Can you ride?" Ethan asks me above the wind.

"A little," I tell him. Now is not the time to explain that my last riding experience was on vacation at a dude ranch in Texas when I was nine.

"Well, just hang on," he says. He lifts me in the air so I can mount the white horse. There's no saddle or anything, so I have to just grab onto the mane and kind of hoist myself up—which, let me say, is not as easy as it sounds. He does the same with Anastasia, putting her behind me on the same white horse. She wraps her arms around my waist.

Then he strides over to the red horse, kind of nods to its horseman, and mounts up. And I admit, watching him leap onto that horse like it's second nature to him—which I suppose it is, since he was born before the automobile and all—is pretty damn hot.

"*Spasiba,*" Anastasia calls to the horsemen. She turns back to me. "Thank you," she translates. Then she pours out some more Russian at Ethan.

"She says they know the way," he tells me. "The horsemen have taught them. They're not bound like Baba Yaga is—not bound by the magic. She thinks Viktor doesn't realize this, that it's something he didn't anticipate."

"That's what Baba Yaga said in my dream too, but is she sure?"

Ethan shrugs. "Does it matter? There's no other way."

"Next time I do something like this," I say, "I'm doing it with someone who knows all the rules before we start."

Ethan doesn't comment. He just guides his horse around to stand in front of ours, digs his heels in, and makes a soft clicking sound with his tongue. The horse begins to trot away from the hut. Behind me, Anastasia makes the same sound and kicks at our horse. It follows Ethan's horse.

But then the black horse—the one without a rider—breaks away from its horseman, who's still standing alongside it. It trots quickly ahead of Ethan's horse, then picks up speed and leaps over the gate. It comes to an abrupt stop, snorting, whinnying, and pawing at the ground. Without warning, Ethan's horse and mine both follow it. My heart thuds as we leap over the gate, and Anastasia grips me even more tightly around my waist.

And then—nothing. The horses don't move.

A few seconds later, I understand.

Viktor, only a few feet ahead of Baba Yaga's disembodied hands, comes tearing out of the forest, eyeballs us all for a second, and leaps onto the black horse. The hands clap together—hard—then fling themselves skyward. Behind me, Anastasia breaks into an angry stream of Russian. Some of it sounds like swear words. But there's no time for Ethan to translate. All I can do is cling to the white horse's mane, gasp as it gallops to the front of the other two horses, and ride.

Thursday, in the Forest

Ethan

Looks as if we're all leaving Baba Yaga's forest together.

Anne and Anastasia's horse takes the lead. The two girls sit together on the white horse, their hair streaming behind them in the wind. My horse and Viktor's follow. Their hooves pound the forest floor beneath us, crushing the dead leaves deeper into the soil. That sickly sweet smell of death permeates everything.

Above us, the howling begins. A deep sobbing sound—mournful, weeping, gnashing at the air in its misery. "Anastasia," howls the wind, which whips around us fiercely. "Do not leave me. Do not leave your Auntie."

Her iron teeth gleam through the darkness of the forest as she cries out. Her eyes glow with madness.

Suddenly she's standing in front of us. Her gaze fixes on Anne. "To save or to sacrifice, girl. Which will it be?"

She's gone before we can even cry out, but her words freeze in my ears. *Sacrifice.* Hasn't there already been enough of that?

I urge my horse to gallop faster. We're nearing the edge of the forest. I cannot risk thinking about what will happen—to all of us—if we don't make it.

And then it occurs to me: I have no idea how to get us back.

Even if I did, where would we end up? On a runaway El train?

We gallop out of one last stand of trees and come to a stop in front of a stream so small and thin that it's barely visible in the dim light. If there is a way back, it's beyond this stream, but the horses dig in their hooves. They'll move no farther.

It seems entirely possible that we've come this far only to be trapped. Perhaps Viktor was right about me after all.

Above us, Baba Yaga whirls through the sky, stirring the air in her mortar. "I can't help you, girl," she shrieks to Anne, "but you can help yourself! Round and round and round. Choices, my girl. Think carefully! It is not as simple as it seems. Where do you want to be?"

The horses line up in a row. One, two, three; side by side, they stand in front of the stream.

"Move!" Viktor shouts to them in Russian. He slashes his hands through the air commanding a spell to compel them as he compelled Baba Yaga so long ago. But they do not move. Our magic is still useless here.

"Get off!" I shout to the others. "We'll need to go the rest of the way on foot."

"No! *Nyet!*" Anastasia waves her arms at me. "Wait. Please." Her voice is loud and clear. "Wait," says the tsar's daughter. "Watch. It will come."

"We can't wait anymore," I say. I start to swing myself off the horse.

"No, Ethan!" Anne shouts to me. "I think she knows what's she's doing! Hold on! Please!"

"My God," Viktor thunders. "Are you crazy? We need to make a run for it."

"Ethan," Anne says, "you really better hold on. Look!" She points to the ground below us.

"*Koshka*," says Anastasia. She reaches into her pocket and tosses some crumbs to the ground. Between the narrow stream and the horses, the black cat—the one that led us through the forest—walks slowly, delicately, and stops to nibble on the crumbs of bread or cake that Anastasia has dropped to the ground.

I grab tight to my horse's mane. The others hold on tight as well. The cat arches his back, looks up at the three horses, and hisses, baring his razor-sharp teeth and flicking his pink tongue. The horses whinny in fear, rear back, then paw at the ground. They back up some more—step by step as we cling to them. Back and back we go.

"Choose now, young Anne!" Baba Yaga's voice fills the air, the forest—everything.

The cat hisses again. The horses bolt forward, racing to the stream. *We're going to jump over it,* I think. But then they balk. All three stop dead at the foot of the stream. I close my eyes. Anne, Anastasia, Viktor, and I—we tumble over their heads, across the stream, and out of Baba Yaga's forest.

When I open my eyes, though, we're not back on the El train. We're rolling in a heap out the front door of the Wrap Hut, tumbling onto Second Street in the middle of afternoon traffic. When I finally sit up, I'm staring at Java Joe's.

And then something else begins.

THURSDAY, 2:35 PM

ANNE

S HE'D TOLD ME TO CHOOSE, SO I DID. I CHOSE TO GO HOME, and it looks like it worked.

"We did it!" I shout to Ethan as we all sprawl in the middle of the street. "We did it! I can't believe it was that easy. I guess Baba Yaga really did want to help us. She told me to choose, so I thought of home. Well, I thought of here, anyway. It was the first normal thing that popped into my head. Java Joe's. The Wrap Hut. The Jewel Box. Normal stuff. And it worked, Ethan, it worked! I can't believe it really worked!"

I grab Anastasia's arm and pull her to her feet. She says something to me in Russian, but I'm too busy avoiding the speeding soccer moms in their SUVs who clearly think we've all rolled into the street just to piss them off on their way to Pilates or something.

"Don't be afraid," I say to Anastasia. "It'll all be okay." I haul her with me to the sidewalk in front of Java Joe's. She looks a little terrified—and why not? She left this world in the long-skirt-and-corset days, survived like a hundred years in a witch's hut, and now some suburban Botox queen almost mows her down trying to make it to the head of the carpool lane. I haven't even told her the price of a double latte at Java Joe's yet!

I glance up at the huge clock on the bank down the block near Miss Amy's. It's just a little after two thirty in the afternoon. It feels like it's been a lifetime, but school isn't even out for another thirty minutes. And if it's still Thursday, my mother's got the afternoon off, so if I'm living right, she's not across the street watching me dodge through traffic with the last living grand duchess of Russia.

Things are looking up.

And then I remember what's supposed to happen once I've saved Anastasia.

Ethan. He's made it out of the street to Java Joe's. So has Viktor. They're standing a few feet from us, kind of weaving back and forth.

"Ethan," I call to him, but he doesn't answer. He doesn't even look up, especially not once he begins glowing. Yes, glowing, right there on the sidewalk of Second Street in front of the plate-glass windows of Java Joe's.

Viktor too, and he doesn't look very happy about it.

My gaze swings back to Ethan. He looks at me, but I don't think he really sees me. Light's shining everywhere—in his face, his hands, his hair, his eyes—like this big spotlight is just beaming down on him.

He stiffens. His hands clench into fists, then open. His eyes—those bright blue eyes—close. The light about him grows even brighter. Pure white now, it pours into him. He throws his head back, opens his mouth, and seems to just sort of gulp it down. His eyes open—two blue crystals shining.

And then it's over.

He turns, starts to stagger toward me, then sinks slowly to his knees. Right there in the middle of the sidewalk in front of

Java Joe's, Ethan's life returns. A mortal life—and eventually, a mortal death.

Just like he was meant to have.

I kneel down next to him and watch quietly as he studies his hands, clenching and unclenching them as the last shreds of light drift away. He covers his face with his hands. His shoulders start to shake.

"Ethan," I say again. I touch my hand gently to his shoulder. He lowers his hands from his face and looks at me with those blue eyes, now wet with tears.

"Anne," he starts, and for a second, it's just the two of us here on the sidewalk. "Anne, I—"

But he never finishes whatever he's about to tell me—maybe something like, *Hey, I'm really eighteen now, so let's do something normal together like get a Mocha Madness at Java Joe's, or catch a movie, or anything not involving a life-and-death scenario.*

I stop feeling so smug about having rescued Anastasia and figured out how to get us back. In fact, all of a sudden, I don't feel very well at all.

In the sky, a huge bank of black clouds rushes in and swirls over Second Street. A bolt of lightning rakes through the sky and slams into the roof of the Wrap Hut. The building ignites in seconds, flames leaping everywhere. People start racing from the restaurant. A young woman lurches out screaming. Her clothes are on fire. She rolls on the ground to put them out.

"Ethan!" I yell. "What's happening?"

Anastasia is screaming too. Viktor calls something to her in Russian. Like Ethan, he's still kneeling on the sidewalk, his body glimmering.

283

Another bolt of lightning streaks over our heads, rips through the roof of a parked car like it's just a tin can, and then powers its way into the asphalt. The street cracks. A minivan with a mother and a couple of kids buckled into the back seat skids into the fissure, one front wheel jammed in the opening, the car tilted at a crazy angle.

Everywhere, people are running and screaming.

The third lightning strike aims itself at Java Joe's. Ethan hauls himself up off the sidewalk and grabs me. He screams something in Russian to Viktor and Anastasia. We race back across the street and make it to the front of the Jewel Box just as white-hot destruction shatters the plate-glass window of Java Joe's, sending shards of glass everywhere.

Something makes me turn around. My back to the street, I peer through front door into the Jewel Box. Mrs. Benson is standing at the counter, staring open-mouthed at what's going on outside. She doesn't seem to register my presence on the other side of the door. Behind her, there's a flash of motion. She turns and says something I can't hear.

Sometimes, you just know what's coming next. Sometimes, you do everything in your power to prevent it. But sometimes, there is nothing you can do.

My mother runs out from the back of the shop. She comes to a halt at the counter next to Mrs. Benson and looks out toward Second Street. Her eyes meet mine. She moves toward the door to come for me, probably to get me inside where she thinks it's safe. In that moment, I don't hear or see anything else. Not Anastasia or Ethan or Viktor. Not the people running and screaming, or any of it.

Nothing but my mother coming to help me.

Ethan shouts something. I'm fighting against him. He keeps pulling, dragging me away. I'm shrieking, although I can't even hear the sound of my voice. Some distant part of me registers that Viktor and Anastasia are following to wherever Ethan is forcing me to go.

When the lightning sears through the roof of the Jewel Box and the roof collapses, I'm in the middle of the street, screaming for my mother.

ETHAN

S HE WASN'T SUPPOSED TO BE THERE!" ANNE SHOUTS AT ME. She pounds her hands on my chest as I try to hold her. Rain streams from the sky, huge drops of water pelting down on us. The fire on the restaurant sizzles out—one small blessing in all this destruction and chaos. We've rescued Anastasia and escaped from Baba Yaga.

But the witch has come after us. And the magic has gone wrong.

"We have to help her!" Anne shouts at me. She breaks from my arms, dashes back to the jewelry store, and starts digging through the rubble, pulling at hunks of roof and ceiling tile and dry wall. Even through the blinding storm, I can see the glow of her hands.

I hurry to her. Only part of the roof has collapsed. *There's a chance,* I think, *if we get to her soon.* Through the hole where once there was ceiling and roof, Baba Yaga swoops down through the clouds in her mortar.

"Anastasia!" she shrieks. "My girl! Anastasia!" Her long hair is wet and matted. Her voice is hideous.

I whip my head around to look for Viktor. He's just standing where we've left him, staring up at Baba Yaga.

If Anastasia hears the witch calling her name, she doesn't look up. She's too busy kneeling next to Anne, searching for Anne's mother.

"Her mama," Anastasia says in Russian. *Mat.* I have no idea how she knows, but somehow she does.

"Oh God, Ethan." Anne's eyes have gone blank. She pulls at the pieces of broken roof and tells me what I'm already thinking.

What we've both understood too late.

"We should have realized," Anne says. "It's the threes, Ethan. Three drops of blood. Three horses. Don't you see? There were only supposed to be three of us. You, me, and Anastasia. I think that's how it was supposed to work. But there weren't three. We were four. Viktor made four! And now it's all wrong. The magic's screwed up somehow. And my mom may be—"

"Over here!" Anastasia says. "Come quickly!" Even above Anne's screams, above the storm, above Baba Yaga's cries, her voice rings out clearly.

I go to where she's frantically pulling at a heavy piece of tile. The store owner coughs and groans, but sits up when we free her. I lift her in my arms and carry her out to the street.

She's too dazed to speak, but she's alive and moving. An older man with a jagged cut down one arm takes her gently by the shoulders and walks her down the street toward the bank building. It's still in one piece. At least for now, it's a place of safety.

I run back to the store. Anne and Anastasia are bent together over the rubble. I step over the broken pieces of the roof toward them. They're moving in unison—the princess in the torn white dress and my princess in the battered denim jacket, two young women who deserve more than this.

"Mom!" Anne cries.

"Mama!" Anastasia says.

But only one of their mothers is still alive.

I move over to help carry Anne's mother—bleeding from a shallow cut on her forehead, but breathing and in one piece—from underneath the fallen tile.

"She's unconscious," I say to Anne, "but she's alive. That's all that matters right now. We'll get her to the bank. But then you have to stay with me—stay focused. We've got to stop Baba Yaga, stop whatever's happening, and I know I can't do that without you."

Anne nods. "Okay," she says. She bends over and kisses her mother on the forehead. I see now that one of her arms is hanging at an odd angle. "You'll be okay, Mommy. Just hang on. Please."

Her mother's eyes flutter open. She gazes curiously at Anne. "What are you doing here?" she asks. Her eyes close again, but she's still breathing.

Anne turns to me. "Let's get her to the bank," she says. "Fast."

THURSDAY, 3:20 PM

ANNE

You're right," Ethan says tersely. We're huddled under the overhang of the bank building. My mother's lying on a makeshift bed of coats and jackets inside.

I'm trying to do what Ethan says. I have to see this thing through, but I'm just not that brave.

I look at Anastasia standing there, looking—well, regal, despite everything she's been through. How could it not have broken her? How could anyone have thought that keeping her trapped there all this time would have solved anything? And how the hell could I ever have thought I was special enough to do something about it?

There's always a choice, my mother had said to me the other night, when I mentioned Lily to her. My mother—the woman who's lying in there unconscious because of me.

Choose, Baba Yaga had told me.

They were both right. There's always a choice. But how do you stop yourself from making the wrong one?

"What am I possibly right about?" I put the question to Ethan. The rain continues to pour from the sky. Baba Yaga circles and howls. Anastasia is a few feet away from us, saying something to Viktor. Another lightning strike hammers into the strip of stores a block down. The Gap sign shears off from the store's façade, smashes into the sidewalk. I can see the flashing lights of emergency vehicles a few blocks down, but they don't seem to be getting any closer. Something—real or magic, I don't have time to figure out which—is keeping them from us.

"The three. You're right. I should never have missed it, Anne. Don't blame yourself. I'm the one who should have seen it." He pushes some wet strands of brown hair off his forehead, then clasps his hands together, the two thumbs against his lips. It looks like he's praying.

"Whatever," I tell him. There's no point in playing the blame game. We just need to figure out what to do to make this all stop. "I know it's all screwed up somehow, because four of us came out. But I don't get it."

"It's her." I hadn't even noticed that Viktor, with Anastasia behind him, has moved over to us. He points up to Baba Yaga, who's howling Anastasia's name.

"Explain," Ethan says. His blue eyes lock onto Viktor's face. His hands clench at his sides. "If you knew that this would happen—"

"No," Viktor says. He raises his hands briefly in the air, as if to signal his innocence. "I'm guilty of a lot of things, but that's not one of them. But I think I understand what's happening." He looks skyward, and I'm shocked when he pulls Anastasia behind him as Baba Yaga swoops closer.

"It's the original spell, I think," he says. He's shouting now over the wind, the storm, all of it. "The ancient magic we used to compel Baba Yaga to do our bidding. She didn't want to. You see," he points again to her, "how strong she is. How

290

powerful. The words, the events, they had to be just right. It's like building a house of cards—one slip and it all comes falling down. The magic—I think they were built around one of us, you, Ethan, or me, or another brother—going with the girl into the forest. Three of us would be coming out. I never had to really think about the end of it, but I suppose that's what would finally break the hold—not only to free Anastasia, but to reverse it all."

"And so it's not reversed?" I think I finally understand what Viktor is saying. "You mean she's still compelled to take Anastasia?"

"Even if she *wants* to free her," Ethan says. He turns to Anastasia, fires off some Russian, listens to her response.

"She agrees," he tells me. "The witch wants to give her up. She's the one who called the horsemen to help, set things in motion to let her free. But I don't think she can. She's got to protect a Romanov, whether she wants to or not."

"I will go back to her." Anastasia stands up straight. Her blue eyes—even bluer than Ethan's—are clear and strong as they look at me. The grand duchess, telling me what she wants to do.

"No!" Of all the things that are making me absolutely hysterical at the moment, this one seems somehow to be the worst of all. "No!" I say again. "Tell her, Ethan. Tell her in Russian so I'm sure she understands. She can't go back—not after all that's happened, all we've done. She just can't!"

I don't even wait for him to say what I've asked him to. I put my hands on Anastasia's shoulders. I have to keep myself from just clutching at her wildly. "You can't do that!" I scream at her. I'm not sure if she can understand me, but the words pour out of me anyway. "You're only seventeen! You didn't have a chance. You've been stuck there all this time. You've got to stay here. You've got to live. You've got to do the things you've always wanted to do. Please, Anastasia!"

"Let her do what she wants." Viktor's voice sounds tired and angry at the same time. "You think she cares what you think?" He grabs my arm and yanks me away from Anastasia. A cut on his cheek is bleeding freely. He's mortal again, so his wounds will be around for a while. "You—you've destroyed everything! Look at all this! Look at her! You think she can survive in this world? You think you've really helped her? I told you—"

"You stupid son of a bitch!" Ethan's fist connects with Viktor's jaw so hard that Viktor staggers backward. Ethan grabs him by the collar with one hand, then punches him again with the other. The second punch sends Viktor sprawling to the wet ground.

"Stop it!" I yell. "This isn't solving anything! It isn't going to help us stop Baba Yaga."

"*Nyet!*" Anastasia shouts in Russian. No!

Maybe she really doesn't understand, I think. *Maybe she doesn't realize how much Viktor has betrayed her.*

"You can't protect him!" I scream at her. "Not after what he's done to you! To me too! Do you know why it's me? Because I exist through him. I'm his blood too. That's why it's me. He had a daughter, and I'm descended from her! I'm one of you too! Part Romanov. And I'm telling you, he's the bad guy!"

"Do you think I do not know?" Anastasia says. "Please. Let me do what I must! Let me end all of this."

So I back away, and Ethan does too, and we both let her do what she has to do.

ETHAN

"YOU SAID THAT YOU WOULD HELP." ANASTASIA STANDS IN front of Viktor, still the grand duchess, even with the rain whipping sideways at us as we press against the building. She's speaking in Russian, so I translate quickly for Anne. "That you would keep us safe. But you didn't really do that, did you, Brother? You never planned on doing it."

"But I did," Viktor says to her. So many emotions are crossing his face—anger, denial, regret, perhaps even love. It's like he's seeing Anastasia for the first time, not just as a pawn to use to get what he wanted, but as a person. "I did. I wanted you to live." As he says it, it's like he's there again, and for a moment, I almost believe him.

Anne moves to stand next me. I listen, and watch, and translate for her as best as I can.

"Do not lie to me, Viktor," Anastasia says to him. "I will know." They both step from the protection of the bank's overhang out into the driving rain. In an instant, they're both soaked once more by the storm, the wind swirling around them.

"It is no lie," he says to her. "I wanted you to be safe. I wanted to help."

"But then, my brother, you wanted something else, didn't you?"

"She really does know, doesn't she?" Anne says. "She knows what he's done—why he's done it."

I nod. It is between them now, between Viktor and the half sister he has betrayed—just as he betrayed me, and Anne.

"Look at you," Anastasia cries at him. "You look exactly the same. You have not changed. You have not aged. How is this possible? Am I the price you paid for that?"

"Anastasia." Viktor attempts again to say something, but she's already told him that she knows, so his words could only be lies.

"Your jacket, Viktor. It is leather, is it not? And a fine leather. I can see that. Your shoes—look at your shoes. I know good quality, my brother. I am a grand duchess of the Romanovs. I know what it is to have the very best. And I know he denied you that. So what did you do, Viktor? Did you really use me to gain this jacket, to buy these expensive shoes? Tell me, Viktor!" She's shouting now, her voice echoing even over Baba Yaga's howls, even over the torrential storm. "Tell me the truth!"

Viktor stands silently. The rain is streaming over him, running down those fine clothes, soaking those fine shoes. And even through the storm, I can see he is doing something I never expected him to do. He's weeping.

"They killed them, one by one," Anastasia says. She clutches her arms around her as though she's in that room once more. "Mama. Papa. My sisters. Even Alexei. You told me it would be all right. But it wasn't! They were slaughtered! Their blood spattered over me as they died. I knew it was all wrong then. That I shouldn't have listened to you. But it was too late. They were dead—and I was not. You said I would save the Romanovs, but the only one you wanted to save was yourself!"

Viktor's face has become a study in anguish. He seems to grow smaller: the powerful Brother Viktor, bowed by the truth.

"Then she"—Anastasia points to the sky, to Baba Yaga— "she took me away. Because you made her. You compelled her. She didn't want to. Do you know that, my brother? Do you know that I was reaching for my mother's hand when Baba Yaga grabbed me?"

"I'm sorry," Viktor says to her. "Oh, God. I am so very sorry."

"You must let me go back," she says to him.

"To be trapped again? No. I cannot."

Anastasia's blue eyes burn into Viktor's face as she studies it. "He was right," she says finally. "You really are not worthy of being his son."

She reaches back and slaps him—hard—across the face. I can see the red imprint of her hand on his cheek. "To the world, I am already dead. Do not destroy any more lives because of me! Please. I am begging you. Let me go."

As though she has heard the girl speak, Baba Yaga swoops closer, reaches down with those hideous hands.

I'm not prepared for what happens next, even though I should have realized it was coming. People sometimes surprise you—perhaps surprise themselves. I can't say that it changes anything. It doesn't bring back the dead. But it's something, just the same.

"Witch!" Viktor pulls Anastasia aside and stands to face Baba Yaga. I can see the distorted reflection of his face in her iron teeth as she smiles at him. "You need a Romanov, do you not?"

For one terrifying moment, I think he means something else. I reach out for Anne. He's going to give her to the witch, trap her forever.

But I'm wrong.

"Take me, then!" he says to her. His voice is as terrible as Baba Yaga's smile. He reaches up to the jagged cut on his forehead, swipes his fingers over it, and holds them out to her—stained red with his own blood.

"It's in me too!" he tells her. "Romanov blood." He shoves his hand into her face. "Smell it, Baba Yaga. Know it. I am one of them. So take me! Stop this thing! But do not take the girl. Take me instead."

For a moment, it's as if everything around us is holding its breath—the rain, the thunder, Baba Yaga herself.

And then she smiles. "Ah," she says. She runs one enormous finger over the blood on Viktor's hand—brings it to her lips, runs her tongue over it.

Viktor turns around to look at us. He opens his mouth, about to speak. But whatever he might have said, we never get to hear. Baba Yaga's hands wrap themselves around him. He doesn't even scream as she lifts him into the mortar.

She whirls away with him, up toward the black clouds. Her eyes are glowing in the dark sky, each pupil a smiling skull. Her iron teeth are shining.

"Peace be with you, Brother," I say. But I never know if he has heard me, because then they are gone.

Thursday, 4:20 pm

Anne

THE THUNDER STOPS, BUT THE RAIN CONTINUES TO FALL. IF possible, it's raining harder. The street is filling with it.

"She is crying," Anastasia says. Well, actually she says it in Russian and Ethan translates it for me, but it's still what she says. "Auntie Yaga. She is weeping."

I don't ask why she's crying, if, in fact, that's what she's doing. The answer is pretty clear. She's crying for Anastasia. Like a mother, I realize in a rush, crying for a lost child—or at least for a poor, motherless girl who just wants some piece of what she has lost.

I'd thought of Baba Yaga only as a witch. It never occurred to me that she might be more than that.

I peer into the door of the bank. My mother is still lying where we've left her. I press my face against the glass until I see the movement of her chest. She's breathing. I need to go to her, but I can't—not yet.

"What do you want?" I ask Anastasia. I reach over and smooth my hand down her wildly tangled hair. Then I take her hands in mine. They're warm. Even out here in the damp, her hands are warm. Anastasia—my distant relation through circumstances I'd never have believed even a few days ago.

I could be friends with her, I think, *if things were different. She and I and Tess.*

"What do you want to do?" I ask her again, because I think that if we can help her do it, then it will be all over. It's the one last thing Baba Yaga needs.

Anastasia hesitates. She pulls her hands from mine, but our gazes stay locked. When she answers me, it is in Russian. I'm not sure why, but I think it is easier for her because she knows that her words will hurt me.

Ethan translates. "She wants to go home," he says. His voice is very tired and sad. "Back to Russia. Back to when it happened. Anne, she wants to die like she was supposed to. It's the only thing she really wants."

"Die? But she can't! I—Ethan, how can she want to—?"

I don't even finish protesting. I may be a lot dumber about some things than I ever knew I was, but I understand that sometimes, you just have to let go. There's an order to things, to life. Viktor had broken that order. Maybe he'd done it out of selfishness. Maybe he'd done it for vengeance. Or maybe a little part of him—the part that knew Anastasia loved him—did it to help her. But none of that mattered—not even Ethan's personal sacrifice for so many years, not anything that I had done.

It only mattered that it was broken, and we had to fix it if we could.

"Can we do it?" I ask him quietly. "Is there a way? Do we have any magic left? Maybe together or something?"

"I don't know for sure," he says. "I would think right now, you've got a lot more than I have, but we won't know until we try."

I look at Anastasia. She's pulled the small, wooden doll from her pocket.

"She's pretty," I say to her.

"She is my *matroyshka*," she says to me slowly in English. "It means 'little mother.' My mama told me to hold on to her. No matter what. That if I did not let her go, she would keep me safe. And she has. She has kept all my secrets." Anastasia pulls the doll apart, shows me the other smaller dolls tucked inside. "Even as I was hidden away like this."

I watch as she clasps the pieces back in place, and I wonder how a doll can keep you safe, but I don't say anything. It's amazing enough that she's kept this doll with her all this time, with everything she's been through—things I don't even want to know. She's still kept this link to her home, to the person she used to be.

"May I see her?" I ask Anastasia. I hold out my hand, palm up. She hesitates, but only for a second. Then she places the doll in my hand.

I suppose I can always think that what I hear then is just my over-stimulated imagination. Or I can choose to believe that the doll really says something to me. I mean, it's not like those pretty, red-painted lips actually move or anything. Still, a little voice whispers in my head.

Hold me between you, the voice says. *Both of you think about where she'd like to be. Imagine. And if you can hold that thought—together— then you can send her home.*

I don't really know what to believe. I'd thought of home when Baba Yaga had told me to choose, and that hadn't gone well at all.

But somehow, this feels different.

Professor Olensky's dying words come back to me. *The book doesn't matter,* he'd said. *Not exactly.* He'd said that I already knew what I needed to, and maybe he'd only meant about using my blood to get to Anastasia. But maybe I knew something else too.

My mother had given me the answer when she'd handed me the lacquer box and told me the story—the one I'd read the rest of on my own. About Vasilisa the Brave and her magic doll. The doll like this one, that Tsarina Alexandra had given to her daughter Anastasia.

"Yes," Anastasia says. "I hear what you hear. And I think it is the way."

"It's the doll," I say to Ethan. "That's what will send her back."

"Are you sure?" he asks.

But we all know the only way to be sure is for us to try. So we do.

We stand together, Anastasia and I. Between us, we hold her *matroyshka,* my hand on one side, and hers on the other.

I take my other hand and place it over my heart like I've learned in ballet—the universal sign for love. Can I love someone I've never really known? I guess it doesn't matter. All that matters is that I can do this.

The air around us sparks with light.

I don't flinch when, like in my dreams, I see what's in her head. I know it's just part of the connection we have with each other. So when she sees that basement again, I don't push the image away.

But then—well, it's like it always is for me in my dreams, when things shift without my permission. I just can't help myself when all of a sudden I think of one last thing I'd read when I was researching Anastasia—about the wonderful Easter her family had spent together in 1911, when she was almost ten. It was the Easter her father had commissioned this really fantastic Fabergé egg with all the children's pictures on it to give to the tsarina. They all looked so happy—and so unaware that a few years later, their lives would all end.

So there I am, trying to think about death—but all I can think about is life. And Anastasia—well, she looks over at me. Her hand's still on the doll. So is mine. And she smiles. It's a great smile—and it even reaches her pretty blue eyes, the ones I know Tess would want to fix up with a little mascara and some shadow and all that.

"No," she says to me softly. "Not then."

Our fingertips touch across the doll. The image we're sharing shifts back to the basement. No matter how much I want her to live, it turns out that it's not my choice. I can only stand and watch as the shooting begins and Anastasia, the last grand duchess of the Romanovs, slowly fades and disappears.

Thursday, 5:00 pm

Ethan

ANNE STUMBLES AWAY FROM ME INTO THE RAIN, SOBBING. "Anne," I say. I follow her. We stand in the street, the rain soaking us. "Anne, stop. Please, stop. Don't cry. It's over. You did it. It's going to be okay."

I wrap her in my arms. Her body shakes against mine.

"What difference did I make?" she weeps. "I was supposed to save her, Ethan. That's what you told me. And I couldn't. That poor, innocent girl—trapped for all these years, and now what? She's dead. And there's nothing I can do about it. I have all this crazy power, and for what?"

She pounds her hands against me over and over until I grab them and hold them tight. "You told me I could make a difference," she says, her voice ragged with pain, "that I could save her. But I didn't. Not really. I just helped make a huge mess of things. I didn't save anyone."

I hold her tighter. "Don't you see?" I tell her as the rain streams down our faces. "You did save someone." I slide my arms from her and then cup her face in my hands, look into those warm, brown eyes so filled with pain. "Look at me, Anne. I'm still here. You did save someone," I tell her again. "You saved me."

I bend and press my forehead to hers, half-expecting her to pull away. But she doesn't. She reaches up, links her arms around my neck, and touches her lips to mine. And then I kiss her—really kiss her, like I've wanted to for a while. And as the last of the clouds disappear, and finally, the rain stops falling, she kisses me back.

Chicago,
A Few Weeks Later

ANNE

THERE'S NO HEADSTONE YET ON ALEKSANDER OLENSKY'S grave—just the freshly turned earth and a few flowers I've placed there, the thin, white ribbon around them fluttering in the cool breeze.

It had been a small, graveside service. Turns out the professor really had no family left. Just Ethan. And me. And so many students who had loved him, but whose questions about his death will have to remain unanswered—because, honestly, what would we tell them?

So many secrets, I think as I stand here holding Ethan's hand. *So many secrets.*

"How's your mother doing today?" Tess asks. She'd wanted to come with us to the cemetery, as if seeing the grave would help make it all seem more real.

"She's good," I say. "Real good. She'll have to keep that cast on her arm for a few more weeks. And she's going to have to have some physical therapy. But she's getting stronger. And she's eating and starting to bitch at me." I smile. It's not quite the grin I'd like it to be, but as with my mom, it's taking a while to get back to what had been.

It's still so strange to me how people explain what happened on Second Street. Freak storms. Tornados. Flash floods. No one mentions a giant witch. Or a girl who was there and then disappeared. I guess people just see what they expect to see—or what their minds can handle. Even if it's an illusion. I suppose that's what keeps us all from just hiding under our beds some days: our own illusions that cover the secret truths and make them easier to bear.

I've got a lot of secrets these days. I still haven't told my parents what really happened. I think someday I will, because the bloodline I share is not just mine. It's my mother's too, and someday, when the time is right, she'll need to know.

Ethan squeezes my hand. "We'll need to go soon," he says to me. I can see the sadness in his eyes—those eyes that are still as blue as ever but hold a new sorrow that never quite disappears.

I nod. It seems impossible that I've only known him just a short time—not even a month. We've been through so much together, it feels like I've known him forever. I don't know where we're going with that part either—that thing that started when we kissed each other out there in the rain, the day that Anastasia went back to die but Ethan got to live. That thing might be something—but it might not.

I need time to think about it—time when we're not running for our lives or trying to save someone who, it turns out, just can't be saved; trying not to screw up the world even more than it already is.

"I'm ready," I tell him now.

We turn and start up the gravel path toward his car. Ethan is still holding my hand on one side of me, and Tess, close enough that she keeps bumping up against me as we walk, is on the other. But even the warmth of both of them doesn't block out the wind. I pull my jacket a little tighter around me. Like so many things, I guess, the cold is inevitable. It comes whether we want it to or not. But it doesn't last forever.

There's one more secret I'm holding—one I share with the two people crunching the gravel path alongside me.

Lily, my birth grandmother, might be searching for the daughter she had given away. If I can find that woman, Nadia Tauman, who wrote to Professor Olensky, then maybe I can track her down—if, that is, she wants to be found. But I know how that goes now too. It's not always easy to find someone—or keep them around once you do. Things don't always turn out like we hope they will.

Right now, I've got to do something else. Something that I've been dreading since he first told me a few days ago. I've got to say good-bye.

Ethan is leaving—not forever, I don't think, but for a while. He's going back to Europe, to Russia—back to his homeland, his roots. He's free now, and I know he's got to come to terms with what that means, with who he is—and more importantly, who he's going to be, now that he can live out his life as he chooses.

"I have to do this," he'd told me. "I've been one thing for so very long. I need to see what other paths there are."

We've reached the car. Ethan and I climb into the front seat. Tess hops in the back. "Remember I'm back here," she says. "Don't you two start groping at each other up there and forget about me."

"Hey," she says when we both turn around to glare at her, "someone had to cut the tension around here, so I volunteered myself. And by the way, you're welcome."

Ethan rolls his eyes and gives me a lopsided smile. Then we settle in our seats, and he turns the key in the ignition.

He'll come back to me, I tell myself. *He has to.* But as I keep learning, there are no guarantees.

Ethan guides the car through the cemetery gate and onto the street. He reaches over and clasps my hand in his. Underneath my skin, where no one can see, sparks dance, then ignite.

Acknowledgments

Many, many people have helped me along this journey. A profound and hearty thank you to:

Wonder agent, Jen Rofe, who took me on literally in the middle of Hurricane Ike and who has kept me sane with her intelligence, wit, and wicked cowgirl skills.

Editor Lyron Bennett, who, when he's not having a computer apocalypse, has scathingly brilliant ideas. You knew Anastasia needed a journal. And you had a soft spot for my poor, clueless Ethan. This book would not exist were it not for you.

SCBWI critique partners Suzanne Bazemore, Dede Ducharme, Bob Lamb, and Kim O'Brien. You've been there since Anne was just a voice on half a page. You were always willing to tell me when I sucked. And thrilled for me when I didn't. Your love and support never fail to energize me.

The Class of 2k9—how lucky am I to have gained over twenty new writer friends with whom to share this journey. You are gifted, generous of spirit, and amazingly supportive.

My school family at Oak Ridge High School—I hope I'm making you proud. Now go do your homework! And a special thank you to my very first readers, including Kara—who told me Ethan was swoon-worthy and made sure I worked to keep him that way. You rock!

To my friends—I am truly blessed that there are more of you than I can name here, but especially to Sandy, Deborah, Wanda, and Beth Ann—yes, you are my people.

Finally, to Rick and Jacob, the two who know my heart the best of all—you kept telling me I could do it. And you were right.

About the Author

Joy Preble grew up in Chicago, though she moved to Texas and inexplicably began listening to country music, which she claims she didn't like until then. She has an English degree from Northwestern University, and she teaches English to high school students. *Dreaming Anastasia* is her first novel. She can be found online at www.joypreble.com.